TYLER'S ROAD

ALSO BY DARREL SPARKMAN

The Apocalypse Chronicles

Shepherd's Fire

Blood Justice

Broken Arrow

Shepherd's Sword

Chrysalis

After the Fall

TYLER'S ROAD

An Anthology of Western Stories

DARREL SPARKMAN

WOLFPACK
PUBLISHING
— EST 2013 —

Tyler's Road: An Anthology of Western Stories
Paperback Edition
Copyright © 2024 Darrel Sparkman

Wolfpack Publishing
701 S. Howard Ave. 106-324
Tampa, Florida 33609

wolfpackpublishing.com

Paperback ISBN 978-1-63977-352-7
eBook ISBN 978-1-63977-351-0
LCCN 2024933656

To my wife Sue and our family
for their understanding and patience.
To the numerous advisers along the way.
To the late Dusty Richards,
who started me down the trail.

He lived, the impersonation of an age that
    never shall return.
His soul of fire kindled by the breath of the
    time he lived in.
Now, a gentler race succeeds, shuddering at
    blood.
The effeminate cavalier.
Turning his eyes from the reproachful past
And from hopeless future,
Gives way to ease and love,
And music,
His inglorious life.

—*The Knights Epitaph*—
The Poetical Works of William Cullen Bryant, 1878

The following characters did not exist,
but their time, place, and circumstances certainly did.
These are their stories.

TYLER'S ROAD

TYLER'S ROAD

HOLY SABBATH MORNING

On the Holy Sabbath morning of June 26, 1870, I went to church and prayed to the Father—took communion at His table. I was at peace. Today, I'm going to kill a man.

The back of Trinity Lutheran Church became crowded with congregants anxious to get home for lunch, a picnic, or other plans they had made. Seems the faithful come slowly to the altar and then quickly leave all in a bunch, piling up like cattle in a chute.

Enduring curious glances as I waited by the door, I stood patiently to let them through. Some spoke in a friendly manner, most ignored me. It takes a long time for a lawman to build trust. Given the divides in the community, that time may never come. There was no hurry now, and the air coming through the open windows and back door was fresh and inviting. Laughter drifted on a honeysuckle breeze as I waited. A deep, slow breath of it calmed me. Finally, there was no reason to delay as the last person walked out.

Pastor Schuler was an older man with steel-gray hair

and a kindly look about him. He met me at the bottom of the steps where he'd shaken hands with all who came to his service. Except for a few young boys who shinnied through a back window to avoid the line, thinking themselves undetected. They were not. We both saw them and gave each other a knowing smile. I knew they'd get a talking to later by the pastor. He'd catch them at school and have a friendly, gentle, and straightforward conversation.

Since I was the last to leave the church by normal means, we had a moment to talk.

His voice was soft enough that I had to lean toward him to hear. "I almost didn't give you communion today, Jim. You have a look about you that worries me. It's customary to be at peace with God when you take his Holy Supper. Commanded, in fact. You must put away all hatred and ill feeling toward others. That includes offering forgiveness."

"If it's written in your Book, it must be so. But that's a mighty tall order. I doubt there's many mortals in your flock that could do that." I kept my voice mild and noncommittal as I buckled my gun belt. I'd left it on a peg just inside the door and carried it outside with me. I'd once worn it during the service because I'd heard someone had, on occasion, stolen the collection plate. Pastor Schuler admonished me for it, saying there was a greater punishment awaiting the thief at his appointed time. Pieces of silver were not worth someone's life, even that of a thief—and it was a poor church, not worth the effort.

Reining in my drifting mind, I continued. "And to put your mind at ease…I'm at peace with what I'm going to do today. It's necessary."

His gaze mapped my face, knowing every line of quilt

and reason found there. "You're a rancher at heart, not a gunfighter. And I know you are a good man. It's a sin to kill someone like this. That's premeditation. Your anger is gone. Find another way. Will you give the man a chance to surrender?"

"I will give him as much chance as he gave that young girl." My voice echoed my surprise. "How do you know about all this?"

"Half my congregation is Cherokee, along with other tribes. You have friends, and they are worried."

Strange things come to you while trying not to answer a question. The squeal of a windlass drawing water from a well, a mule braying at a cursing hostler—whispering wind through tall grass, and a yearning for a simple day. Just one simple day. Was my confidence stealing reason away? Were these last memories imprinting on my soul?

I shrugged the doubt away. "I'll make some people angry, and some will find closure with what I do. There is no good ending with this. But in the end, my friends need not worry about me."

Schuler gave me a concerned glance. Knowing the man, I knew he had to try, though my mind would not change. His voice reflected a sadness I was sorry to inflict on him.

"Your friends worry when they don't understand. I can sympathize with retribution and understand the need for a reckoning in this matter, but I cannot condone what I think you have planned. The final ending of this man is not your job."

I settled my hat, watching him for a moment. "I guess we'll have to disagree on that one." With a small smile, I continued. "I'm sure that does not surprise you."

Shrugging, his gaze pinned me again. "Let's talk of

something else for a moment. What will you do about Betty? She's a good person. We all make mistakes, Jim. Some are greater than others. Human frailty guarantees it."

I gave this relentless man a long look. "And what do you know of that particular problem? Is there anything going on around here you don't know?"

"Oh, I'm sure there is." The pastor smiled for a moment and then glanced down at his folded hands, clasped across his belly, the cross hanging just above them. "She came to me early this morning about daylight, seeking help with forgiveness—yours and God's. Her guilt won't let her enter the church, although I encouraged her to worship with the rest of us sinners. The frailties of our church would make quite a book, but she was quite forceful in denial."

I nodded at that, didn't expect it, and wondered why she bothered. "That's real interesting, Pastor. But I'm not in the business of forgiveness, that's your calling." Pausing a moment, I shook my head. "Still...help her if you can. As for me, I have a job to do. A duty."

His voice stopped me as I left. "You can give up the job. It's temporary at best."

Looking back at him, I gave his words a moment's thought. Shrugged. "You're correct, Pastor. I can give up the job and give it to someone else. But the responsibility? I cannot."

I gave him a somber look. "Nor the betrayal."

———

Two days ago, I sat on a rickety chair in front of my office. The day was warming nicely—if you call boiling a warming trend. I couldn't decide between the somewhat cooling breeze outside or the stifling heat inside the office.

Down the street, the blacksmith was taking considerable anger out on his anvil. I couldn't fathom how much the man had to eat to maintain his large body, considering the boiling heat of the day and his own fire agitated by a bellows. Add a heavy leather apron, and his sweat must fill his boots to the top.

Some nights are better than others. Last night, the Bar M boys rode into town, hoping to exchange their hard-earned money for a little fun and excitement. We don't offer a wide menu of entertainment, but our beer parlor and restaurant did the best they could. One notable exception to the festivities was Latigo Johnson. He could not hold his whiskey, and when he switched to rot-gut, or Indian whiskey, the bartender sent for me. I did ask him if his momma named him Latigo, but that was after I'd put a knot on his head with my pistol and dunked him in the murky water of the stock tank. Befuddled and wet, he didn't give a coherent answer.

When I walked out of the office at daybreak, I almost stumbled on the half-eaten carcass of a rabbit. I kicked the remains toward a dog stretched out against the building. His tail thumped, but he didn't raise his head. His uncertain ancestry gave him a large, bony, red-bone and brindle body with a black, wide head too large for his structure. Friendly in nature and too slow to catch a sunburn, I doubted he'd caught the unfortunate bunny and wondered if he had a bobcat bringing him offerings.

A free breakfast made the work of putting the eatery back together after the Bar M blew through it, but the tables and chairs were sturdy. Any breakage was already paid for with apologies from all concerned. By the time I returned to the office, Betty had come and gone, leaving her temptations of the day.

Swatting Boney's cold nose aside, I reached down into the paper bag sitting on the shady side of the chair and rummaged around for a cookie. If the bag were on the sunny side, it might catch fire, and overdone cookies were not acceptable. There was a dried apple pie inside on the desk, safe under a tea towel keeping the flies away. A certain lady was trying to get my attention, and I'll admit to not putting up much of a fight. If I played my cards right, she'd catch me soon, and I'd probably gain fifty pounds.

The sign on the wall behind me read *Jim Schmidt, Sheriff of Howard County, Kansas*. I thought it was a bit much, too big, and colorful—more like a circus billboard with multicolored fancy lettering. The businessmen in the community presented it to me for doing my job, possibly thinking a big sign would make me feel important enough to stay on permanently. If I stayed, it would better the town's chances of becoming the county seat.

And the sign was pretentious. Some would bet on the county being split in two sometime soon, with more organized counties on both sides. The Federals were busy reallocating land after the war and naming things after Union Generals. Sitting on my chair in Howard City, of Howard County, I was confident the names would change soon enough. But the people would not change. And none could decide where to put the county seat. Some wanted it in our town, others in Langdon or Elk Falls. All the officials and organizers were lining up to feed at the Union trough. Most people I knew wanted the government as far away from them as possible. Government oversight and management was the surest path to failure I could think of.

Their fancy sign wouldn't make me stay. But stay, I would. It was time to stop traveling. I felt neither young nor old. I'd learned a few things in my years on this earth and had the scars to go with that education. The days of having to prove my manhood were long gone, along with my adolescence.

When I walk into a saloon, I don't care how I appear to the shady denizens holding court at tables or the bar. Unlike characters in a dime novel, I couldn't care less who has the fastest gun hand—the fanciest rig, or who demands the most respect. Most of the rough crowd I dealt with would learn those things don't matter. If they lived. They weren't bad men, just rough around the edges.

There was a bullet hole in the top of my hat, a reward for facing trouble head-on. That's all anyone needed to know. The real reward was that someone shot high, and I didn't.

The shine hadn't worn off my new badge when some men rode into town to make an unauthorized withdrawal from the bank. Most folks didn't have any money to put into a bank, but it was my responsibility to keep the meager amount of funds intact. I'd watched them ride in, knowing at a glance they were up to no good. They were a motley lot, riding with studied casualness. Some still wore Confederate butternut and gray, while others wore patched-up Union clothing of blue and gold. There were Indians with them as well, but with hats pulled low, who knew where they called home. Even five years after the war ended, we were long on renegades and discontent.

I grabbed a ten-gauge double-barreled coach gun loaded with buckshot and went to greet the travelers. Within a few moments of their arrival, we had a short and loud discussion that prompted them to leave without money. Well, some of them did. A couple remained in the street. Those two would not move until the mortician brought his wagon. I got a hole in the crown of my hat and the promise of a better one from the bank. I wasn't sure if they meant the hole or the hat.

The only respect I wanted was from the hard-working men and women of the community. People who produced things and made a difference in the lives around them. These were salt of the earth folks. The roots they put down would endure long past any endeavors of the troublemakers, card sharps, or slick-talking politicians.

I'd been home for over a year this time and figured this was my last stop. The things I wanted most and learned to cherish were here—friends and, God willing, a wife and home. I'd taken the job as a part-time county sheriff because my ranch hardly made wages. It would come around, but it takes a while. There was a herd to build, both horses and cattle. Even had some goats if the Cherokee boys would leave them alone. Somehow, they had contests for goat-roping, and now the goats hide in the barn. Saw one standing on the rafters when I went inside to get Red. Scared the hell out of me.

So far, the ranch was long on gophers and coyotes. I lived in one room of my disrepaired house while working on the rest of the ranch when time allowed. The barn and corrals had to come first, but I was gaining ground on the work.

This was an interesting part of the country. The confluence of borders between Missouri, Kansas, and Oklahoma was a melting pot of people from other places. Seemed a lot were always traveling somewhere, in about any direction. I was as likely to see a Chinaman pulling a cart as an Irishman laying track or a Welshman in mining

clothes mingling with any number of Indian tribes—
Cherokee having the most numbers. German farmers
were surveying plots outside of town, and straighter
fences I'd never seen.

An English lord rode through with his entourage,
hoping for a shot at a Pronghorn antelope or buffalo. No
one told him he was too far east. Way too far. If he was
looking to impress anyone with all his finery, he had to
be disappointed. Folks treated their cavalcade with all
the dignity of a carnival—entertainment is where you
find it.

Before the attempted robbery, I was a necessary
encumbrance to the daily goings-on in a small town. I
figured the best job a lawman could do was to be invis-
ible to honest folk and relentless toward the others. I
would make the drunks hold the noise down, run off
card sharks, and try to keep the peace between miners
and cowhands. People would get quarrelsome, but not so
much that they wanted a knot on their head or to spend
the night in jail. The jail was an old root cellar next to
the office. Nobody wanted to go there, including me. I'd
opened the door once and peeked in—the spiders looked
hungry. I closed the door. For now, things were calm.
Our town was small, and the work was not too hard.
Most of the bad things happened over toward Joplin, and
they could have it.

I'd about decided to go inside and pour some tepid
water over my head to cool off when an old Indian
approached riding a small paint pony. Either the man had
long legs, or he was riding a paint donkey—and I'd never
heard of one of those. The man's feet nearly touched the
ground, and his face looked like twenty miles of rocky
trail. He stuffed his gray hair under a floppy and faded
black hat pin-cushioned with feathers. He sat loose as a

bag of beans on the horse as he stopped, and I made a bet with myself he wouldn't be any shorter if he dismounted. He didn't get off his horse but stared at me until he was sure I noticed him.

How could I not? He'd painted his face red and black and did the same to the horse. We didn't see that much nowadays. Most of the warpaint was farther west. There were still bad feelings between the tribes and whites locally, and I couldn't blame them much. Both sides did bad things to the other. I supposed it would always be that way. Since our town was just north of Indian territory, it put us in the middle of the discourse.

Even worse was the animosity between the tribes. They didn't like each other any more than they liked whites. Never had. The wars between them started long before the whites set foot on their land. Politicians were afraid the tribes would unite against a common enemy, but I'd bet against it. It would be the same as those same politicians in Washington uniting for a common cause. Unlikely.

A crow in the distance counted cadence with the blacksmith. Both were similar in making raucous noise. Ticking off a few seconds to myself, I waited. When he sat there staring at me and didn't speak, I grew tired of waiting and tried English.

I held up the bag. "Care for a cookie?"

The man shifted on his horse and looked around. There weren't many people on the street, and no one paid attention to us.

"You Smit?"

That was close enough, and I nodded. Most folks cannot pronounce my last name. The old man's pronunciation was closer and more kind than some I'd heard.

"Yeah, I'm Smit."

"John Proud Bear say you come to his home. You come now."

That set me up straight. If this were an urgent message, my vision would be of the Indian flogging his paint and arriving in a cloud of dust shouting for help instead of sitting on his horse watching me like I was some curiosity.

John was a Cherokee and a good friend of mine. My folks had left me a small ranch west of town. When I say left, I mean it. After I got back from the war, they gave me a hug and left for Texas, leaving me with a worn-out house and a barn leaning with the wind. I hope they made it. I haven't heard from them.

John and his friends helped around the ranch when I was away being a sheriff. Most days, the money was better coming from the county job. We made expenses on the ranch, and that was about it. I paid them with very little money, but they knew the cattle represented food for them anytime they needed it. All of them. It seemed to be enough. I could get cranky about the men feasting on my cattle but couldn't stand to see the children going hungry. To be honest, wild game was scarce, and a barbecue held once a month seemed reasonable. My friends always invited me, and I appreciated the hospitality. I never asked the obvious.

We hadn't talked in a while, but a summons was not his style. To send someone for me was out of the ordinary. It didn't take much to know something was wrong. This was not an invitation to supper.

Some called these Cherokee white Indians, or one of the civilized tribes. A few of the other tribes disliked them because they seemed to take up white ways. Or so they thought. I knew that to be a lie. If anything, small ranchers and farmers gained ideas from the Cherokee.

They had farms and cattle long before the whites set foot on their land. If they saw a better idea, they'd take up with it. We all do that.

Gazing at the messenger, I didn't ask the old man's name, and he didn't offer. It was their way. I guess one of the reasons I got along with them was that I didn't try to interfere with how they wanted to do things. They had their way, I had mine. It worked most times.

As I stood, placing the bag of cookies on the chair, Milo Hamilton came toward me. He was a portly man wearing a broadcloth suit and vest, something I'd have shed on such a hot day. Maybe it befitted his station in life. Our town wasn't large, but he owned half of it. He walked around town like a gaited mare stomping snakes. A blind man would know he was coming by the vibrations on the boardwalk.

"We need to talk about this county seat issue, Sheriff. Say—what's that Indian doing in town?"

My glance took in the Indian and settled on him a moment. I detected the start of a smile on his face before he shut it down—I'm sure he spoke English as good as me. Or, it could have been bad lighting on another wrinkle. It was hard to tell.

"Looks like he's minding his own business to me." I turned my attention to Milo. "Are you volunteering to mind his business for him? It would probably require a lot of riding."

If the businessman didn't loosen his collar soon, he was going to blow up. He stared at me a moment before he continued. "I thought we had an understanding that they would stay out of town. It scares people and is bad for business. They don't belong here."

I almost laughed. People flooded into the western lands from origins unknown and then set themselves up as experts on ownership. Seems I spend half my time mediating between factions that consider others different. The Indians had their own way of life and a point of view that was slow to change. The whites looked at the same things, the same problems, with a different view, mostly from a position of ignorance. It was an uneasy truce.

I tried to keep anger from coloring my voice. "They don't belong here? Try this for size. The Federals got this land from the Little Osage by hook or crook—some called it a treaty. Now this town sits in the middle of land you bought from the Federals, who didn't have a deed to it in the first place, and then you sold city lots to businessmen, giving them a deed backed up by the government's deed. I don't need to be a fancy lawyer to think your claim is on mighty shaky ground."

His color wasn't getting any better as he sighed and shook his head. "I guess we should expect that. You're always taking their side on things."

By now, a few more people had come to see what the commotion was about. I longed for my bag of cookies and wondered where the day went wrong. Wrinkle-face was starting to grin again.

"Now, that's not true, and you know it. I kept your bank from being robbed—"

"Your money was in it!"

"True, but I wouldn't have missed that twenty dollars. When those boys drove a bunch of cattle down Main Street, didn't I stop them? Only one longhorn ran through the saloon, and he was dying of thirst. Once he grabbed a beer, he was gone. What about when some Indian women wanted to buy cloth in your store and you tried to run them off? Didn't I intervene and stop a bad situation—take them to another store that was more tolerable and had a better choice of goods?"

I don't think he got my jab at him. More than likely, he never would. My gaze took in the small gathering as I shook my head. "The big problem is you think of different folks as *those* people instead of just people. Although some of us look different, deep down, we're all the same. We want the same things. Hearth and home, family, and friends, and to be left alone to forge our own destiny. It's not complicated, just the ways and means are different."

Milo wouldn't let it go and pointed at the Indian. "Why is he all painted up like that? Is that warpaint?"

Frustrated, I gave up. Words would not change them, only time and generations. "That's where I was going before you interrupted me, to find out about that. Maybe he and his horse are going to a party. Now you folks can stand around here in the heat and complain all you want. I have a horse to saddle."

As the man stomped away, I shouted after him. "I thought you wanted to talk about the county seat?"

"Go to hell, Sheriff."

"That was rude, Milo."

———

SADDLING old Red was always tricky. I was lucky this time. He was in the corral on hobble strings. If I let him loose in that corral, I'd never catch him. I'm not much of a roper and was always glad to supply entertainment for onlookers. I don't know how they knew, but there always seemed to be a crowd for the event. The varied and ribald advice I garnered was enlightening. I swore the men and boys sitting on the rail were passing notes and suggestions. No one could think of all that on their own.

After the horse tried to bite me and missed imprinting a horseshoe on my boot, I led him out of the stable. I finally saw a smile from the old man and knew he'd stayed around to see if I got my butt kicked.

"Horse make good stew someday."

I couldn't disagree with that. Maybe sooner than later. Maybe a monthly barbecue? Now, that was a vision I could live with.

As we rode south out of town, Betty Connor stood waiting on her porch. Her home was an addition to the church school, close to the Lutheran church. It was handy for her. I stopped, and the Indian rode on.

She shaded her eyes as she gazed after the man. "That's the smallest horse I've ever seen anyone ride. Is that your bag of cookies?"

I turned in the saddle and looked at the man as he rode away. He didn't look that quick, and I'd never seen him leave his horse. That was a dandy piece of cookie thievery. "Why that old…"

"Don't worry." Betty laughed for a moment before continuing in a mocking tone. "I'll make some more for you. At least he didn't get your pie."

I wasn't sure about that. If I didn't see him steal the cookies, who's to say he didn't get the pie too? Even more baffling was her lack of comment on war paint.

She continued. "Thought you were coming over for lunch? What's going on?"

My stomach growled at the thought of it. If there was a better cook around, I'd never parked my feet under their table. "Well, I was planning on that until the old man came and got me. Says John needs to see me right away. I can't imagine why, but I'd better see what's going on. He's never sent anyone like that before."

She stood, wringing her hands on her apron. "Oh, I hope no one is hurt. Should I go with you? I can be ready in a few minutes. Now I'm worried about Sarah and the girls."

"I don't think so. He'd bring them in if they were sick or hurt, although this is a bit mysterious for him. There's no telling what's going on, so I'd better go alone."

Nodding, she shrugged. "Okay, then. But let me know what you find out. Now you've got me curious. Will you be back for the box supper and dance tomorrow?"

Box suppers are always fun. Since most people knew we were seeing each other, every single man there—some loosely called friends—would bid for her box just to rile me up. It didn't work, but it was a fun time.

I sat on my saddle, wishing I had time to get down. "I should be back for that. It depends on what's happening with the Cherokee. Sometimes it gets complicated."

"It's always complicated." She shaded her eyes with her hand to look at me. "You be careful. Since you won't get off Red, consider yourself kissed."

Never one to shy away from needful action, I vacated my saddle, doffed my hat, and took care of that problem. It took a few moments because I like to be thorough, and Betty gives as good as she gets, but it was time well spent. There are rules about school teachers showing public affection, but neither of us cared. School wasn't in session, and I figured to end her employment with a better job soon. All I needed was the guts to ask her.

We'd been seeing each other for about six months. She showed up on the stage one day and went directly to see Pastor Schuler over at the church. When she started teaching at the church school, about every unattached male for miles around came to see her during her off hours. She was that kind of pretty, with blue eyes and black, shiny hair, along with the shape to make any kind of clothes look good. Mostly, she wore dresses. Out at the ranch, when no one was around, she wore pants. I favored that.

Somewhere, she'd picked up some Cherokee language. Once that was known, the school grew in numbers. It was something to see kids no bigger than a pound of soap riding two or three to a bare-backed horse, coming to school. She had to throw them back on when they left. I never saw one fall off, going or coming.

Re-mounting, I gave her a smile and a half-salute. Maybe it was time to quit straddling the fence and see if she'd like to pull a double trace. She was on my mind a lot.

"I'll check in when I get back."

One of the things I loved about her was that crooked little grin. "I'll be waiting for you."

The old Indian was long gone, but I knew the way. The land was all rolling hills of short-grass prairie and tree-lined creeks. It was pretty country unless you were hunting for strays. Sometimes I thought cattle loved the game of hide-and-seek. Except for them, it was running around the bottom of the hill as you went over the top. Or running across the creek and hiding in the brush. Some men were good at rounding them up, and they had my respect. I was not. I blame it on my horse. And I rely on my Cherokee friends. There were some real brush-poppers among them.

A couple of hours later, I walked Red up to John Proud Bear's house. Surrounded by shade trees, it was a wood frame structure of ill-defined plans, as he'd added rooms when needed. He'd whitewashed parts of it and left the rest to nature's aging process. I never figured out why.

There were at least twenty people scattered around the front of the house, mostly men. Including the cookie thief, and he wasn't looking grateful. I didn't want to do it because everyone was watching, but I took the thong off my pistol. I didn't like this at all. There were some salty men in this bunch, and all were stony-eyed and grim-faced. They carried weapons, mostly rifles, but that was normal. Hell, even the kids carried pistols for rattlesnakes and varmints. Somehow this seemed special.

Like I told Betty. Complicated.

The crowd turned and watched as I dismounted and tied Red to the hitching rail. The only smiles and nods I saw were when the horse tried to kick me. John met me on the porch.

"What's with the paint on all these folks? Looks like you're going to war."

John Proud Bear stood tall in homespuns with a checkered shirt and cowhide vest. With his long hair stuffed under a hat, he looked like most ranch hands you'd find in this part of the country. Of course, he wore soft knee-length and handmade moccasins. For that matter, so did I. His wife made them, and they were far more comfortable than store-bought boots.

He met my gaze. "Depends. We just might. I'd hate to take a vote on it right now."

I gave him a puzzled look as we shook hands.

"Come inside. We got trouble."

He led me inside to a bedroom filled with women and subdued voices, including his wife and two half-grown daughters. As if by command, everyone parted to show a woman lying on the bed, covered with a sheet. I couldn't tell her age. Her face was too bruised and swollen. I've been around enough to know a beating when I see it. I'd given a few and been handed some.

I looked at her for a moment, and my shoulders slumped. Cussing would have made me feel better, but I knew John's wife would bounce something off my head if I started. I'd read something about depression in an old newspaper from back East. It may not have been worth any more than wrapping paper, but it was interesting. They talked about depression as being a female malady. After a long sigh, I convinced myself that it was contagious and I was getting it. For a moment, I felt light-headed and chilled at the same time. The men outside were mad—not far removed from a killing. Now I knew why.

This wasn't some floozie lying on that bed or a broken flower who met up with a bad man in a whorehouse and got beat for her trouble. This would get small notice over in Joplin. I tried to rub away the cold knot forming in my belly before I caught the gesture and stopped. No woman deserved something like this. Given the people she was with, I figured her for a normal girl, just living her life and minding her own business.

Except she was Cherokee, and at this day and time, that put a whole different twist to the story. She didn't need this. None of us did.

The hostile gaze of the women washed over me, even the young ones—John's daughters included—and they were friends. I was grateful most of the guns I saw were outside as I nodded somberly and then turned to John.

"Tell me."

John gestured toward the door, and we watched the women leave, except his wife Sarah. She appeared calm and self-assured as she stood by the bed. But then, she always seemed that way. It was like her to stay and give support for the girl—and not to leave when her husband said go. That brought a small smile to my face.

I often told John he married up. Way up. The blue gingham dress and white trim set off her dusky skin, and I noticed a blood spot on the front. Seemed I'd seen her wear that dress to church and hoped the spot would come out. She came over, patted my arm, and kissed me on the cheek before pulling me to the bed.

The girl turned her head away as Sarah pulled the sheet from her upper body. The girl shook her head, clutched at the cloth for a moment, and then let go. I tried to be polite and turn away.

"Look at her, Jim."

Her clothes were torn, leaving gaps of skin showing. There were bite marks and scratches, and a couple of deeper cuts on her shoulder. I had no idea what did that. They didn't look like knife wounds.

"We didn't clean her up much. I thought it would be better if you saw her like this."

I looked at her for a moment, trying to figure out what she meant. There's always that hidden message in what people don't say, and I didn't like where this was going.

"You thought I'd need motivation? You know me better than that, Sarah."

She covered the girl with the sheet, and then her gaze burned at me, ignoring my comment. "It's like an animal got to her, Jim." She nodded toward the door. "The women agreed to keep this from the men, at least how bad she looks. The men know she was hurt, that's all. I don't know how long that can last. If they saw her like this—"

John interrupted in a soft voice. It didn't fool me. He was mad clear through. Being a big man, things generally moved or got broken when he was angry. And he was hell-on-wheels in any kind of fight.

"Here's another little wrinkle. This girl's name is Fawn. She's the daughter of Ten-Wolves."

"Stumpy?" His nickname might fool some people. Born with one leg shorter than the other, he was still a warrior and a big man in the Cherokee community. I was starting to get a first-class belly ache.

John continued. "Yeah, and it won't take much to set him off. He reads the white man's Bible, but mostly the Old Testament. Says he can relate to them better, and he ain't much good at forgiving."

He nodded toward the bed. "This girl was bathing alone by the creek on the backside of our place. There's a nice limestone pool, and we all go there on occasion to swim. She was about to leave when a man rode up and caught her before she could get away."

Sarah glanced at us for a moment with tears in her eyes and then looked away. She smoothed the girl's hair like she would a child, crooning something to her in a soft voice. I couldn't make out the words, but the cadence sounded like a medicine song. I hoped it was for healing and not revenge.

John continued. "When she resisted, he beat her—knocked her out. When she woke up, he was raping her. She started screaming and fighting again. He finally stopped, jumped on his horse, and rode away."

I stood with my back to them, hands on my hips, looking out the window. Most of the men outside were in a tight knot surrounding Ten-Wolves. It appeared the ladies hadn't kept their secret for long, and I couldn't blame them. It was an odd sight seeing men dressed like local cowmen and farmers with faces painted in streaks of yellow and black.

Their rifles had feathers adorning the barrels and jagged designs painted on the stocks. Brass tacks nailed into the wood reflected in the sunlight and caught my attention. I'd heard a couple of townsmen discussing the tacks after they'd seen one of the rifles. They thought the tacks represented counting *coup*, or some great deed carried out by the man—often embellished out of proportion—and they laughed about it. For their own peace of mind, I did not correct them. The truth? Each tack was a man killed. There were a lot of tacks out there, and Ten-Wolves' rifle was the most adorned of all.

A good part of these men rode with Stand Watie. The Cherokee general combined the first and second units of the Cherokee Mounted Rifles and formed the Confederate Indian brigade in the late difficulty. There was little doubt they'd know how to use their weapons. Given a leader, they'd sweep through the country with little to stop them. If something started, it would be a lost cause and disastrous for both sides. But they could sure make our lives hell for a while. We didn't need this kind of trouble—Whites or Cherokee.

I turned back to John, the one man I needed to keep neutral in this. He was the leader who could command troops with deadly precision and was respected by all the tribes.

"Description?"

Sarah spoke up. "Fawn said he was dressed all in black—everything black. She remembered silver decorations on his belt and holster. The saddle was the same, all fancied up with silver."

"Sounds like his gear costs more than any of us make in a year. I'd like to see him ride through Apache country in that get-up." It was a throwaway statement, buying time while I tried to get my head around the problem. I felt odd talking about a girl like she wasn't there under blood-spotted sheets. Once in a while, the girl would jerk and groan in pain. We could only guess at her injuries.

"She noticed a lot."

Sarah shrugged and nodded toward the girl. "You tend to notice things when you think you're going to die. Besides, all that silver was digging into her. He didn't even…" She stopped, wiping a tear from her eye, and looked at John. "It could have been one of our daughters."

"Was this a white man?"

I needed to get my mouth under control. In times like this, folks pick at every word and look. I'd seen it before, done it myself. People start thinking of what you should have said or done. Hindsight. And it was a needless question. If it wasn't a white man, John wouldn't have sent for me. The man would be dead or stretched out on an anthill somewhere. Or, more likely, his skin stretched on a tanning rack. Other than a pointed look, they didn't acknowledge my voice and were right. It was a dumb question.

I glanced at the girl on the bed, her face streaked with tears leaking from closed and swollen eyes. She'd heard everything we said, and I regretted ignoring her. She wore her embarrassment and pain like a mantle. But I couldn't help her bear it. No one could. I prayed she was a fighter, and deep down, I hoped she had the strength to get past this.

Walking up to the bed, I stood next to Sarah. "Fawn, I'm sorry this happened to you. Right now, you need to let people take care of you and not worry about anything else. I'll bring this man to justice. You have my word." I paused for a moment. "When I catch him, would you recognize him? Point him out for sure?"

Her nod was a faint movement, but I saw it. I reached out to touch her shoulder, and she flinched away. I couldn't blame her. Her opinion of men must be pretty low.

"You've got my promise, Fawn. There will be a reckoning. I'll make it happen."

I looked at Sarah, asking a silent question. It had to be on everyone's mind. Would the girl be alright? Could she walk among her friends again with her head held high? Sarah knew I didn't want to ask the question out loud, so she shrugged and then nodded. I hoped she was right. A young girl's journey is hard enough without something like this happening to her.

"One more thing, Jim." Sarah's voice was soft. "She marked him."

Nodding, I waited her out—and got impatient when she didn't speak right away.

"And...?"

She glanced at her husband before answering. "She had a big chunk of skin under a nail. He'll have a good-sized wound."

"Face? Back? Arms?"

At her glance, I backed away a step. Murder shone in those gentle eyes for a moment. Just long enough to remind me of the wildness that lurks below the surface in all of us. Most keep it inside, and we call it being civilized—like whistling past the graveyard. I recognized it because I've fought that devil before. I wasn't always successful.

"His face. She said he didn't even take off his gun belt."

I wasn't sure what to say about that, couldn't get my head around the mechanics of it, so I remained silent. I'd already made one foolish statement and didn't want to add to my list.

Turning away, John and I stood by the door. His daughters and a couple of other women were about to run us over coming through the entry. Over their whispered comments, I could hear the drone of conversation from the men outside, and none were speaking English. Another bad sign. These were good people, but even the best of us can do bad things when we're mad. That these were very capable and dangerous men made the situation worse...if that was possible.

Knowing the background of this group of Cherokees, the town folk would be anxious when they heard of the trouble. The town was full of ex-soldiers from both sides. All of them knew the reputation of the Indian Brigade. That would make them jumpy and have a bad outcome more likely. We didn't need anyone to get trigger-happy on either side. Violence would divide the existing factions more than they already were.

My sigh was long and loud as I turned to my friend. "Other than the obvious, what do you need from me?"

He stood, rolling his hat brim for a moment. "Talk to these men. We trailed the man's horse until it hit the main road. If he keeps going the same direction, he's in Silvertown. Providing he stops, of course."

The name of our town was kind of a running joke with the locals. After the war, the county was renamed, along with the city. But years ago, someone dug out the start of a mine. Looking to turn a profit, he seeded it with enough silver to get a good price for it. No one thought to get his samples assayed to see if the silver came from the area—and yes, they can tell. Someone with get-rich-quick fever stepped up and bought the mine. The owner promptly skipped the country. A town sprung up like a lot of them do. It would have faded away, but by then the surrounding ranchers and farmers were using the stores, and the town grew to permanence.

I gave him a quick glance. "Anything more? Broken horseshoe, three-legged horse—anything?" It was a joke to lighten the moment. Not in good taste, considering the circumstances, but we were friends and could do that.

His grin was quick, but he sobered fast. "What more do you need? She just about gave you a picture of the man."

We went out on his porch and stood before the gathering crowd. I could feel their reluctance to hear what I had to say. It was like facing a lynch mob, and I hoped they weren't looking at me to be their first customer. I singled out the biggest problem, not that he didn't have cause.

"Ten-Wolves, I'm sorry this has happened to your daughter. It's a bad thing."

The man raised his rifle, shaking it above his head. I was pleased to see there were no scalps on it. Yet. "We will go to Silvertown and find this man. He will face Cherokee justice."

I knew he was trying to save face, and I hoped raiding our town was the last thing he wanted. It was the last thing anyone wanted if they weren't crazy. If the Cherokee rode into town in a large group, an angry group, some hothead would say something, and the shooting would begin.

"Ten-Wolves, I am the law in this county, and this is my problem to deal with. If this man is in town or anywhere else, I'll find him and see he is punished. The last thing we need is all of you riding into town and scaring the hell out of folks. Next thing you know, we'd have the army riding around in circles, stirring up a lot of dust, and attacking the Osage."

There were a couple of chuckles from the men, and I could tell that appealed to some of them. There was no love lost between the Cherokee and Osage. Ten-Wolves shouted them down and turned to me.

"What will we do? White man's law doesn't care about the Cherokee."

Complicated. And he was partly right. If the Cherokee kept holding themselves separate, there would always be a rift, but I was not going to voice that opinion.

"It may seem like that. But you all know me. I care about the Cherokee. Who stood up for you when the Federals wanted to take your farms? Your land? I did. I'll still do it the best way I can. You need to trust me on this."

The grumbling was starting again. "Now, hold on. If I need any help, I won't send for the army. You know that. If I need a posse to chase this man, I'll send for you. We all know you're the best trackers around. I'll let John know if you're needed. Give me a few days. Will that work for you?"

They didn't seem to agree, but the shouting quieted down. A slow migration of men started for their horses. I took that as a good sign.

"Ten-Wolves, take care of your daughter. If you need anything, like medicine or a doctor, let me know. I hope she gets well."

He started to argue again, but at a headshake from John, he relented. His shoulders slumped, and his gaze went to the open door. "This I will do."

We watched as he walked past us and into the house. I couldn't imagine how helpless he must feel. Some days, you want to shoot something just to see it blow up. I ran across that once during the war. After a battle, one of our men walked up to a wounded soldier who fought for the Union, shot him in the belly, and then crouched down in front of him. Crazy things happen in war. Seems they knew each other before the war, and their families were feuding. When I asked him about it later, he looked at me like I was the crazy one and told me he hated the man and just wanted to watch him die. No remorse. No guilt.

I hoped the Cherokee wouldn't take up that school of thought.

———

A FEW MINUTES LATER, I stood with John under the shade of a live oak. A hot breeze ruffled the leaves above us as we watched the last of the men disperse. Sarah and her daughters would take care of Fawn. She was in good hands. It was my job to take care of her assailant. And I was having bad thoughts.

He looked at me with concern. "What's banging around in that head of yours? If you need help, I'm your man."

"You'd be the first one I'd ask. No, it's deeper than that. You know the problem. I can arrest this man, but what then? I can't hold him long without a warrant, at least not legally. With all the new lawyers around, he'll get off free. If I arrest him and just hold him, who knows when the circuit judge will come. The troublemakers will want him to go free. The rest of the town will want him out of jail and away from here to avoid trouble."

I looked at him. "And the Cherokee need their pound of flesh."

"So, he gets away with it? Is that what you're thinking? We will not allow it. That could start a war."

My gaze measured him for a moment. We had a checkered past, and I'll admit, his was more honorable than mine. As children, we'd torn up the countryside with our antics. I'm sure our parents were ready for us to leave the nest if we ever grew up. I left and kicked around the country some. Made some mistakes and did not always make good decisions. Then came the war. John stayed home, finally joining up with the Cherokee Brigade. I went south and joined Hood's Texas Brigade. When we came home, we were both surprised to see the other alive. Pleased, but surprised.

I couldn't keep sadness from my voice. "We've been friends, John. A couple of times, we broke bread with the devil and thumbed our noses at him on the getaway. We have history that can't be undone. Are you threatening me?"

His gaze broke first. "You know I'm not. It's not personal. But you have to be aware of how we feel." His grin was quick. "Besides, my wife likes you better than me. I couldn't chance making her mad."

If I were drinking beer, it would have come out my nose. I settled for a sneezing snort that made my eyes water.

"My friend, you're out of your mind. Look, here's what I'm going to do. One day won't make a difference in this, so I'm going to ride over to Mindenmines to see Judge Ritter. He'll give me a warrant so I can arrest and hold this man all legal-like, maybe move him to Joplin or Carthage. The extra day won't hurt anything as long as we know where the man is, and that will give Fawn a day to heal so she can point him out."

It took a minute for his answer. "All right, I can see the sense in that. What can I do?"

"You need to go into town and find this guy. Don't do anything to spook him. Just watch him. If he leaves town, follow and send word back on your whereabouts. No matter where he goes, how far he goes, you follow him. Tell the men I'll find some way to pay them for their time."

"Pay with what? You're about out of beef." He shrugged and grinned. "We have him spotted already. The boys are taking care of it. That was the first thing I did."

The boys he mentioned would be the men who helped at the ranch. They were a tight-knit bunch and not given to talking. I gave him a hard look. "No shooting. Understand? I know you can roll him up and make him disappear. But if it ever got out, there'd be hell to pay. There would be a ton of heartache for just a little revenge."

His anger was seeping through again. "Yeah, I got it. No killing of whites by red men. Don't cause trouble. I know my place."

My hand gripped his shoulder. "Your place is by my side as my friend. My best friend—"

"Only friend."

"Yeah, well, there's that. Anyway, let's be smart about this. There's enough trouble in this world without us making more. There are good people in town and on the ranches. No one would condone what's happened. Not if they think about it. But it just takes one hothead to blow it up."

Hoping I was getting through to him, I continued. "One other thing. You need to think about my offer to become my deputy. It would go a long way toward keeping peace with the tribes. You'd do a good job."

"Or put a target on my back." His head was shaking. "Maybe. We'll see."

Like always, he wasn't much interested. We shook hands as Sarah walked up to us, holding out a package.

"What's this?"

She shrugged. "Some food for your journey."

How did she know I was leaving?

John laughed. "See? I told you."

Dividing her gaze between us as she walked away, she finally stopped and stared at her husband for a moment. "Stop it."

I envied what they had. Closeness and sharing. It was like they were always of one mind. With a grateful nod to her, I stuffed the package into my saddlebag. Whatever food it held was better than the salted-down and dried-up beef jerky it was replacing. With everything strapped down tight, I waved and rode toward Mindenmines. I'd bypass Betty's house, but that couldn't be helped.

———

THE ROAD WAS WELL-TRAVELED, but when the moonlight was gone, I cold camped until dawn. When I unwrapped Sarah's package, I was pleased to see she remembered I loved fried chicken. I'd have to rub that in when I talked to John. Maybe she did like me. As I savored the cold meal, I thought of their big red and black rooster that tried to flog me whenever I visited. I hadn't seen it around today—maybe the crowd ran it off.

The town of Mindenmines rose from the strip-mining operations for lead and its by-product zinc. The miners called it Jack, and that's where the money was because they used it to make metal hard and paint last longer. Other than hearing the blacksmith pounding on his anvil, I had no experience with metalworking, but I was doubtful of the paint. Most paint would flake off in the Kansas sun, no matter how good you made it.

Getting close to town, the land looked turned upside down. I pictured a giant groundhog burrowing around, looking for roots to eat. Most of the smelters were over toward Joplin, so ore wagons were moving south like a trail of ants. I don't know who was getting rich off what, but a man could do well selling wagons and mules. Watching the activity, I pondered turning in my badge and opening a supply store. Something peaceful and less complicated.

It was well past daylight when I rode up to Judge Ritter's building. He was just starting his day, and my news surely didn't make it better. It didn't take long before I figured my ride was a waste of time. I sat in his office and explained what had happened, my thoughts on it, and my need for a warrant.

"Judge, you know my history better than anyone. If you hadn't set me on the right path a few years ago, I'd be sitting in one of your cells or dead. I'm trying to do the right thing and avoid bloodshed."

He'd had breakfast brought in and was eating as my stomach grumbled. He nodded and waved his fork for me to continue.

"I'm walking a fine line between the Cherokee and whites. This matter needs to be as legal as possible so there isn't any blowback from the townspeople and done fast so the Cherokee feel vindicated in their trust of the law. Not to mention their trust in me."

He sat for a moment looking at me, and then dabbed at his lips with a napkin. With his mustache and beard, it was a chore and enforced my penchant for being clean-shaven. Too much mess.

"Well, of course you'll get your warrant. I have a good enough grasp of the situation, so if any complaints come back this way, I'll know how to deal with them. But let's think past the arrest. Have you thought this through? Do you think for one minute you can get a conviction? It doesn't matter where you move him, the situation will be the same. You'll be holding a stick of dynamite with both sides striking matches and trying to light the fuse."

He thought for a moment and then pointed his fork at me again. "You can't set the Cherokee on a jury. It'd be legal if you did. But right or wrong, most folks wouldn't stand for it. A few years down the road...maybe. But not now. If this man has the money for some jack-leg lawyer, he'd get off easy. And there's no direct witness except the girl. Correct?"

I'd take the word of an Indian tracker any day, but I could see the rabbit hole this conversation was diving into. "That ain't right."

"That's the way it is. Do you see it differently?"

I thought for a moment. "We have a good description. She marked him. They trailed him. Once I round him up, she can identify him."

"You're beating a dead horse. It's all hearsay with no actual proof. An Indian girl's word against a white man, despicable though he is, will not carry the weight you need to sway a jury."

Judge Ritter got busy writing as I slumped in the chair. "So, what now? Discounting the Cherokee aspect, hell, no matter who he raped, I can't let the man get away with something like this."

He leveled his gaze at me. "Of course not."

After waving it in the air to dry the ink, he handed me the useless paper. I thought about tearing it up.

"This warrant, in my real pretty handwriting, will give you all the excuse you need to go get him." His gaze settled on me. "Your job is to make damned sure he resists arrest."

I hoped my confusion wasn't as clear to him as it felt to me. "So..."

"If this happened to some rancher's daughter, a white family, the rapist would be found, gelded, and hung. No questions asked. And yet, we ask the Indians to abide by our laws and not do that. Do you think they would be afforded the same courtesy from society looking the other way? I don't think so."

"I agree. But still..."

"Jim, don't quibble about this. Sometimes the law can't do what's right. Everything we hold dear says that a man deserves a trial by a jury of his peers where he faces his accuser. That's the law. Do you see that happening here? All it will do is humiliate that poor girl and anger the Cherokee, and he gets to go free. We can both imagine how that would turn out. Innocent people would die on both sides. All for some scum of the earth bad man not worth the powder to blow him up."

The judge continued. "And you're right. It's not fair. We both know it. But that's why we have an elected county sheriff with more power given to you than a federal agent. You represent the people in the county that elected you. All of them. Whether they realize you're doing it or not."

He shuffled some papers for a moment, making a tidy pile, and then glanced at me from under bushy eyebrows.

"Oh, I'd love to have a trial on this—make all the big papers with the publicity. Politicians from all over would flock to your town, trying to take credit for the trial. Lawyers would line up for the chance at this, and dignitaries from Washington would be here. It'd be a real circus, and you'd lose control in a hurry. You'd be standing in the street wondering what the hell happened. It would blow this part of the country apart."

We stared at each other for a moment. When I didn't respond, he continued.

"You need to keep control in your hands. Most people are good and decent. Don't subject them to this. Once in a great while, when you can't guarantee the decision people will make, you must take that opportunity away from them. I expect you to take care of business, Sheriff. Do what has to be done."

"I've sworn to uphold the law, Judge. I don't take that lightly."

He nodded, stirring his eggs around. "I understand that. I do. That's why I trust you."

His fork-pointing was getting to be a habit.

"You've sworn to serve the people. Sometimes that puts you square in the middle, holding two factions apart. That's just the way it is. Besides, we don't need a small Indian war to muck things up around here. If the Cherokee start shooting, it won't be long before the rest of the tribes join in just for the hell of it. Don't risk that. I'd just as soon let all the Indian wars be fought west of here."

That wasn't the answer I was looking for. I wanted an easier way, a legal way—maybe for someone to take that cup from me because I sure didn't want to drink from it. Now he'd placed the problem right back in my lap, and I felt I'd wasted time. The only advantage was the judge. Some might call him old-fashioned, but if push came to shove, I knew he'd have my back, provided it wasn't full of holes. We shook hands as I prepared to leave.

I didn't need much out of life. What I really wanted to do was go back and watch my cattle grow, if there were any left after the monthly barbeques. Maybe watch some children running around if Betty was willing. It didn't seem like a lot to ask. I clamped my hat on my head as he spoke again.

"Thanks for coming, Jim. And thanks for the warning. I appreciate it. Now, you go and get some breakfast instead of trying to shame me into giving you mine. I heard your belly growling before you walked in the door. Send me an official letter sometime to let me know how it turns out." He pointed the fork at me again. "There's a good place to eat right next door."

"The next letter you see may be my obituary, Judge."

He shrugged, returning to his meal. "I'm not worried. Only two or three men in this country could stop you, Jim. We both know that. But don't take a chance with your own life, this peckerwood isn't worth it. Shoot him while he's in bed if you want to, but this man needs to be put down like a rabid animal. Make sure that happens."

As I left the building, Red and I looked at each other. If I rode him hard, we'd be back late tonight. He might be meaner than a snake shedding its skin, but he always got me where I needed to be. I'd miss seeing Betty at the box supper and dance, but I'd get half a night's sleep and be fresh in the morning. I had a feeling this situation needed to be resolved damn quick. Ten-Wolves wouldn't wait, and neither would his friends. If they took the notion to kill the man they thought raped Fawn, no power on earth would stop them—certainly not John

Proud Bear or the duly elected county sheriff of Howard County.

I flipped a dollar to the man running the livery to find some oats for the horse. It was next to the café and handy. Seeing the man scurry away, I grabbed a quick breakfast and drank a half-pot of scalding coffee. The cook must have been a retired drover because the brew resembled tar and barely poured into my cup. But it would keep my eyes open and kill the worms. If it caused a few stops along the way to water the bushes, it was worth it.

A few miners and merchants were having a late breakfast while I rested, gazing out the window and watching Red munch in a feed bag. No one seemed interested in talking to a man with a badge on his vest, and I had nothing to say. All my thoughts were about the problem at hand.

Once Red finished and I kept him from bloating on water, we hit the road. I think he felt the urgency because his foot stomp was only halfhearted as we settled into a trail-eating trot. It was a well-traveled road, and we made good time. There were too many gopher holes to be riding cross-country unless you were watchful, so any shortcuts were out of the question. I didn't need a lame horse, although I contemplated that for a moment. Payback?

———

AFTER SUNDOWN, instead of another cold camp, I gave Red his head and let him go while dozing in the saddle. He could see a lot better than me and never hesitated. It was after moonset and dark as ten feet down when we approached the edge of town. The only way I could tell we were on the road was the hard sound of Red's hooves on hard-packed soil. The few lanterns hanging on eaves only served to disorient you if watched too close.

The men must have been listening because John met me at the edge of town. He had his own lantern he'd flagged me down with and now held it up high.

"Jim, you look plumb tuckered out. Your horse ain't much better."

I had to admit, I was looking forward to some sleep. It would be days before I could take the horse out again. He'd done his job, but Red was sucking wind.

I patted him on his lathered shoulder. "We had a hard ride. Who's watching our man?"

It's hard to see his expression in the lantern light, but it seemed he avoided looking at me. He handed his lantern to one of the men and eased his horse close.

"He's easy to find right now. I got some bad news for you."

I was afraid they wouldn't wait and felt guilty wasting my time with the judge.

"You killed him, didn't you?"

"No. All things considered, maybe we should have. Waiting was a mistake." He hesitated a moment. "Look, Jim. There's no other way of saying this. He's at Betty's."

Weariness and lack of sleep had slowed my mind, so it took a moment for that to sink in. All I could do was stare at him. A rapist at Betty's? What the hell? How could they...? I started to rein Red around and found myself surrounded by men on horses. I realized they must have planned this. Most of them I recognized as men who helped on the ranch and, if not friends, were good acquaintances. They settled my horse down, staying close. One of them grabbed Red's bridle to hold his head down. They had me ringed so tight I couldn't get off my horse or even pull my feet from the stirrups to try. I didn't realize I was holding my breath until it came out in an exasperated sigh.

John grabbed my arm. "I can't let you go there. Not like this. Listen to me. She knew him, even introduced him around. His name is Rob Timmerlane, from over at Joplin."

"Dammit, Jim." He shook his head, glaring at me. "You got any idea how hard it was to not kill that man? He showed up at the box supper, and once he saw Betty, he stayed close to her. They danced together. She didn't look happy and kept looking around. I'd guess looking for you. I don't know what was said between them, but she didn't turn him away."

I threw my hands up in exasperation when one of the men ripped the reins away from me. "Some friends you are. Why in hell didn't you go get her?"

"I know you'll hate me for this." Shaking his head, John continued. "To be honest, I didn't think much about it, even with him being a bad actor. We were watching him close, and they were just dancing. She danced with other men too. You know how these dances are. Every unattached man around was looking to kick up some dust and impress the ladies. Betty is always on every man's dance card. There wasn't much of a way to get to him without starting something. Since she knew him, I couldn't see the harm. You know the town folk let us watch the dance, but not much else. If we tried to separate them, it would have been a fight."

"So. Like you've never been in a fight?" I booted Red's flanks, still trying to get through that circle of riders. He didn't quiver.

"Jim, I am sorry. They caught us flatfooted. We

figured he'd leave after the dance was over, and we'd follow. When they went back to her house, I didn't know what to do that wouldn't start a shooting. Finally, I sneaked up to her window. I swear, if we'd heard screaming or fighting, we'd have gone in. There was no light, but I didn't hear any protest. If she was fighting, I couldn't hear it."

I stopped trying to get through them and gazed into the darkness. We weren't far from her house. How could I get my head around this? We were close. I thought we had an understanding.

"She knew him? What the hell?" Once again, I tried to break free of the encircling horses and men. They held tight.

"I know. What was I supposed to do? We made a mistake, and then I didn't know how to fix it. Jim, it was harmless while we watched, and then they were gone. I'm sorry, but if you're thinking of saving her virtue... there's nothing to save. Not tonight. We figure it's over and done. We'll get him tomorrow. He didn't kill Fawn, so I doubt he'll kill Betty."

He kept his grip on my arm until I settled down. If she was a willing participant, there was no point in going in and making a fool of myself. It seems there are some things I didn't know about her. Some? More like a pot full of things.

I took out my pistol and checked the loads by feel. "All right. You can let go of me. I'll be fine now. It was just a shock."

A hand streaked for my pistol, and I slammed the gun back into its holster before they could grab it.

"Yeah, sure you are." John still gripped my arm. "I can understand. I feel terrible about this. We all do. I don't know what I'd do if..." He shuddered for a moment. "Did you get the warrant?"

"Oh, I got it. We've got enough men. How about we just sidle quiet-like over there, bust in the door, and grab him? Let's get this thing over with."

John shook his head. "We don't know this man. If he's a light sleeper, she might be killed. And a shoot-out in the dark? I think we all know better than that. This kind of polecat would hide behind her. You need to wait until he's by himself, cut him out of the herd."

I couldn't stop the bile from boiling up. It wasn't like I was a stranger to killing or blood. But this? My last meal was breakfast, but if there was anything left, it was surely coming up. My voice sounded strangled in my ears.

"Whores get caught in the crossfire all the time. It's the company they keep."

The slap caught me unaware as his face loomed in front of mine when he leaned over.

"She's not a whore. We don't know what's going on, but she'd not do that. Do you think Sarah would have her for a friend if she was a common whore? Do you?"

At least I lost all thought of losing breakfast. With watery eyes and as gently as I could, I took his hand away. The slap had done its job.

"John, you're going to ruin my shirt. I just bought it."

When he relaxed, I continued. "All right, I'll serve the warrant tomorrow, unless something happens sooner. Maybe they'll sleep in long enough I can make the church service."

I heard a grunt or two. Maybe stifled laughter? But these were my friends, and none of us were gentle souls. A deep breath helped to calm me.

"John, you make sure he doesn't leave early, and that

will give you time to send a rider and get Fawn into town."

I looked around at the shadowed faces. "That suit you fellas? Good. Guess I'll go home now. I need the rest. You boys can go on."

He gave me a pat on the leg. "A few of us will stay here and watch the house, just in case." He gave me a sad look. "It's not that we don't trust you, but you don't mind if some of the men ride along with you? Just to make sure you make it home? And stay there? They'll be sure and get you up early for church."

I looked around, and they were all grinning at me. It didn't look like I had much choice. They knew me well. Of course, they didn't like it much when I turned down the street and stepped off Red in front of the sheriff's office. There was a bunk in there—just one.

Handing the reins to one of the men, I smiled. "Take Red to the livery and turn him loose in the corral. Tell the hostler to give him a good rubdown tomorrow. He needs the rest."

The man's eyes got big, no doubt thinking of what that spectacle would be like and wondering if he could sell tickets.

Going inside, I took off my gun belt and boots. It was dark as an inkwell as I lay on the cot and stared up where I knew the ceiling to be. Not that I would get any sleep.

I heard the complaining creak of wood bending as someone leaned against the door in the back. The same happened with the front door, as I heard men clumping around on the walk, grumbling about sleeping on boards.

Concerned friends? Or was I their prize fighter just waiting for a contest? Would they place a bet on me?

I sat up and felt around the table before I laid back down. The pie was gone. I smiled in the darkness, thinking of an old man riding a sway-backed paint and harboring a serious sweet tooth.

———

BETTY STOPPED me as I walked away from my talk with Pastor Schuler. Sitting on a picnic table under a shady elm with her feet swinging free of the ground, she was a beautiful woman who made my chest ache. Her soft voice carried to me.

"Jim, aren't you going to talk to me? Please?"

I stopped, glancing at her, trying to control my breathing. The first thing I noticed was a bruise on her cheek. Her eyes were puffy. Crying? Or a gift from her lover. I didn't want this conversation. A quick cut to sever the ties between us would be a better ending.

Any education about life will cost you money or pain. Someone told me that. The realization that I loved this woman beyond all reason hurt. It wasn't supposed to be like this—love should be joyous. Another part of my education was that you can't just turn it off. My mind seemed mired in quicksand, struggling to make sense of its own indecision.

Now? To talk it over seemed like twisting a knife buried in my gut. But why not? Might as well get it done and finished. Maybe I'd become accustomed to the pain. Someday.

I'd heard of a Chinese torture called *dying of a thousand cuts* and wondered if it was a female who invented that. Or if we somehow inflicted this upon ourselves.

I moved over and stood in front of her, reached up, and cupped her face with my hand, brushing the bruise with my thumb. For a moment, she leaned into my touch. The gesture turned more intimate than I intended.

"So, how was your night? Make any new friends?"

Her eyes widened as she flinched away, her face turned so pale it made her eyes look black.

I watched her for a moment as her gaze searched mine. Before last night, there wasn't anything I didn't like about this woman. She was on a pedestal barely within reach, and I'd placed her there. I never felt worthy of her attention—reveled in it, yearned for it.

But my friends would not lie to me. About their prowess with guns and horses maybe, or how many women they'd had...not this. My voice wasn't as steady as I'd like when I spoke again.

"Rob Timmerlane."

I don't know what she was going to say, but that name hit her hard. She seemed to shrink and withdraw, aging in an instant. Her gaze wouldn't meet mine. When she didn't speak, I turned to leave.

She came off that table, and her hand reached out for me, stopping just short. "Wait. How did you know? Can I explain?"

I couldn't keep the anger from my voice. I was mad at both of us. My anger at her was simple and direct. There was a clear cause and reaction. I could understand that part. The anger at myself? That was murky water. Looking at her and knowing I still want her, still love her? Back to the twisting knife.

"Does it matter how I found out, Betty?"

"No. I guess not, although I can guess." Her gaze finally met mine. Tearful. Bloodshot. "When we started seeing each other, you never asked about my past."

My eyes searched the street before us. John Proud Bear sat in front of the mercantile playing mumbletypeg.

Pastor Schuler stood by the church, leaning on a porch rail and watching...waiting. For what? I felt like we were in a stage play—the audience waiting for us to do something while I'd forgotten my lines.

I brought my wandering attention back to her. "I didn't figure our past mattered much. You didn't ask about mine either. I thought we both had a fresh start going here."

Tears leaked down her cheeks, and she wiped them away with an impatient hand. She gave a grimace that wouldn't pass for a smile.

"I suppose you're right. It was certainly a fresh start for me. But I guess we were foolish not to talk. Well, it sure matters now, doesn't it?"

She gestured at the table. "Can we sit? My legs are about to give out."

My gaze drifted up the street again, waiting for some sign. Maybe lightning or the sight of some sort of pestilence on the horizon—and an angel on a cloud? Something to guide me. My stomach was just short of embarrassing me.

"Go ahead. I'll stand."

Stubbornness must run in her family. She didn't sit. With a deep breath, bloodless hands gripping at her waist, she started again.

"I knew Rob in Joplin. That's where I'm from. I guess you'd say he was a good customer." Her cheeks turned ruddy as she glanced at me. I saw blood on her palm from those clenching fingers. "You know what I mean? Do I have to say it?"

I did, although it was a surprise she was involved. Wholesome and clean wouldn't begin to describe this woman. But I knew. Joplin has more bawdy houses than outhouses, and that's a quote from their newspaper. If a lone woman didn't cook, clean houses, or have someone to take care of them—there wasn't much else to do, unless she could haul ore from the mines. I knew all that because my own past did not involve sainthood.

"I understand."

Her head shook hard enough for tears to spot my vest. "No, you don't. I doubt any man can fully understand. It was that, or starve. Can you understand that? My folks died, leaving nothing but debt. There was no money, no way to leave unless I started walking. Maybe I should have. That death would be more merciful than this."

She paused to look at me, but I turned to watch the street again. Eyes are a window into the soul, all that we hold dear. I didn't want her to gaze into my hell.

A slow sigh brought my attention back. "I finally saved enough money, even stole some, and left all that to make a new life. I thought I'd done it. A clean break. I was so proud of myself."

She shook her head again. "When he showed up yesterday, I didn't know what to do. You weren't here. When he told me to put him up for the night, I just let it happen. I didn't want to, and I shouldn't have. It was like being on a runaway horse. I felt helpless and don't know why. Then, I thought if I didn't make a scene, no one would notice. Maybe it would be alright. Maybe the whole thing would go away."

I hardly recognized my own voice. "Didn't you know I had friends around? Anyone of them would have killed that peckerwood for bothering you."

Tears were flowing again. "I couldn't think, Jim. I was so scared. You don't know him. He's killed people." She paused a moment. "I watched him beat a woman to death. I knew her. When he came to her, she told him no because he'd hurt her the last time they were together. It was like he went crazy once he started hitting her. Another time, I saw him walk up to a man playing poker and put a knife in his ribs. He killed him, then wiped the blade on the man's coat and walked away.

"Once inside my house, he didn't take no for an answer. I'm so sorry." She shuddered and rubbed her cheek, wincing at the touch. "I thought it would be easier to let it happen. That you'd never know. It didn't last long. If I'd been stronger…"

My laugh was more of a bark, releasing pent-up emotion. "Well, surprise. I found out."

"You were watching me?" She stood with her mouth open for a moment, then sadness veiled her expression. "You didn't trust me while you were gone, did you? Why?"

"Seems well founded."

She took those words like a body blow. How can I feel anger and shame at the same time? I reached out and touched her arm for a moment before taking it away. The day was warming, yet she trembled. Fear? I hoped not of me.

"Sorry for that. But no. You weren't watched on purpose."

She gave me a tearful look. Both her hands were rubbing her temples. "I don't understand."

"The Cherokee were watching him for me, so he wouldn't get away."

"Him? Why? What's…?" Her level gaze bore into me. "What did he do?"

"He raped a Cherokee girl."

Clutching her chest, she gave an anguished cry. "Not Sarah's? Oh, please…"

"No. We don't know her. A girl named Fawn, daughter of Ten-Wolves."

My mind couldn't get around the fact I'd allowed all this to happen. I wasn't sure I'd ever get rid of the guilt. If I'd taken care of business, he or I would be dead, and this thing would be over. It wouldn't be the first time I got my hands dirty. And Betty wouldn't have had to go through—whatever kind of hell that was backlighting her eyes.

"I wasn't here until late last night because I went to Judge Ritter in Mindenmines for a warrant to serve the man."

Betty stared at me for a moment and then slumped back against the table, shaking her head. "I don't know what to do. How can I fix this?"

And there was the question that churned my belly. Do we fix it? Did I want to?

"I don't know. What's done is done. We can't go back. You gave that man something you wouldn't give me. I'm having a difficult time getting around that."

She gasped and stood straight before me. "Give? I...I gave him nothing. My god, Jim. He took what he got, nothing more. And all you had to do was ask. You must know that."

We were both too old to be innocent. I could accept that. Before I could form an answer, John was standing before us. I hadn't seen him approach.

He spoke in a quiet voice, sharing a glance between us. "He's at the stable, saddling up."

I nodded. What would Rob bring to the game? Was he experienced? There's always someone smarter, someone faster, with their hands right around the corner. Would this be the time? Did it matter? There was an old saying supposedly told to King Henry's knights at the

Battle of Agincourt. *All waiting is at an end. The battle is before us, and an old man is a pitiful thing.*

"Thanks, John."

She grabbed my arm. "No! Please? Not for me. I'm not worth it. I know you're angry. I can't imagine how mad you must be. But if you must hurt someone...hurt me. I deserve it. I don't want you killed. I couldn't stand...please, Jim. Don't go. Don't risk your life for me. Don't risk anything for me!"

I looked my question at her.

"You don't know him. He's fast, Jim. I heard someone say he's all spring wire and quick as a bear trap. Dammit, he hires out to kill people. Don't you understand that? Nobody gets close to beating him. You could ask anyone around Joplin—if you want someone to die, see Rob."

I looked at her for a moment, my anger settling. Hurt her? Not in this lifetime. And his reputation? Well. He wasn't in Joplin anymore.

"It's not about you, Betty. And no matter what you've done, I could never hurt you. It's just not in me. You should know that."

Not being about her? Well, that was sort of a lie.

Glancing up the street, I saw dust settling around a group of riders. They rode their special horses, battle-trained and hardened. Not an ear twitched or a tail swatted at a fly. The men sat loose on their mounts, waiting. Red and black paint, and matching circles on the horses—rifles adorned with feathers and brass tacks, butted against their hips, and pointed to the sky. It looked like a skirmish line from a war long past. I didn't hear a sound from them, but in my mind rose the war cry of the Cherokee. They stretched ten across the road, three rows deep, chosen by rank and age, but the last man in the back row would be more of a warrior than this town wanted to handle. And if I knew the leaders, there would be a similar group at the other end of town...waiting. Not a brigade, but close enough.

———

THE STABLE WAS a few hundred feet away, and it didn't take long to get there. It was a dusty walk between buildings needing some of that zinc paint. The man was cinching his fancy saddle and making a poor job of it with a horse full of water and feed that didn't want to go anywhere. I stopped a few feet from him.

"Rob Timmerlane. You're under arrest."

He turned and pinned me with a gaze and then looked around for anyone else helping me. Seeing none, his expression was curious.

"Am I? What for?"

Dressed in black and silver, he had a red streak on one cheek. Appearing relaxed in the morning light, he had a taunting look in his eyes. His gun was in a low-slung holster in a way some dandies were sporting, with part of the front cut away for a faster draw. John was right. Fawn had painted me a picture.

Hoof beats and the squeaky wheels of a wagon came up behind me and stopped. I couldn't break my attention from the man, although footsteps approached behind me. I had no doubt Rob would back-shoot me given the chance.

John spoke up. "She is here."

I didn't take my gaze away from Rob. "Fawn, is this the man?"

After a moment, John spoke again. "She said it is."

Rob shuffled his feet, hanging his thumbs on his pistol belt while he grinned at us. "What is this? What are you trying to pull? I don't know any of these people."

I ignored him for a moment. "Fawn, I need to hear you say it. Is this the man?"

Her voice was weak but strong enough to hear. "Yes. That's him."

It was enough. I had what I needed. "Thank you, Fawn. Y'all can go on home."

The creaking wheels of the wagon faded as they moved away and then stopped. After a few moments, the street was quiet. It didn't last long. I knew people lined the boardwalk behind me. Most would know by now what this was all about as the muttering and whispers started, making a low drone of sound. I drew a deep breath and tried to relax.

"Rob Timmerlane, you're under arrest for rape and assault. Raise your hands and turn around." I wanted his pistol to stay put until I got my hands on it. I'd seen lawmen tell people to throw down their guns. But too many go off when they're dropped.

He took a wide step away from his horse, still sporting that insulting grin. "I don't think so."

I had to keep my gaze locked on him because he had his hand on his gun. "John, if you're behind me, get people out of the way."

Stray bullets have no sense of right or wrong. Innocent bystanders are often hurt. Shuffling footsteps told me some of them were moving, but I'd bet a few stayed. There are always people with more guts than sense. They'd move close to a train wreck just to see the sparks fly.

The weasel in Rob came out when he started talking. I figured he made his reputation as a backshooter, attacking from dark alleys or doorways. I'd heard of men who wanted to be known as a bad man to take credit for killings done by other people. Maybe he was one. I knew killing that man with a knife didn't take much courage. But it didn't matter. He was worried, and that trickle of sweat had to sting the scratch on his cheek.

He tried again. "It was just some Indian girl. You can't arrest me for that. Nobody cares."

I stared at him for a moment, thankful for the admission, and then spoke as much for the crowd as him. "Do you understand there's a warrant for your arrest for an assault on a woman last night and for raping a young girl yesterday? You understand all this?"

He was looking around, smiling at the crowd of people, playing it up like he was the star of a show. Maybe this was what he lived for.

"Yeah, I understand all that. So, what? None of these people would convict me of anything, and you know it."

My shrug was slow, painful with intent. "You're not going to trial."

Eyes wide, he watched me for a moment, stirring things around in his head. Finally, his eyes lit up. "It can't be the Indian. No one cares about that. It must be the woman. She's yours? Forget it. She didn't want to…I made her. For old-time's sake. She'd seen me kill a couple of whores already and was scared out of her mind. She knew the same would happen to her if she tried to call out. Besides, what's a whore to you…one way or another? That's what this is about? A whore and an Indian?"

I nodded, more to myself than him. Just for the judge's peace of mind, I had witnesses and a confession. To Rob, I might seem addled as I kept repeating his charges—clarifying where we stood. What he didn't understand was that the spectators would be my judge and jury, not his.

"You raped and beat a young girl. We all care about that. It's time to pay."

He shook his head, smiling at me. "You're going to force me to kill you, Sheriff. I don't want to. Hell, it's Sunday. It'll bring me bad luck. Maybe Betty didn't tell you, but I make my living with this pistol. Ask anyone around Joplin."

"A killer of whores and defenseless people. I'll put that on your tombstone."

I watched his eyes—saw it when he made up his mind. His hand was already on his pistol. When his elbow moved, I shot him. He backed up a step, his pistol firing into the dirt before dropping from nerveless fingers. His mouth spasmed in a rictus of surprise and pain. The horse shied away, its saddle sliding under its belly as it trotted a few feet down the street before someone caught it.

"Nobody...who are you? I never heard of..."

"You should have stayed in Joplin. There are men that could take me down without breaking a sweat—you ain't one of them."

He crumpled like a sack of potatoes, trying to stand straight. I hoped he was headed to hell, dragging his soul like a chain behind him, but that was not my decision.

The echoes of the shots had silenced everyone. After a moment, Pastor Schuler came and kneeled with Rob, doing whatever preachers do in a whispering voice, trying to comfort a soul detaching from its body.

I turned to see the Cherokee riders moving away. I don't know what I expected from their silence. Fanfare? The hoof beats of thirty horses played a syncopated, dusty rhythm as they disappeared around a corner. A man and woman sat in a two-seater buckboard, holding Fawn between them, while their driver snapped the reins over the backs of the horses. Outriders rode at the point and flanked the wagon. No finer guard could be assembled, even if the wagon carried gold. These were my friends. Most had a tough way to go, but I knew they'd be fine. They had strong families and faced their problems straight up and proud. I envied them for that.

A couple of women from town stepped off the boardwalk, their bonnets flopping in the wind. The cavalcade stopped for a moment as the women talked to Fawn and her mother, reaching out to them in comfort, and I hoped for a budding friendship. Ten-Wolves chose that moment to glance back at me with a short nod. Maybe a better kind of healing was on the way? That would solve many problems down the road.

In moments, Betty stood before me again, speaking with a hoarse voice I strained to hear because of the noise of the gunshot. For a beautiful woman, she'd cried herself into a mess. Staring at her, looking beneath the tears and smudge on her cheek from rubbing them away, the old Betty was there—the one that made me lose all sense of time while staring into her eyes. Her hand started clutching my arm and ended up rubbing my shoulder. It was like she had to touch me for reassurance that I was unhurt. She stopped just short of a hug.

"Jim, I'm so sorry. Seems I can't stop saying that. I was weak and afraid, failing the one person I'd die for. I should have told you of my past, but was afraid I'd lose you. I don't know what to do. How do I make it right? Is there any chance for us now?"

I started to laugh—I caught myself as I glanced at the body of Rob—and finally settled on a more appropriate sigh. "Well, I may have omitted telling a few things about my past too. And I should have. We're both too old and trail-worn to play the innocent."

Standing in that dusty street, I felt the need to hold on to something, like the ground beneath me was moving. I'd experienced that once in the quaking swamps of Louisiana, and I'd been scared the first time I'd stepped on one of those hummocks. Horses and men would stand still, afraid to move until someone came to lead them away.

Is that what I needed? A guide? Had I come full circle? I'd given up the life of a gunman, pledged to try to do good with my abilities. A sympathetic judge gave me a chance to do that. What I had done was an execution, plain and simple. And as the pastor said, premeditated. I knew the killer would choose to shoot it out, and I didn't give him any other choice. In the eyes of God, that was murder and one of the Shalt Nots. Was there forgiveness for that?

I knew, deep down, that Fawn was only a small part of why I made it happen. Betty held the larger portion. And pride. And anger. Seems I could hear the hammer ringing on wood as it drove more nails into my soul's coffin. I'd done the things I considered right. But justice had cost me something today. Was the price too much?

"How can I trust you, Betty? Will someone else come riding up someday? We're not married, so what you two did last night was your business. But it can't be without consequences. We had an understanding. At least, I thought we did."

"We still do, Jim. I still love you. That won't change even if you send me away." She stood a moment in thought, staring at me. "All I can say is that now that we know each other better, we can protect one another. There is no fear of you finding out hidden secrets. And it shall not happen again. I'll swear that on Pastor Schuler's Holy Bible."

Her words bounced around in my head. Intentional or not, she used the word shall. The word *shall* is a covenant, while the word *will* only states intent, leaving wiggle room for a different intent or outcome. Her statement carried weight but brought us back to trust. Lost in thought, I didn't respond fast enough, and she dropped her hands while walking away crying. I reached out to her, but it was an empty gesture—arrested in mid-thought as I dropped my hand to my side. Equal parts of anger and sadness fought for my soul. I couldn't put this off. The decision would be made today.

As if on cue, Pastor Schuler stood by me, his gaze burning as he locked onto my eyes. "You gave a lie to me this morning. I don't appreciate that. Now that it's over, can you tell me? Are you still at peace?"

Well, there was the skunk thrown through the church doors. I had no answer to give him. Two things died this day. One was a bad man who deserved what he got. And yes, I considered him a thing—not a human. Like the judge said, he was rabid, and I put him down. The other thing lost was that magical connection between two people called love, for want of a better expression. But did it have to be that way? Could we build on this shaky ground and get it back? Somehow, that old man echoed my thoughts.

He shook his head, his gaze never leaving mine. "Who did the greater sin? She broke your trust, although pushed into it by fear. You killed a man in anger, fearing the people of this town would let him go and you wouldn't be able to extract payment for what he did. Fear pushed both of your actions."

Schuler continued in a soft voice. "Jim, understand

this. If you ask forgiveness for yourself, you must forgive her. You cannot have one without the other, and you can't stand alone—neither with your soul nor your life. Don't come back to the communion table until you settle that."

I watched without passion as two men showed up and rolled the body into a tarp, lifting it into the bed of a small, two-wheeled wagon. There was enough silver on the body to take care of his burial. Neither man looked at me or spoke. Lawmen are used to that. Everyone slaps your back in friendship until you do something they cannot, something drastic that shocks them, sometimes the very thing they hire you for. Then you become as much an outlaw in their eyes as the one you protected them from.

Schuler was right.

Standing alone in that street was awkward. My mind whirled with unconnected thoughts, and my feet seemed mired in the street. A hot, fickle wind kicked up dirt that hit my eyes, peppering my face and causing me to flinch. That one instance broke my malaise.

In the distance, I could see John and Sarah standing with Betty. Sarah's arm was around her—I suppose in consolation. They turned as one and looked at me.

I don't know how long I stood in the street, but their gaze never wavered as they watched me. I waited past all reason. Most men in my position would be tipping back a brew at the local saloon or clothed in the brooding darkness and safety of a quiet place.

And still, they stood, watching.

The first step toward redemption is the hardest when you're mired in anger and self-righteousness. But I took it. The second step is easier when you've rid yourself of those encumbrances. I knew my decision was made when I realized the thoughts bouncing around in my mind would be better discussed with her. Without her forgiveness, moving forward in my life held little meaning.

We met in the center of that street with enough force to leave bruises, her hands digging into my back hard enough to draw blood. It was a small price to pay for my future.

John Proud Bear and Sarah stood close, watching us. When I looked at him, he nodded.

"Welcome home, Jim."

COMANCHE MOON

Becker smelled the dust in the air and reined his horse under the feeble shade of a twisted mesquite. He eased himself into the saddle and slowly took off his hat, wiping his brow with a faded red bandanna while looking at the earth in front of him, dimpled and churned with the passage of horses. Enough of them were unshod to have Comanche written all over them, and he cursed softly. This was their land, and he'd hoped to pass through unnoticed. The tracks pointed west, and he was headed north, so he didn't give it much thought until he noticed the heel tracks of someone being dragged on a rope behind a horse. A few feet more, and he could see where the person had regained their footing. He swung down from his horse and kneeled to study the small tracks of feet that barely sank into the churned earth. *A woman or a child.*

The more he thought of it, he knew it must be a woman. The braves would throw a child on a horse to keep from slowing them down, and the captor would be solely responsible for making them keep up. A woman would ride too, for that matter. *They must be mad at this one and not planning to take her far.*

Reading the trail was a simple thing for him. Raised by a fiddle-footed trapper and sometime wolf hunter who always wanted to see the other side of the mountain, he hadn't seen a town larger than a few adobe huts until almost grown.

Following the trail a bit, he chuckled. The woman had dug in her heels hard, and a few feet further, he saw where her captor had hit the ground. *Feisty.* He'd bet good money the Indian got tired of holding the rope and tied it around his waist. *She must have seen that and took a little revenge or tried to get away.* Right about then, he knew he had to take a hand.

An hour later, he was trailing the Indians in lengthening shadows as the sun moved toward the horizon. He figured five at most, which still didn't give him very good odds of helping the captive. And he was getting close to them, real close.

A few minutes later, he heard a short scream from ahead, an angry scream that didn't sound like there was any quit in it. Score one for the little lady. She wasn't giving up.

He eased up through the brush and saw the group in a small clearing. Four of the Comanche were laughing at her, pushing and pulling the girl between them while sharing a bottle of whiskey. A fifth worked at starting a fire. A cold knot settled in his belly. That wasn't a cookfire.

The men were too busy tossing the girl around to notice him sitting on his horse, wishing he were somewhere else. She looked Spanish or Indian, with long black hair and a petite build, incongruous in a voluminous dress that hampered every move she tried to make. But her voice was all Texas, and she was fighting mad, spitting at the men, and cursing them with every shove they gave her. One glance told him she was a fighter.

He had two choices. He could cut and run, which he figured was the smart thing to do, or try to snatch her out of there. If he shot into them from where he sat, they'd kill her and likely get him too.

Surprising himself as well as his mount, he spurred his horse into action. Not used to such treatment, the gelding fairly leaped into the clearing. Becker rushed the group with a wild yell and leaned over the saddle, reaching for the girl. She didn't need an engraved invitation, and using his arm as a pivot, she swung up behind him like a circus acrobat. They were gone in a cloud of dust, with her digging her own heels into the horse, urging it to more speed.

He could not believe they made it. *Of all the harebrained things to—*

He heard the shot from off to the side just as he felt his horse bunch under him. Urging the animal toward a buffalo wallow he saw just ahead of them, the horse suddenly went down in a loose pile of lifeless flesh and bone, and they were pitched sprawling to the ground. Rolling between a couple of prickly pear clumps and leaping to his feet, he grabbed the voluminous dress, hoping the girl was still inside it, and tossed the whole thing into the protection of the wallow. He heard her land with a muffled thump and an indignant-sounding shriek. His rifle was pinned under the horse, and his searching hand found an empty holster at his side. He ran to the horse and tried to free the rifle, with bullets thumping and whining around him. Finally, giving it up, he scrambled to the protection of the wallow.

I can't believe I did that. Becker shook his head and wiped sweat and dirt from his eyes, muttering, "Damn."

"Not too bad." Her soft voice was butter smooth, with the lazy drawl of Texas and country all rolled into one.

He looked at his rifle, trapped under the saddle on his dead horse about fifty feet away, and shook his head again in disgust. *His prized yellow boy Winchester was as far away as next year's wages.* "Dammit."

"There ya go. Put some life in it."

He could tell this young girl was laughing at him, but somehow, he didn't seem to mind. He glanced at the horse again. "Son of a—"

"Hey. Whoa, now. Let's not get carried away. I ain't that worldly."

Becker glanced at the girl's dirty-faced grin, framed by the blackest hair he'd seen this side of Mexico, and quickly revised his opinion. This brown-eyed beauty was no young girl. She was a lot of woman in a tiny package.

He took off his battered hat and edged up to the lip of the buffalo wallow. Dirt splattered into his face before he heard the shot and whine of the retreating ricochet.

"Why don't you shoot back?"

He turned and looked at her. "Lady, if I had a gun—which I don't—you'd be seeing the fanciest shootin' this side of anywhere."

"You don't have a gun?"

He could see a barely concealed smile behind her hand and heard the laughter in her voice. Trying to keep his own peevishness from his voice, he answered softly. "No. I don't have a gun. My Winchester is still on the saddle, under the horse, and I lost my pistol when those Comanche braves shot my horse out from under us. He was a damn good horse, too."

"You dropped it?" She gave up and laughed outright. "What kind of hero are you? You dropped your gun?"

"Look, lady, if you...what's your name, anyway?"

"Mandy Jakes. Pleased to make your acquaintance, Mr....?"

He eased up to the rim again, and a bullet knocked his hat, spinning it into the wallow. "John Becker, ma'am. Look, you may think this is funny, but we're kind of in a situation here."

"I assure you, Mr. Becker, I don't find this situation funny." She paused for a moment. "I find you funny."

"Well, I'm happy to be so damned entertaining. If you can keep from laughing yourself silly, you might look around for a club or something to defend yourself." He took a quick look around the wallow. "Okay, maybe a rock. I don't know what got those boys out there so riled up, but they seem just a bit unhappy. They shouldn't be trying so hard to get you back. Skinny thing like you...well, small, I mean, wouldn't make a good squaw. They like their women strong—to haul wood, do the skinning and such. Hell, you couldn't even pick up a lodgepole."

"I'm not skinny. And what kind of rescue was that, anyway? Didn't you have a plan?"

"Oh yes, ma'am." He started edging up to the rim again after retrieving his hat. "I had a plan. I had a great plan. My plan was to ride up to Kansas and maybe ride the rails. A man told me that a train could go forty miles in an hour. I didn't believe him, him being drunk and all, but I thought I'd take a look."

"I sure hope we get the chance to see. I've never seen anything like that."

He caught the tremor in her voice, looked at her cautiously, and then grinned at her. He couldn't help himself. Her humorous outlook was catching. "We? That's kind of a sudden engagement, ain't it?"

She shook her mane of black hair, and her voice turned angry, losing some of the drawl. "When that stage full of Indian fighters I was riding with took off, I figured my time was up. I sure couldn't see much of a future, except being beat with a stick every day and kept in a dirty hogan for all the...well, you know. That didn't happen, thanks to you. The way I see it, anything good that happens from now on is just gravy on the 'taters." She gave him the benefit of a full smile. "I'm thinking you're the gravy."

Before he could answer, a searching shot hit the bank behind them, and then a scattering of shots bracketed the wallow. Becker figured they were trying to keep him from looking around, and there was only one reason to do that. He pulled his heavy-bladed Bowie, wiped his sweaty hands on his shirt, and gripped it firmly. There were two things working for them. This buffalo wallow was a lot deeper than most, and from the short glance he got, all the braves looked young.

A startled bird flew up a few feet away with a thrumming beat of wings, and the first Comanche came over the rim, followed closely by two more. They must have expected to see Becker at the bottom with the girl because they missed him crouched at the rim.

The war cry of the first man over the top turned to a scream of agony as he staggered on by, trying to hold in his belly where the knife sliced through his buckskins like butter. Writhing in pain, the man fell to his knees in front of the wide-eyed girl. The second Indian was already dropping over the side and tried to bring his rifle around to fire, but Becker grabbed it with both hands and smashed it back into his teeth. The Comanche kept his grip on the rifle and came after him with a vengeance. While both men scrambled for possession of the rifle, he saw the last Indian go after the girl.

This had to end in a hurry. If he lost, not only would he die, but the girl behind him would die, or something worse. Knowing Indians generally knew little of fist fighting, he let go of his grip on the rifle and slugged the man in the belly. The brave gasped for air, and his jaw dropped open just in time to meet a looping overhand roundhouse that broke his nose. Following closely against the back-pedaling man, Becker kneed him in the groin and then jerked the rifle from nerveless fingers and fired into the man's body. Levering a new shell into the rifle, he whirled at a shot behind him and saw the last man slumped over the girl.

He came up out of the wallow just as the remaining braves decided to rush. Snap-shooting the Winchester, he peeled one off his horse and then peppered dust around the last rider as he wheeled his pony and fled.

In the silence following the short battle, a gust of prairie wind rustled the sand and brush, and he could hear the girl sobbing behind him. He leaned the rifle against his leg, took off his hat, and wiped his brow with a blue-checked handkerchief. At best, they should be dead. At worst, they could be captive. He offered a short *"Thank you, Lord."*

He turned back to the wallow and saw the girl had all but disappeared under the bulk of the dead Indian, and as he watched, her heels quit digging into the dirt and lay still.

Dropping to the bottom of the wallow, he grabbed the Indian by the hair and pulled him off the girl. She lay limp with her eyes closed. Seeing the blood covering the front of her dress, he quickly unbuttoned the front and looked for a wound. The bloody undergarment ripped apart in his hands, but he still couldn't find a wound. Her breasts contrasted white against the darker tan of her throat and the red blood on her chest. Still looking for a wound, he started to turn her over.

Her voice startled him. "You were right. That was a short engagement. Looks like you've skipped to the honeymoon."

He grudgingly lifted his gaze from her chest to her eyes. "You're not hurt?"

She rose on her elbows and looked at him warily, but made no move to cover herself. A slow smile brightened her face, and she chuckled. "Not yet."

"You're sure you're not hurt?" He used that excuse to drop his gaze to her body again.

"Yep. I'm sure. And I'm just having the greatest day." She followed his gaze, looking down at her ruined dress, and then looked at him with the first hint of tears. "I just bought this dress. It's the first I ever owned."

He fumbled at trying to pull her dress together but couldn't seem to get it right. "I guess I'd better—"

She interrupted with a very unladylike snort. "I guess you'd better."

He turned and searched the body of the Indian, but not without another glance at her. *No, not skinny*. He found a knife and then stripped the other bodies of their weapons. Sweating in the heat, he picked the bodies up and heaved them out of the wallow.

"What'd you do that for?" Semi-dressed, she stood on wobbly legs.

He reached out to steady her. "When it rains..." He paused to look around at the parched earth. "If it ever rains again, this wallow will collect water. No need in ruining it for everyone."

She looked out over the top of the wallow. "Don't the Comanche always come back for their dead?"

"Usually. But I got some lead in the one that got away. Maybe we'll get lucky and he'll bleed to death before he gets back to his camp."

Armed with a rifle and a couple of Sam Colt's cumbersome old horse pistols, he felt a little better. A nagging thought picked at his mind and finally came into full bloom. He whirled around and looked at the girl. "Wait just a minute. You had a gun?"

She held a little pepperbox derringer up for his inspection. "I only had one shot left."

"Where'd you hide that?"

"Well, they hadn't got around to pulling off my *unmentionables* and *nevershows*." She looked at him with a scowl. "They weren't near as quick about tearing my clothes off as you. Anyway, I was just waiting for the proper time, when it would do me the most good. Of course, they were working up to that notion when you came a fogging it out of the brush. That was right opportune, I don't mind saying."

"It may have been your lucky day, but I'm not too sure it was mine." His thoughts turned to the problem at hand. "You could have told me about the gun, you know. It might have made a difference."

She grinned at him. "Yeah, I can just see you holding off those Comanche with a derringer."

He had to smile back. "Well, it's more than I had to work with."

"Not much more. You seemed to be doin' a fair country job with that Bowie." She paused for a moment. "My pappy was good with a knife."

"Where did you come from, girl?"

"Oh, I was raised on a hard-scrabble ranch over

toward the Sabine. It was just Pap and me, and he sure didn't know much about raising a girl. He took off to bring some cow critters back to the home range but never came back. I gave up waiting after a month, headed to San Antonio, and picked up a job with a biscuit shooter too old to ride a chuck wagon anymore. That's about the whole story, mister."

He stood looking at her, amazed she was taking the situation so well. "Oh, that's not all of it. So, how did these Comanche happen to get you?"

"Oh, that was the easy part. That cook I worked for decided I needed to move to his house and was real insistent about it. I thought a better notion was to leave. I was riding the stage with a bunch of tinhorns and whiskey peddlers. The driver stopped to rest the horses, and the next thing we knew, the shotgun guard was down, looking like a pincushion, and we were combing Comanche out of our hair." She paused for a moment to take a deep breath. "They were looking for guns and ammunition, and maybe a little whiskey. Still, I don't think they'd have bothered us much if I hadn't shot that one."

Becker's voice was incredulous, matching his expression. "You shot one of them?"

"Hey, now. I ain't no saint, mister. But one of them started to get a little...what's that French word, amorous? I guess he thought I'd make a fine addition to his wickiup. I was in no mind to do that, so we had us a difficulty."

"A difficulty?" He paused a moment. "Did this love-struck brave have a name?"

"Yep. Of course he had a name. He thumped his chest a lot, strutted around like a rooster, and called himself Spotted Elk."

Becker just stared at her. "Spotted Elk? You killed a Comanche named Spotted Elk?"

"Mister, that Indian had more hands than a bunch of cowboys at a Saturday night fandango."

He shrugged, trying to fight off the cold feeling coursing up and down his spine. "I've heard of him. Spotted Elk was a prince of the Comanche. Real big medicine."

"He's a prince of the daisies right now."

He sighed. "That just tears it. They'll chase us from hell to breakfast."

She smiled at him. "You'll manage."

He shook his head in wonder. "So, they killed everyone and took you captive?"

"Oh, hell no. While the warriors were trying to decide what to do about their fallen chief, those four-flushing tinhorns and wannabe bad men jumped on the stage and tore out of there like their tails were on fire, leaving me standing with my petticoats flapping in the wind. It *was* a bit awkward."

Becker shook his head, trying to hide a smile. He'd been keeping watch while they talked, and he knew it was time to move. "It'll be dark soon. The one that got away will be looking to bring back some friends. You got anything against walking?"

"Well, unless it's a midnight stroll with Mr. Right, I'd just as soon have a horse. Besides, I ain't exactly dressed for marching."

He eyed the dead Comanche. "I reckon we'll have to get you some new clothes."

She glared at him and backed away. "Of all the low down…nope. Not going to do it. You can't make me wear their clothes."

"Shouldn't be too many bugs in them." He saw one of

her eyebrows arch slowly. Chuckling, he held up one hand. "Now, ma'am, you've shot enough men today."

"I can always fit in one more," she said in a menacing voice.

Becker laughed, and he hadn't laughed in a long while. "Where were you headed, Mandy?"

"Anyplace away from where I was." Her tone didn't invite any more questions.

"Well, I reckon that's where I'm headed, too."

———

THEY WAITED until full-dark before they started. He'd gone back to his dead horse, and with the girl's help, he finally freed his Winchester from under the saddle. He threw his saddlebags over his shoulder. Beyond the carcass of the horse, he caught a gleam in the fading light and retrieved his Remington handgun.

His canteen was full, but he knew it wouldn't last through the next day. Their best chance was to make it back to the stage road and catch a ride or find a way station. His saddlebag yielded jerky wrapped in oil paper, a few sulfur matches in a tube sealed with wax, and a box of cartridges that fit both his weapons.

He had an extra pair of pants and a shirt in his saddlebags, but they were hopelessly too large for Mandy. He cut the pants off at the knees and the arms out of the buckskin shirt. She consented to him cutting down a pair of moccasins taken from one of the dead Indians.

She instantly began to strip off the dress but stopped when she saw his astonished look. "Close your mouth before the bugs fly in. You've already seen my *bits*. I guess it won't hurt if you see all my *pieces*. Just think of it as one of the rewards for rescuing a damsel in distress."

"Just one?"

She gave him a long look and then resumed trying to make small clothes out of big clothes.

Later, after she had dressed the best she could, she came to him. Her voice was softly intimate as she sat close enough to rub shoulders.

"How will we be able to travel tonight? It's dark as the bottom of a well out here."

"Comanche moon," he said. "It'll be about as bright as day in a short while."

She watched him for a moment and then spoke in a serious-sounding voice. "Let's stop pretending. Did you think I wouldn't recognize your name, Marshal Becker?"

He'd just swallowed some jerky and nearly coughed it up. "What?"

"I told you, I worked tables at The Bucket restaurant in San Antonio. You know how men talk. From what I hear, it seems like a lot of men die at the places you show up." She chuckled. "Indians, too."

"Too many have died, Mandy. I'm done with all that, except for one last job. After that, I'm heading for a place I know to try ranching."

She shook her head. "He wasn't on the stage."

He turned to look at her, barely outlined against the stars. "What are you, one of those gypsy fortune tellers? You got one of those crystal balls hid out somewhere in those petticoats you took off?"

"Don't get in a snit. Everyone knows you were sweet on that girl. What's her name, Anne?"

He shook his head, and the quiet stretched out. "You're wrong. She was just a friend. A good friend, but that's all."

Mandy gave a little snicker. "Right."

"But she didn't deserve to die."

His mind flashed back to San Antonio. John Dent had killed several men, usually from the back. Most people in the town knew that Becker's job was to bring him in. Anne came to warn him that Dent was laying for him when Dent stepped out of a doorway, firing at Becker. Anne went down, and in the confusion, Dent got away.

Mandy's voice could change from cattle drive loud to boudoir soft at a moment's notice. Now, she had him leaning toward her to hear. "None of us deserve to die, Marshal. But sometimes we have to."

"Have to? What does that mean?"

It was getting lighter, and he saw Mandy give him a look that put him somewhere lower than a prairie dog and just taller than a snake.

"No matter how you felt, I'm betting you weren't just a friend to her."

"So," he said, changing the subject, "John Dent wasn't on the stage?"

"Nope, but his partner was. That Hobie guy."

Becker vented with an exasperated sigh. "And?"

"Hobie mentioned something to one of the other men about meeting Dent in Kansas."

"Where exactly in Kansas?"

"Hobie didn't say."

Becker got up suddenly and started gathering his gear.

Jumping up and matching his sudden urgency, she said. "I doubt we can get there tonight."

THEY STARTED NORTH JUST as the moon spread its bloody light over the landscape. Not as bright as day, the full moon still gave enough light to make walking easy.

"Kind of early for a planter's moon, ain't it?" Mandy panted as she tried to keep up with Becker's long strides.

"Comanche moon. Young men get all excited. Howl at the moon, make a night raid on some unsuspecting settler, steal some horses so they can buy a wife. There's no end to the fun they can have."

"I thought they didn't like to fight at night." She was trying to see behind every bush while she walked.

"If they get killed in the dark, they believe their spirit can't find their way. You'll notice it's not too dark right now. Besides, there are always a few agnostics among them."

"Agnostic? What the hell does that mean? I wasn't exactly brought up in some highfalutin' boarding school, you know?"

"Unbeliever." He slowed his pace so she could keep up.

They'd been walking for about an hour when he heard them. Grabbing Mandy's arm, he pulled her into the shadows of an outcropping of rock. Smart enough to make no sound, she crouched beside him.

Soon, the shuffling of horses traveling on soft ground came nearer, and they watched a party of Indians ride past, silent and deadly. From what Becker could see, all of them carried rifles, and their bodies looked surreal, painted white and black, ready for war. In the bright moonlight, he could see they'd decorated their warhorses with whatever symbols they thought would bring them good luck. Their silence scared him more than anything else did. Wherever they were going, it wasn't going to be pretty when they got there.

Mandy stirred beside him, and he pulled her close, holding his hand over her mouth. She settled easily into his arms and seemed content to stay there.

He waited a few minutes, making sure there weren't any stragglers, before he started to relax.

Mandy bit him.

Becker leaped to his feet with a curse, dumping the girl unceremoniously on her back. "Jesus, woman!" He held his hand up in the moonlight to look at it. "I'm bleeding. What the hell?"

She stood up and brushed off her rear. "I like being held as well as the next girl, but I couldn't breathe. Don't hold my nose next time, and I'll be more likely to cuddle." Reaching up, she pulled his hand down and inspected it. While he watched in astonishment, she put his wounded finger in her mouth and licked it clean. "Hmm. Tastes like that beef jerky you had earlier."

Ignoring a rush of emotion on several levels, he cleared his throat a couple of times before he could speak. "Deer. Deer meat."

She gave his hand back. "There you go. That'll hold you for a while. Let me know if it starts bleeding again."

Starting back on the trail, she turned and said, "Well? You gonna just stand there and let me go all alone?"

"I don't know." He stared at her for a moment. "I just might."

———

THEY WALKED until the moonlight was gone. The early morning stars were bright enough to reach out and touch, and in the distance, he could hear the night birds calling. Reasonably sure they were actual birds, he kept walking—and then fell on his face.

"John?" Mandy leaned over to look at him.

"I found the stage road." He pushed himself up and pointed to the shadowed ruts in the ground, cut by the iron-clad iron wheels of the stagecoach.

"I knew you could..." Her voice dwindled away as they heard shooting carried in the wind. They waited a few moments and then heard another volley, followed by a few raggedly spaced shots. The last round seemed to be closer.

"We have to find a place to fort up, Mandy. Right now."

Though the sun was not up, there was just enough light in the predawn to see. She pointed up the trail toward a jumble of boulders. "There."

"You got cat eyes, girl." His voice was ragged as they jogged to the formation of rocks. "This'll work just fine."

Once they were behind the protection of the rocks and were watching in the direction the shots came from, she spoke softly. "What's got you spooked, John? What are you thinking?"

"Those shots we heard were in a volley. Disciplined firing. That means those Indians ran into an army patrol."

"Good. Why don't we head that way?"

He looked at her, shaking his head. "Those Comanche won't stand up to a pitched battle with the army. They're not stupid."

"But—"

"Mandy, those Indians are going to come back down this trail, and they are going to be mad. Real mad."

"So, we're in trouble."

"Lady, we've been in trouble since I first laid eyes on you. This is just another chapter in the book."

"Don't let them take me, John." Her voice broke, and

then she looked fiercely at him. "I was going to do it before…before you rescued me. I had the gun. But I hesitated, and then they were all over me, and I never had a chance." She shook her head. "Don't leave it up to me."

He looked at her in the morning light, and his heart ached with wanting. She stood there in a cut-down shirt, pants twice her size, a raggedy pair of ill-fitting moccasins, and so much hair she'd never need a hat. In a moment of startling clarity, he realized she represented everything he wanted—hearth and home, children, and a woman to walk beside him.

For a moment, he couldn't speak, and she watched him with a small smile on her face. And that eyebrow thing. He reached out and pulled a piece of cedar from her hair. "They'll not take you, Mandy." He took a deep breath. "Not while I'm alive."

She reached out and touched him, her hand flat on his chest. "Are we having a moment here?"

He shrugged. "It's that damned Comanche moon. They call it a planting moon. Or a marrying moon."

She laughed, rose on her tiptoes, and kissed him lightly on the lips. "Well, I can't say you're just real quick on the uptake. I had this figured out since you threw me into that buffalo wallow. This ain't a land for long courtships and romantic speeches."

When he started to take her in his arms, she stopped him. "Now, I'm not above doing some planting and fertilizing the next time that moon comes out, but right now, you'd better look out yonder."

Becker whirled and grabbed his rifle. Loping toward them on lathered horses, the Comanche warriors carried wounded men in front of them, and several riderless horses followed behind.

Seeing their tracks in the loose dirt of the road, the

band of riders stopped, looking toward the rocks Becker and Mandy stood behind. After a moment, he moved out into the open. One of the men, clearly the leader by his stature, rode slowly toward him. They stood looking at each other for a moment, and then Becker put his rifle in the crook of his left arm. Holding his right hand flat with the ground, he motioned them away.

"Go in peace. I'm not your enemy."

There was no sound, except for a whispering footfall when Mandy came to stand beside him.

Finally, the warrior spoke. "Is this the woman who killed Spotted Elk?"

"Yes," both answered at once and then looked at each other.

The Indian nodded and said mildly. "I should kill her."

"Not going to happen. Besides, killing us won't help you."

The Indian gave what might have passed for a smile. "This is your woman?"

Before he could answer, Mandy interjected. "I am."

The man shook his head. "If we let you live, you must promise to raise your children far from here. We have enough trouble. Go in peace. Spotted Elk was a fool."

The man raised his arm, and the band at his back moved off down the trail. He stopped and turned back. "Your name?"

"Becker."

"I will remember your name, white-eye Becker. You are much man, for this woman to choose you. Somehow, you must find your own voice." The man smiled this time. "The warrior woman cannot speak for you always."

When they left, two horses remained, tied to a mesquite.

"I can't believe they let us go."

Becker laughed. "Don't put too much nobility into that. It probably had more to do with the army patrol coming up behind them. We're forted up pretty good. Although they could have made it bad for us. They left the horses so we'd come out, and the army patrol would have to deal with us. They can't leave us out here."

"That's pretty smart." She stood close enough to breathe his air. "What now, John?"

"Well, I thought I'd want to go to Kansas, but somehow, that doesn't seem too important now."

"You a marrying man, John?" She watched him closely, and he could see the start of a tear in her eyes. He realized this was as close as she would ever come to showing fear.

He chuckled and brought her to him. "I'd be honored."

She relaxed then and leaned her head against his chest. "I'll need some proper clothes. I don't have a dowry. All I have to offer is right in front of you." She leaned back and gave him a quick smile. "And you've seen most of that."

"Then we'd better be finding a sky pilot. That moon's going to be coming up pretty damned quick."

STAGE TO ABILENE

The stage was a dusty whirlwind as it careened along the road, two days from Abilene. Grizzled and wrinkled from age and years of throwing his tough old face into the wind, Frank Drummond shifted his cud of chewing tobacco, stretching his left cheek to impossible proportions as he eyed the figure standing in the road ahead. He started to spit an amber stream over his left shoulder, then abruptly changed his mind and aimed it into the soiled can at his feet. If he spit over the side, it would blow back into the passengers, and that'd about got him shot once.

Frank turned to yell a warning at his shotgun guard, but Miguel was already alert to the figure waiting for them. The guard held his rifle casually, but the business end accurately tracked the stranger in the road as the stage ground to a stop.

There was silence for a moment as the dust chasing the stage caught up with them. Both men riding on top of the stage watched warily as the man lowered his head to let the dust go on by. Slim-hipped and wide of shoulder, the stranger held his forty-pound Texas saddle on one shoulder while his right hand held a new Henry repeating rifle. Frank noticed the man's typical cowhand dress was a little better in quality than most, the boots hand-tooled and solid black. A black gun belt held a Navy Colt in a tied-down holster whose walnut grips were worn smooth with use.

The old stage driver knew the signs and knew the look. The Kansas plains of 1870 were awash with castoff and battle-scarred veterans of war, cattle wars and arguments over water and land rights just as deadly. Ranchers were building barbed wire kingdoms, jealously trying to hold huge amounts of range land, and men were dying. Hired warriors were common occurrences along the Chisholm Trail, and the word *Gunman*, a term being idolized by the newspapers and dime novels produced back East, was on everyone's lips.

The dust swirled on past, and the man's gray eyes came up from under the brim of his hat. Frank saw his face at the same time his eyes caught the glint of the star pinned on his shirt. He had to adjust his first impression —but not by much, but enough to bring a smile to his face.

"Jesus, Gawd. Matthew Bodine! Thought you was over in the Nation."

"Been a while, Frank." Matt dumped his saddle on the ground and grinned at the two men on the box. "I could use a ride."

"What happened to your horse? Injuns?" Frank was turkey-necking all around, trying to see if any hostiles were about.

"Gopher hole. Half a day south of here."

"Nice day for a walk." The accented voice of Miguel Franco was soft and musical.

Matt glanced at the Mexican, noting the familiar way the man handled his weapon. "Not really." He tossed his saddle into the boot at the back of the stage and walked around to one of the side doors. Stopping on the shady side, where he could see into the stage, he paused to look at the passengers. One by one, he met their eyes, and they could see in their reflections—assessments made—opinions cataloged.

Frank came up from behind. "We'll squeeze you in somewhere, Marshal."

"I can ride on top if there's no room. Wouldn't want to crowd anyone."

"Nonsense," one of the women inside replied, "we'll make room."

Matt glanced back into the stage, and his eyes lingered on the woman. He'd thought he knew the voice, and her face confirmed it.

Frank's gruff voice interrupted his thoughts.

"We better get goin', folks." The matter settled, the old stage driver was already climbing back onto the coach. "There's a rest stop about an hour ahead. Be some shade and water. Then we'll push on to Baxter's Crossing."

As Matt leaned back in the seat and pulled his hat down over his eyes, he heard the old bull-whacker pop his twelve-foot blacksnake whip over the eight horses pulling the coach. Frank Frank was a tough old man and had been a lot of things, at least to hear him tell it, but so far, Matt hadn't seen any indication that he was a stage driver. Not unless bouncing his passengers to death was a prerequisite. The careening coach made sleep impossible, and everyone was covered in a fine white dust.

Still, Matt surmised, it was better than walking. He

just hoped his back would last until the night stop at Baxter Crossing.

"Mr. Bodine?"

Matt focused his attention on the woman across from him. "Ma'am."

"You're a peace officer?"

Matthew Bodine III took his left hand and lifted the lapel of his vest. The silver star pinned to his shirt was engraved US Marshal. It also revealed the butt of a second pistol, set for a cross-draw and never far from his hand.

A man sitting across from him leaned over to shake his hand. "I'll introduce you around, Marshal. You've been talking to Mrs. Prescott." He pointed to a man next to him. "This is G. W. Rourke—going to Abilene to buy cattle. My name's Quinn. I sell dry goods to mercantile stores."

Matt held Quinn's eyes for a moment, debating whether to challenge the obvious slur to the woman who hadn't been mentioned. She was sitting beside Matt, and Quinn hadn't even looked at her. Probably couldn't see her around his long Puritan nose. Sighing, Matt decided not to push it.

He didn't need to be told about Annie Holt. When he'd recognized her, a flood of memories had come back to him. A small smile came to his lips as he glanced at her. A few more miles were showing since the last time he'd seen her, but she was still a beautiful woman. Somehow, she was the only one of them who looked unaffected by the blistering heat and dust. Turning slightly toward her, he asked, "How are you, Annie?"

She looked at him, startled for a moment, gratefulness seeping into her soft brown eyes.

"Tolerable," she said dryly. "Just tolerable."

"Who's the Mex riding shotgun up top?" Matt asked.

"Couldn't be better," Quinn replied, not giving Annie a chance to answer. "It's Miguel Franco. No one will buy trouble with him riding guard."

Matt was still looking at Annie, ignoring for the moment the man's reply. She smiled softly and shrugged her shoulders, turning back to look out the other window.

Finally...Matt said, "Heard of him."

"What brings you here, Marshal? Are you going to Abilene?" Mrs. Prescott was at him again.

Matt glanced at her, then at the ring on her hand. Her white-blond hair was piled high in curls and ringlets, her dress buttoned tightly at the collar. Young and pretty, too young to be a widow and old enough to know better, she didn't hide the sudden interest she had in the marshal. A little close between the eyes, Matt thought. He'd had a horse like that once.

"Warrant," he replied. "Man, I want to see is supposed to be in Abilene."

"You're from the Indian territory, Marshal?" Mrs. Prescott asked. "It's not often one of the judge's men get over this far into Kansas."

Matt's quick eyes pinned the woman to her seat. "You make a study of marshals, ma'am?"

Before Mrs. Prescott could reply, Annie interrupted.

"Who's your warrant for?"

"Texas Red Wyrick." Matt's voice was flat, but his eyes were questioning.

"Jesus." Annie's voice was subdued. Her gaze lingered on his face momentarily. Her eyes went from speculation to curiosity and finally settled on sadness. With a slight negative shake of her head, she returned to looking at the scenery outside.

Complete silence permeated the coach. All had heard of Texas Red. Up with the trail herds from Texas, and all the bad ones always seemed to be *up from Texas*, he was known as one of the fastest gunfighters around. Some said he was even faster than Earp or Hickok. In Annie's part of town, he was known as a pig. He was as unscrupulous and profane as he was dirty. He took whatever he wanted and challenged anyone to defy him.

Finally, Rourke cleared his throat. "He's been cuttin' quite a swath around Abilene. Heard he's killed four men in the last month. I even heard he faced down Wild Bill himself." Rourke was taking in the marshal with new and skeptical eyes. "You going to team up with the town sheriff to try to get him—maybe get together a posse?"

"Who is the sheriff?"

"It's Tom Smith, Matt." Annie didn't turn from looking out the window.

"Bear River Tom?"

"Sounds like you know him," Quinn interjected.

Matt wondered if Quinn would ever shut up as he answered tersely. "Nope. Just know of him. From what I've heard, he won't last. I figure on talking to him, but I won't be asking for volunteers." Matt pinned Rourke with a steady look. "Mister, I wouldn't be spreadin' around that story about Texas Red. James never backed up for anybody and isn't likely to."

"Who?" Quinn's voice was puzzled.

"James Butler Hickok. Wild Bill," said Matt. "From what I hear about Abilene, he may even be your next marshal. If he hears that story, he's sure going to be wondering where it came from."

"It's just talk. No harm to it." Rourke tried to shrug it off.

"Your funeral."

"Whoa up there!" The voice of the stage driver penetrated the conversation in the coach. Looking out, Matt could see a grove of trees ahead.

"We'll rest the horses for a half hour, folks," Frank yelled at them from on top of the coach. "Better get out and stretch."

———

THE STAGE DRIVER was busy watering the horses from a couple of buckets he'd filled from the creek, losing half the water as he sloshed and cursed his way back to the stage. He was carefully watching how much he let each horse drink when he heard Quinn's nasal voice addressing Rourke. "All them women should be run out of the country..." It was obvious who they were talking about, so Frank walked around the horses and interrupted. The old stage driver had covered a lot of ground in his time, and not all of it was easy, so he liked to avoid trouble whenever he could.

Walking up close to the men to try and keep from being overheard by the other passengers, Frank stared at Quinn until the man's voice faded away.

"Mr. Quinn, is this your first trip out West?" Frank's voice was patient.

"Why, yes, it is," said Quinn.

"Then let me try and keep you from being killed." He glanced at the cattle buyer. "I'm surprised at you too, Rourke. You're a western man, and you know we don't speak slighting of our womenfolk out here. We show them respect."

Quinn laughed loudly. "Respect? For a—"

"For a what?" Matt had come up on the other side of

the men. "For a what, mister? Are you about to call someone a name?"

Quinn stuttered rapidly. "Well, just what everyone knows. I mean, that Holt woman works in a saloon, don't she?"

Matt reached out casually with a big hand and slammed Quinn up against the coach. Quinn knew this was the West—knew he was expected to fight back and defend himself, but it was also Quinn's first good look into Matthew Bodine's eyes, and something inside Quinn seemed to fold up and set down.

"Let me tell you what everyone knows about Annie Holt, Mr. Quinn. She was dumped out here on the prairie when she was just a little girl. She survived that, and she's made it on her own since then. Maybe not the way most folks would, but then most folks would have died. She did it all by herself, with no help from anyone.

"A couple of years back," Matt continued in a low voice, "cholera broke out on the Missouri-Kansas border at a town called Mindenmines. Miners were dying like flies. People left that place in droves. But two or three didn't, Mr. Quinn. One of them who stayed was Annie Holt. She stayed and nursed about fifty of those miners back to health. She fed them and took care of them, risked her life for them. Now those miners think a lot of that girl, and their friends do too, so you'd best not talk down on her. You just never know who's going to be listening. She's good people, and don't you ever forget it." Matt stood staring at the man for a few more seconds. "Is that clear?"

———

A FEW MINUTES LATER, Matt was standing down by the creek when he heard a light step behind him.

Annie stopped beside him and stood looking out over the water. "I heard what you said back there. I'm not sure you're entirely right, but thanks anyway."

Matt shrugged his shoulders. "It was all true, Annie. Folks are grateful. I'm grateful, and I think you'll find that most people who count are on your side."

She looked over to where Mrs. Prescott was talking to the cattle buyer. "Not everyone is."

Matt turned and looked. Smiling, he said. "What do you know? She's giving up on me already." He turned his steady gaze on Annie. "I said the folks that count, not people like her. Why go back to Abilene, Annie? You've surely got some money set by. Even if you don't, I know many a man who'll give you a stake with no strings attached. Why don't you just walk away? Find some cowpoke and make him happy the rest of your life."

"You think I could?" Annie's voice was skeptical. "Just that easy? I've surely thought about it, but I'm always afraid to try." She glanced up at him. "Anyway, who'd want a retired dancehall floozy?"

He was about to answer when Miguel called from the top of the coach. "Marshal, we got company."

Matt turned to see who was coming and felt a cold knot start in his stomach. Easterners were always asking how to tell the difference between a wild Indian and a tame one. At that time, back east, there were people who hadn't seen anything wild, much less an Indian. They did their jobs during the day, then at night, went to music concerts, strolled along the boardwalks, and tipped their hats to the constable on the corner.

Wild Indians? Some people would say there is no difference. Those people had never seen the Kiowa,

Sioux, or Cheyenne in their own domain. The old-timers would say you feel the difference in your gut. It's the same feeling you get when you're pushing through thick brush and come face-to-face with a mountain cougar or prairie rattler. Matt had that feeling now—that cold knot in his belly—knowing that what he would say and do in the next few minutes could mean life or death for all of them.

Sitting on their horses about fifty yards out into the prairie were three Kiowa. Straddling their ponies like the princes of the plains that they were, they sat loose-jointed and relaxed—and painted for war. Their faces were streaked with red and yellow, and the horses each rode were painted with circles and dots. The horse's manes were decorated with bits of bone, feathers, and medicine bags. Two of the Indians had rifles, and the one in front carried a lance adorned with fresh scalps and eagle feathers. These men were neither downtrodden nor apt to beg. This was their land, and they would control every inch of it.

As the rest of the passengers converged on the stage, Matt told them, "No shooting, unless they start it, but I want every gun we have in plain sight. We're in a bad spot here." Matt looked curiously at the trio. Since they hadn't laid an ambush and simply killed them all, he knew they wanted something. All he had to do was find out what it was without getting killed in the process.

As the three Indians rode closer, Matt stepped out to meet them. They drew up in front of him, and he got his first good look at the leader. His blood ran cold. Matt didn't know if it was good luck or bad that he knew him. Wild Pony hadn't agreed to any treaties and refused to be carted off to a reservation. A few years ago, he'd left a trail of bodies and burned ranches from Texas to the Missouri River.

In the fleeting moments before he spoke, Matt remembered the first time he'd met with Wild Pony. It was in the panhandle country of Texas, and he was forted up in a buffalo wallow with four other cowhands. They'd been busting strays out of the thickets when they were jumped by a band of Kiowa. The cowhands were young, and so were the bucks. The first volley of gunfire had netted nothing for either side. Had the young Kiowa been with older warriors, it would have been a lot different.

The wranglers made it to the natural fortress of a buffalo wallow, all carrying brand-new Henry repeaters and saddlebags full of ammunition. The Kiowa were stubborn—to return home without scalps would be a disgrace—but so were the cowhands.

The battle had lasted all day, with a last-ditch charge by the Kiowa with the sun at their backs. After the dust and gun smoke had settled, two men were left standing. Wild Pony came walking out of the dusty sunset, carrying a slain warrior over his shoulder. Matt rose from the buffalo wallow, half-dazed from a bullet graze along his scalp. Both men were startled to see each other and simply stared—too tired to do anything else. Wild Pony had finally broken the silence.

"It is a battle to be remembered. Many brave men died today. It is enough."

Later, they'd each helped bury the other's dead. The Kiowa on raised platforms, facing the rising sun—the cowboys as deep in the ground as the hard-packed earth would allow.

Matt went to sleep from exhaustion. When he woke the next morning, the Kiowa were gone. Matt's weapons were lined up next to his ground sheet. Wild Pony could easily have taken the weapons and killed Matt while he slept, but he hadn't. Afterward, they'd crossed paths a few times, but had never fought again.

Matt raised his left hand, palm out. His right was resting on his pistol, a fact not missed by the trio of Indians. "Wild Pony is a long way from his lodge. It is good that you come to this shade and water as friends. You are welcome here." The Kiowa looked mildly surprised as Matt addressed them in their own language.

The Kiowa chief looked stonily at Matt for a moment, then replied in English. "The Kiowa will hunt where he wishes. If my lodge is here, then this is my home." A small glint of humor came to the warrior's eye. "The marshal is also far from his home. What does he do on Kiowa land?"

He pointed west. "In the town where cattle are sold is a man I must see. He is wanted by the law and must be punished."

"White man's law?" Wild Pony's voice was scornful.

Matt shrugged his shoulders. "Wild Pony is painted for war. I see in the distance his men are ready to take up the knife." At this statement, the passengers whirled to look at the hills behind them. "Why is Wild Pony ready to break the treaty his brothers have agreed to?"

The Kiowa spoke angrily. "The Cherokee and the Kansa are old women who hide their faces when we come. They sit on their blankets and wait for the White Father to feed them and give them clothes. Our young warriors want to join forces with the Dog Soldiers of the Cheyenne. Together, they hope to keep the whites from our land."

"Then why does the Kiowa wish to speak with me?"

"When I saw you were here, I stayed the hands of my

warriors. They have not seen the numbers of the white man as I have. They think if they kill the whites that are on our land, no more will come. They are foolish, but they are young and will be mighty in battle before they die." The Kiowa spat on the ground. "Soldiers came to our village while we were on a hunt. They burned our homes and took some of our women away. We found the women later. Dead. The soldiers who did this ran away to hide in their fort. The Kiowa is patient. We will wait until they come out. Then we will kill them."

Matt's anger seethed, and he inwardly cursed the army. Of all the idiotic things to do. After a moment, he spoke to the Indian. "Wild Pony knows me. We have fought against each other in battle. You know my words are true. I have never lied to you."

"Wild Pony knows this."

"Then hear me. What Wild Pony believes in his heart is true. The whites will keep coming. They hunger for land so they can grow their crops and raise cattle and horses. These are the ones who will defeat the Kiowa. For each one you kill, two will take his place."

"The soldiers have done a bad thing," Matt continued, "but if you kill the soldiers, it will only make more trouble for you and your people. Your act of revenge would be your death song. It is even possible this bad thing was done to make you angry—to make you do something foolish so the government can take away your lands again and send the soldiers against you. Hear me, Wild Pony. Take your warriors and go home. Move your village farther away toward the sun, so you will be hard to find. I will take care of the soldiers."

"White man's law will not punish them."

"I cannot speak for all places or all people. But here, I am the white man's law. There are no courts here. You have spoken to me. It is enough. If you give me time, I will punish them."

Wild Pony turned and pointed toward his men. "Many of my braves want to take your hair. They are angry and seek revenge. I am their chief and have stopped this. I will bring your words to them." The Kiowa spoke directly to Matt again. "You know I am only the war chief. They do not have to listen to me. Some among them may come against you and test your strength."

"It is the way among warriors. It is their right to come and taste our bullets and blades." Matt spoke without taking his gaze from the chief. "Miguel, I have heard you are very good with that rifle. How far away would you say that herd of pronghorns is from here? Six, seven hundred yards?"

Miguel, too, had noticed the curious antelope. "Nearer nine hundred."

"How about you drop one," Matt drawled as his eyes held those of Wild Pony.

Miguel slowly lifted his rifle, not wanting the Kiowa to mistake his intention. The crack of the rifle startled the horses, and the two Indians with the Kiowa chief quickly turned to see. The herd of pronghorns was up and running, leaving one kicking on the ground. Wild Pony's eyes had not left those of Matthew Bodine.

"Take the meat to your lodges and feed your women and children," Matt told him. "Tell your warriors the deaths of their people will be avenged. When I have done this, I will come to your village to share the pipe and talk with the medicine drums."

The Kiowa chief sat on his horse for a long minute. His thoughts were traced by the fleeting expressions on his face. Finally, nodding his head at Matt, Wild Pony whirled his horse and rode away.

————

THE PASSENGERS WERE LOADED, and the coach was again bouncing down the road toward the night stop at Baxter's Crossing. Matt Bodine had stayed on top of the coach, keeping a watchful eye toward the hills.

G. W. Rourke broke the silence inside the coach. "That marshal is quite a talker. You seem to know him, Miss Holt? Can he fight as well as he talks?"

Annie Holt looked across at the cattle buyer. "Don't ever try him, Mr. Rourke. I've been around a lot of places and seen a lot of good men. Some who claimed to be gunmen, although the really good ones don't strut it around. I've never seen anyone like Matt Bodine."

"You sound as if you admire the man." Mrs. Prescott's voice carried scornfully across the coach. "He's nothing more than a hired killer himself."

"Mrs. Prescott, you're new to the West. You'll learn that things are different out here. Generally, men and women can be just as good or bad as they want to be. The good people try to build something for the future, and the bad ones? Well, there's nothing to stand in their way, except men like Matt Bodine. You always hear about Wild Bill or the Earp brothers, Goodnight and Masterson. But for every one of the famous gunfighters you hear about, there are more that you never hear of, men who don't seek a reputation and just do their jobs. Matt Bodine wasn't given the marshal's job because of his knowledge of the law, Mrs. Prescott, he was given the job because he's fast and tough. If you're looking to find a constable on every street corner, like it is back East, you're going to be sorely disappointed."

"The civilized way would be to talk these matters out, Miss Holt. Surely, even the savages can be reasoned with."

"Of course they can." Annie tried to keep the contempt from her voice. "But only from a position of strength. You may have noticed the marshal kept his hand on his gun all the time he was talking to the Kiowa. That was a message to them, just like having Miguel shoot the antelope. The Kiowa are the greatest hunters on these plains, Mrs. Prescott. Do you think we had to supply them with meat? The marshal wanted them to know how far away we could start killing them before they got in range with their weapons."

"If he's so good with a gun, I'm surprised he bothered to talk his way out of this at all."

Annie Holt looked at her—astonished. "Mrs. Prescott, only a fool starts trouble with Indians."

———

AN OPPRESSIVE LATE-AFTERNOON heat was still hanging on when the coach pulled into Baxter's Crossing. The air was still, and the dust hung in small clouds around the buildings and corrals—shot through with golden streaks from the low-hanging sun. A young boy ran out of the barn and immediately began unhooking the horses, leading them first to water, then to the corral for a rubdown.

Matt was the last to leave the coach. Stepping down into the dusty lot, he took off his hat and slapped at his pants and shirt to try and rid himself of the dust. He thought the passengers had all gone inside until he heard a quiet chuckle behind him.

"Won't do you much good," Annie said. "You're just making more dust."

Matt grinned at her. "I'd just jump in the creek, but all this dust would turn to mud, and I'd sink like a stone."

"More likely you'd just dry up all the water," she said lightly.

Matt leaned against the stage, knowing she hadn't come to him for idle chatter. She was skirting around something that was bothering her.

"I know Texas Red. We'd been together some before I left Abilene, Matt. I wanted you to know that."

"You're his girl?"

"He might think so."

"That doesn't answer the question."

"No. I'm not his girl. Never was, really." Her chin came up, and she looked at him steadily. "But I was with him. I stayed too long with him." Her face turned sad as she reflected inward for a moment. "He uses people, Matt. He hurts them, and then he laughs at them. And after he's through, he discards them."

"I've heard that." Matt's voice was puzzled. "So what's the message?"

"Just this. He knows you're coming. Not you in particular, but someone. I don't know how, but he does. He's waiting for you, and he won't be alone. He'll have help."

Matt sighed, suddenly feeling tired to the bone. "Yeah, seems like they always do."

"Then don't go. Just let him be, Matt. Someday he'll come to the Territory. You can get him then."

"Trying to protect him?" Matt was getting angry, and he didn't really understand why. Or maybe he did...

Annie turned away from him, then turned back. "I've seen him fight, Matt. He's all spring steel and leather. I've never seen anything so fast. It's like he keeps all his energy bottled up inside, then it just busts loose and explodes!"

"I'll keep that in mind."

"Then keep this in mind, Matt Bodine. How long have you been doing this? Ten years? Longer? How many bullets have you taken? More than the three that I know of? What's the odds, Matt? When's it going to happen? How long before the day comes that you'll be a shade too slow, or you slip on a rock just as you draw? You've been at this too long, Matt. The odds are getting bad." Annie stood looking at him, shaking her head. "And you think I should start a new life?"

Matt just stared at her. Finally... "I don't know, Annie. Maybe I just don't worry about it. Besides, if I go down, do you know how much difference it will make? Like pulling your finger out of the water and trying to see the hole you left."

Annie Holt watched him walk away, knowing deep frustration and sudden longing. She didn't want him to die. He was a good man and one of the few who didn't look down their noses at her. Most people knew she worked in saloons. What they didn't know was that she wasn't one of the girls made available to everyone for a price. She gambled with the men, cajoled them, made them buy drinks from the house—sometimes at double the price. But, in her way, she had her pride too. Her jaw tightened with resolution. He was too good a man to die at the hands of Texas Red Wyrick.

———

THE NOONDAY SUN WAS BOILING, and the world had turned one click into the afternoon. Marshal Matt Bodine was forking a chair in front of the L. Sammis Mercantile, hoping to stay on for the ride in the only shade offered on the main street of Abilene. Leaning back on his cane-bottomed mount, he surveyed the bustling street of the busiest cattle town in the West. Just this morning, he'd heard someone say the Kansas Pacific Railroad had packed over a hundred twenty-thousand head of cattle out of here in one year. That was a lot of beef.

His eyes were on constant alert as he absent-mindedly rubbed the back of his neck. He'd sprung for a shave and haircut and paid his buck and two-bits, but now his neck itched. That barber should have sharpened his razor a little more.

Matt was waiting. When he arrived in town, he'd cleaned his guns, then got a good night's sleep. Early this morning, he'd checked in with Bear River Tom and showed him his warrant for Texas Red Wyrick.

"No business of mine" was the town sheriff's only comment. "You want him, you can have him."

It was well past noon when Matt saw Texas Red come out of a saloon up the street, step precisely to the center of the dusty street, do a left-flank, and begin walking toward him. Texas Red was a tall man, well set up and wide through the shoulders. His petulant face was partly hidden in the shadow of the high-peaked Texas hat pulled low on his forehead. Walking slowly toward Matt, his Spanish spurs punctuating each step, he was a man who knew everyone was watching—and liked it—and preened for it. Every step he took was a practiced move to make himself look good to the crowd.

Matt shook his head, sighing to himself. It looked like Texas Red had been reading too many dime novels about gunfights. Have it your way. Levering himself out of the chair, Matt slipped the thong off his Colt and stepped out into the street. He wasn't worried about Texas Red. At least, not yet. Texas Red could be counted on to do his talking first and shooting later.

Matt's eyes were searching the crowd and shifting to the windows in the buildings lining the street. He didn't like it. There were too many people—all wanting to see who got killed—eager to see the blood. Mixed in the crowd would be Texas Red's hole card...or cards. How many men would he have?

"It doesn't have to be this way, Red." Matt's voice carried easily along the street. "You can come peaceably, and we'll go see the judge."

"The Hanging Judge?" Red Wyrick laughed. "Not likely. Won't be any lawman taking me in, least of all you. You never saw the day. Man, I've watched the best of them! Hardin, Hickok—I'm faster than any of them. And, if you were any good, I'd have heard of you." Texas Red looked at him scornfully. "I just ain't never heard of you, lawman!"

"Then I guess it's time."

"You called it." Red's hand was streaking for his gun, the same malicious smile on his face that he wore all the time.

No one saw Matt Bodine draw. Some claimed he must have had the gun in his hand all the time—although they hadn't seen it. But in the still noon air, in the quiet of a hundred indrawn breaths, they did hear a sibilant whisper of gun metal clearing hard leather. Matt's Colt fired one time, and then, before the echo had started down the street, he whirled at a sudden movement to his left. An unkempt, bearded man had his pistol just half out of its holster...and was staring into the bore of Matt's Colt. Slowly, the man took out the pistol, dropped it to the boardwalk, and raised his hands. As Matt slowly started to relax, he was startled to hear a shot behind him.

Whirling in desperation, Matt saw a man stagger from the crowd. Taking two steps, the man fell full length into the dust. Behind him, he saw Annie calmly putting a small revolver back into her purse. Their eyes met for a moment across the open space of the street, then she turned and walked away.

Frank Drummond stood at the door of the saloon, sipping his beer. Miguel disgustedly dug into his pocket for a silver dollar and handed it to Frank. The old stage driver laughed. "Miguel, I love to take your money."

Miguel laughed ruefully. "Between you and staking that girl to a couple of horses, I don't have any money left. Say, didn't I see her talking to you, too?"

Frank cursed softly, then grinned. "That gal hit me up for a loan, too. Guess she was bettin' on the same man as me."

The street was suddenly full of people, all trying to crowd around the marshal and shake his hand. Matt shouldered them off and walked toward Texas Red. The man Annie had shot was lying in a tangled heap—half on the boardwalk. It was obvious he'd never bother anyone else. Red Wyrick was lying on his face, the ground around his mouth painted red. Matt didn't have to look. He knew where he'd placed the bullet. Giving Texas Red's body only a cursory glance and continuing on down the street toward the stable, he saw two horses being led out.

As Matt came up to her, Annie shrugged and smiled. "Thought you'd need a horse to go with your saddle."

Matt smiled. "I count two horses."

"You said a girl could start over. Two could try that, Matt." Annie's soft brown eyes were brimful of unshed tears, waiting for an answer.

"Why, Annie, I think you may be right."

"What about Wild Pony?"

"I made a promise. I'd not go back on that."

"No, you wouldn't," Annie said. "I wouldn't expect you to."

Matt gently raised her chin with his hand, then kissed her for a long time. When they finally broke apart, Mrs. Prescott was standing there watching them.

"Well, I never!" she said as she flounced away.

"No, ma'am. Likely not." Matt's voice was cool as he mounted his horse and followed Annie down the street.

THE LAST WARRANT

A column of smoke and the hope of a good meal led Marshal Luke Randall toward a flat-roofed building sitting on the prairie, with nothing around it but a pole corral and water trough. Drying racks set up next to the cabin told him it was a trading post, although the only thing locally he could think of to trap would be muskrats and maybe squirrels. One of the racks held coyote and fox pelts. Guess that's why he wasn't a trapper. He'd starve.

It was common for places like this to crop up every few miles in the Indian Nation or Oklahoma Territory. Folks were divided on what to call this part of the country.

He rode up to the store with a prisoner in tow and tied to the horse behind him. Lem Hawkins wasn't a bad man, just not particular about ownership when he needed a horse. To give him credit, he'd come along peacefully when found. Most would have fought it out, knowing a hanging was possible for stealing a horse.

Naturally, Lem would try to escape, given any chance, and probably take Luke's horse with him.

As they stopped, a couple of dusky men dragged a body from the ramshackle building made of mud and saplings. A cookfire burned inside but didn't need a chimney. There were enough holes in the roof to let the smoke out. A piece of canvas sufficed for a door and wouldn't last any longer than the building in the next windstorm.

"What's happened here?" The Indians ignored his question, not unusual for the place and time. Whites weren't well-liked in the territory, especially those who wore a badge. The men looked Choctaw, but he wasn't sure. Their long hair was braided and stuffed under flat-crowned hats, both with a single feather. Other than that, they looked like any other cowpoke loitering around a store. Everyone dressed about the same, and the tribes mingled freely.

Finally, one of the men gave him a sour expression. "Taking out the trash."

Luke dismounted with a grunt, his hands at the small of his back, trying to stretch the kinks out. He pointed at Lem. "You stay put. If I so much as hear your horse pass wind, I'll come out shooting."

Shaking his head, the horse thief grinned and hooked a leg over the pommel of his saddle. "Go do your duty, Marshal. Bring me back a biscuit or something. I'm hungry."

Inside the dim interior, another dead man lay on the floor with his pockets turned inside out. Luke leaned on a counter made of rough-cut planks laid across wooden crates. Looking closer, he decided to put his elbows some other place. Fresh pelts graced one end, and they were leaking.

The same two men came in and grabbed the body, one man to a leg, and dragged it out the door—head thumping as it went across the threshold.

A bald, fat man holding a dirty apron came out of another room with a woman. Daylight wouldn't be kind to either of them. He'd read a short piece a while back, published in a paper from back East and written by a man named Poe. It was frightful. These characters leaped from his story.

Luke moved the front of his vest aside to show his badge and pinned the man with his gaze. "Are you the owner?"

Baldy gave a wary nod but offered nothing else.

Luke kept an eye on that back room. This wasn't a place where you'd turn your back on anything. "So, you got a story to tell me?"

The bald man shrugged and grimaced at the effort. "Not much to tell. Man came in and robbed me. Got forty dollars in gold and took a bottle of good whiskey. Then he hot-footed out of here."

Nodding and trying to see into all the dark corners, the comment struck him as odd. Which was worse? Losing the money or the whiskey? "If it's so simple, how'd those unfortunate souls get dead?"

"Well, Johnny took a shine to Ella and wanted a quick visit with her in the back room. Those gents that died had already paid their money and objected."

The dim interior hid more than it revealed, and what it did show wasn't too likable. One end of the room had shelves with dried goods and those new air-tight cans, mostly peaches from the looks of them. A couple of tables with chairs graced the floor. Luke went to a table and sat down with a sigh. "You called the shooter Johnny. Do you know him?"

The motley pair moved toward the table, and he wondered why they were so skittish. It was a tossup whether they'd stay or bolt from the room.

Baldy finally spoke. "Yeah, it was Johnny Ruskin. He's been through here a time or two, always bragging it up how bad a man he is. Never expected him to rob us. I thought we were friends."

Ella moved closer, and her fragrance was not something to brag about. Her face was graced with spots and a big nose that eclipsed her other features. Limp, dark hair fell to her shoulders, and the unwashed odor assailing his nose didn't help her appearance.

"You going to get that money back, Deputy? Half that forty dollars was mine."

Luke pulled a blank warrant from an inside pocket and smoothed it out on the table. He took a quick glance at the woman. "You charged twenty dollars?"

She shrugged. "They had money to spend, and I was in a mood to take it. It's what they call a seller's market." Smoothing down the front of her low-cut dress, showing a freckled chest, she gave him a pointed look. "You're a good-looking young man, got some size on you too. I'm still in the mood, and I might cut you a deal on that price."

He glanced at her—good-looking he was not. The scar under his right eye and crooked nose might pass for an interesting face at best. How crazy and hard up would he have to be to go down her road? He'd heard a man screaming once as a doctor gave him the cure for something picked up from a local soiled dove. He shook his head, not surprised at his sudden chill.

"Thanks for the offer, but I'm going to pass on that."

Finding the witness portion of the warrant, he pointed to the man. "What's your name?"

Scuffing his moccasins on the dirt floor, Baldy finally glanced up. "Ed Pearce. Her name's Ella."

"You told me that already." Luke sighed and looked at her. "Do you have a last name?"

"Yeah. Somewhere. I'm easy to find if you need me." She rolled her eyes at the question, trying to adjust something under her dress and give him a show at the same time.

After looking at her, he wondered if he could wash his eyes. "Do either of you know the names of those poor departed souls your men took outside?"

The two conspirators glanced at each other before Ed gave a grudging answer. "Nope. Nothing in their pockets, either."

"Well, that's kind of odd, don't you think?" Now he knew why they were nervous. Staring at them a moment, Luke shook his head. It didn't take much imagination to know where all the earthly goods belonging to the dead men went. Guess it didn't matter too much. If he arrested everyone here, he'd be leading a parade around the country. He'd put it down as burial expenses. He wrote down Johnny Ruskin at the top of the paper, followed by the murder of two unknown men.

"What's this Johnny look like?"

Ella sidled up to him. "He's about your size, wears all black clothes—prettiest brown eyes you ever saw and real soft hands."

"You got a description I could use in a saloon without getting the daylights beat out of me?"

"Well." Her thought process looked painful. "He's slick. A smooth talker, you know?" Her gaze settled on him. "Not like you. I mean, you got those blue eyes, broad shoulders, and square chin going for you, but you're hard-looking—like you bit into something sour. Maybe you need to relax some. What about a free ride?"

"Ella..." The bald man's head swiveled so fast he risked breaking his neck. "She didn't mean that."

If he'd stepped into someone's rehearsal of a poor one-act play, it might have been funny. So far, it gave him a sour stomach. Folding the warrant, he stuffed it back into his pocket.

"I'll see what I can do about your money, but don't stay up nights worrying about it. I suspect you've already made a profit this day."

He walked outside and stared into the distance. Decisions you make every day can form your future or come back to bite your ass. Sometimes both. Sighing, he shrugged and turned to Lem. "Give me your hands."

With a surprised look, Lem leaned down and shoved his hands forward. Untying the man, Luke rummaged around in his pocket and found two dollars. "Here. That'll buy you a meal somewhere. Enjoy your freedom."

"What's going on? Why are you letting me go?" The man rubbed his wrists and didn't seem to be in any hurry to leave. He sat loose in the saddle as he took a drink from his canteen.

Luke shrugged, glad to be rid of him. "The murder of two men trumps horse stealing in my book. I need to travel fast. It's that simple."

He shrugged. "You shouldn't have taken that horse. You know better."

Lem wet a bandanna and wiped out the inside of his beat-up hat. Something had taken a bite out of the back of it, but with the way the day was going, Luke was not going to ask.

Finally, he answered. "Yeah, I know it was wrong.

First horse I ever stole." He grinned. "But it's a fine horse, and I was in a damned big hurry."

Taking Lem's pistol and cartridge belt from his saddlebag, he handed them to him and smiled. "Next time, don't cozy up to a married woman. Husbands tend to frown on that. Besides, it was the judge's horse, and you stole it right in front of his window. If I catch you again and take you back, you'll either hang or get shot—depends whether the judge or husband gets to you first."

The horse thief grunted and then gave him a sober look. "She didn't tell me she was married, and between you and me, that was a well-traveled path to her door. Besides, you ain't gonna see me again, Luke. Lots of country west of here."

"Good. And just for conversation, I have a little horse ranch west of Springfield. If I see you around there, I might jump to conclusions."

Lem shook his head. "Changing my ways, Marshal. I've seen the light."

"Make sure of that. Since the judge neglected to put a brand on his horse, you might get someone to write you out a bill of sale. It should be good anywhere west and north of Fort Smith and keep you out of trouble."

"That's good advice. Think I'll take it."

"See that you do."

"And, Marshal"—He held out his hand to shake—"You made a friend today. I appreciate what you're doing for me."

Luke shook his hand and gave him a wry smile. "I doubt we're going to be friends. Just make sure you take advantage of my gift."

As the horse thief left, Luke looked around one more time. This was a story that got played out a lot in Indian territory. The only law was what the deputy marshals brought out of Fort Smith, Arkansas. It wasn't well received. Nobody wanted the law around until they had a problem. As soon as the trouble was over, the lawman was treated like a leper. Many a deputy never came back from trying to keep the peace.

He'd heard Johnny's name before and knew the man didn't have any conscience that would keep him from being a ruthless killer. This was one more checkmark on a long list of things he'd done. It was time to put an end to that.

Making a circle around the sutlery, he found the trail of a lone rider heading northeast. Since the trail was fresh and he knew it wasn't Lem's, he pushed his horse hard. Big Cabin was west of them, and he expected his quarry to head that way, but the trail took them away from that town.

———

TWO DAYS LATER, Luke almost caught him in Galena, but the outlaw went out the back of a saloon as he came in the front. He learned the man had friends and considered the chase a game to be played. But the town constable in Galena was not his friend and told Luke the outlaw was partial to Joplin and their painted ladies. Added to the general direction he was riding, his best bet in finding him was in the city ahead.

He'd been to a lot of places, but never to Joplin, Missouri. He knew by reputation it would be hard to root out the outlaw once he got there. Most wanted men ran to wide open spaces, hoping to lose anyone chasing them. This one headed for a city where the crowds could hide dangerous men lurking in the shadows. Things were not simple anymore.

In the distance, columns of smoke rose from the factories outside of Joplin. He'd heard the smelters never shut down, and mining operations went all day and night. Of interest to him, neither did the saloons or gambling halls. It narrowed the search somewhat. Johnny wouldn't be found in church.

As they crossed Shoal Creek, he tightened the reins on his horse to keep his head up so he wouldn't drink the water. Typical of April, it had rained hard the night before. The runoff from the detriment and earthen heaps dominating the landscape turned the water dirty brown. The ugly water in the creek was belly-deep on his horse. With a gravel and limestone bottom, it was a careful ride. Not that he wasn't looking forward to a bath. A mud hole would be cleaner than the water they were crossing.

Still an hour's ride to the main part of town, he passed through low, rolling hills dotted with tents and covered wagons used for homes by the miners—and there were a lot of them. Cook fires smoked from green firewood and were tended by wives or kept women while their men worked. Half-naked children played between the homes in the makeshift shanty town, and he couldn't believe the filth. Some of the children stopped and gave him an empty-eyed stare as he rode by. It looked like a brutal existence, and he wondered how the lure of any amount of money could make that kind of life worth the hardship.

The prairie was behind him, clean and open, with air you could breathe. He almost stopped and turned back, a compulsion hard to resist and one he'd been thinking of a lot. He had enough money saved to stock his ranch with horses. It was all there waiting for him. Why was he doing this? The miners had a squalid existence, and he realized he'd just answered his own question about them. He was doing the same thing, except he was killing people and getting shot at. And for what? Money. It was time to end it.

Riding onto the main street was an eye-opener. It was a good thing he rode a fair-cutting horse. They dodged freight wagons, handcarts, and an occasional buggy, mounted and pushed by demented men hell-bent on running over anything that got in their way on the narrow streets.

His city of choice was Kansas City, a spread-out cow town with room to breathe, if you discounted the smell of the stockyards. This town was...he shook his head. He didn't know what this town was.

Standing at a water trough, making sure the horse didn't drink too much, his mind started ticking off things to do. Once he had Johnny locked up, there would be decisions to make. Should he stay in service or go home? Could he give up the excitement of the chase? Last, but yearning to be first on the list, a bath and haircut.

Uneasiness plagued him as he gazed up and down the street, yearning for something he couldn't pin down. The sun seemed dull, and shadows looked deep, showing no detail. The end of his string was near. He knew that. What wasn't clear was how it would play out. Johnny might take care of the problem. His hand caressed the worn, walnut handle of his belly gun. That surprised him. He didn't remember reaching for it.

Dropping his hand to his side, he chided himself. Getting lost in thought was a sure ticket to hell, and Johnny, or someone like him, would send him there.

The imposing two-story brick building in front of him had a bank stenciled in every window, along with Patrick Murphy, Proprietor. It must take a lot of building to hold all that money from the mines. A small office next to the bank had a hand-painted sign that read Town Marshal. As he walked toward that door, a small, dapper-looking man rose from a chair and stopped him.

"Friend, I wouldn't go in there just now."

The cussing and yelling inside the office rose and fell in cadence with the whining, high voice of a man berating someone, with words becoming more inventive by the minute. Maybe he should take notes—some phrases were that good, if there was some way of scoring profanity.

The man standing in his way stuck out his hand. "James Donnelly."

He looked the man over as they shook. James sported a black bowler hat pushed back on his head, a light-colored suit coat and checkered vest on a hot day, and shoes Luke could see his reflection in.

"Trouble inside?"

"You might say that. The town marshal doesn't take disappointment well. I didn't catch your name." The man's face was openly curious.

"Are we holding hands for some reason?" Startled, the man let go and stepped back.

"I'm Deputy Marshal Luke Randall."

James nodded, rocking up on his toes and then back down again—a habit some short men had. "I thought so. You were in Kansas City once at the Cattleman's—right after a shooting at the stockyards. So, what are you doing in our fair city?"

Ignoring the question, he wondered how James got his teeth so white. It didn't look natural. "So, what's going on inside?"

The man shrugged and smiled. "Oh, the marshal is pitching a fit because Wyatt left."

He'd never heard of anyone else called by that first name. "Wyatt Earp?"

Up the street, two wagons had locked wheels. Tired of lashing their mules, the drivers turned the whips on each other. A laughing throng of people were shouting encouragement to both men.

He turned back toward James. The last he knew, Wyatt was out in Kansas. He couldn't be called a good man—just one you wanted on your side in a difficulty. They weren't friends, but he was sorry he missed him. Those who wore a badge often traded information about people skirting the law.

He heard a bottle smash against a wall and more cussing. "Sounds like quite the tantrum. Guess it's not a good time for a visit. Is there a good place to eat around here?"

"Couple of choices. You could go to Jack's Palace, across the street. It's famous worldwide for a lot of things, food among them. A much quieter choice would be Mrs. McBride's boarding house just around the corner. She serves up a hearty meal."

He didn't have to think about it. This place was too noisy already, and his dusty clothes wouldn't do for fine dining. "I'll go for quiet."

The man pointed the way and fell in step with him. "I'll buy your lunch if I may. I'd like to interview you for the Herald. I'm a reporter."

Luke stopped and gave him a level gaze. "No."

The rejection did not faze James. "If you're in town on business, I know a lot of people. Perhaps I can help."

He shrugged and started walking. "It's your money."

————

THEY WERE SEATED in a quiet corner of the café by a young woman sporting a clean white apron. She had a natural rosy complexion, or she'd been cooking over the hot stove. Her dark blond hair was held back and tied with a ribbon. He resisted the urge to stuff an errant curl of hair back behind her ear when she smiled at him. At least she looked clean. He had an aversion to taking food from anyone who looked as if they'd cooked with dynamite and got caught in the explosion. She interrupted as he started to ask for a menu.

"I have beef and potatoes on special today. Maybe some fresh biscuits to sop up the gravy."

"Milk gravy?" He'd had a bad experience with old gravy.

Her left eyebrow rose as she gave him a look that made him feel like a schoolboy caught pulling pigtails.

"It's fresh, too."

Anything was better than his own cooking. "What's the special tomorrow?"

She pretended to think for a moment, and he liked the laughter in her eyes. "Potatoes and beef. Leftover biscuits."

He inclined his head and smiled. "Add a pot of coffee and trot it out. That's my kind of food."

"And the same for me." The reporter smiled at her but didn't get one in return.

They were about finished with the meal when James started. "So, why do you like being a marshal? I've always been curious about that, given that longevity is not in your job description." He smiled at the scowl he received. "Sorry, it's what I do." He sat up straight. "Wait. You're not going to shoot me, are you? I've heard you don't need much of an excuse."

Luke sighed. He'd run into this before. Maybe the

reporter would give his words a true accounting. "And where did you hear that, James? Look. People like to talk. You should know that. The more they talk, the more they embellish the story. It's always easier to make up something than get it right. Truth is rarely exciting."

The reporter wrote on his pad and then glanced up. "Point taken. I always try to get it right. So, what's the punch line on that? How does that apply to you? If you'll forgive me, embellished tales or not, you're not known for being a gentle soul."

Luke was distracted for a moment as he sipped the black tar that passed for coffee at McBride's, wondering if she'd been raised on a ranch cooking for cowhands. It was just how he liked it. He glanced back toward the kitchen. There were several things interesting about her.

Centering his attention on the reporter, he gave the best answer he could. "Mr. Donnelly, I don't go into every situation expecting to shoot someone. Far from it. But you need to understand, I'm not sent after people who are inclined to come peacefully or want to repent for their misdeeds. Most of them know I'm coming, or someone like me. Their choices are often made long before I get there. That gives them an advantage. While I'm wondering what someone is going to do, they have no indecision to slow them down."

James's pencil broke, and he fished another from an inside pocket. "You've killed men, some brand you a killer with a badge. From talking to you, that seems unlikely, but still...how do you square that with a good conscience?"

Staring out a window, Luke ignored him for a moment and then finally replied. "Oh, there's no squaring it. Most deserve it. Hell, we all deserve it at one time or another. I'm sure my time will come."

He looked up as the woman filled their cups, leaving the fresh pot and picking up the empty. She had a chipped nail, and one finger was scratched. What looked like a small burn on her wrist had healed into a red welt. He'd banged enough pots and pans around a cook stove to know the cause. This was a girl used to working.

Her voice was as soft as her eyes. "Then why do it? There are other ways to make a living." Her face turned more red. "Sorry, I couldn't help but overhear."

She wouldn't stop trains or start wars with her beauty, but she had an honest and straightforward manner to her. When she looked at him, he didn't want to disappoint those eyes.

"Do you have a name?"

With a startled smile, she seemed puzzled for a moment. "I'm surprised James hasn't told you already. I'm Sarah McBride. This is my place. I own this little corner of the world."

A thin gold band on her finger reflected the morning light, and he hoped his disappointment didn't show as he shook his head. "Your husband is a lucky man."

Her gaze was curious for a moment, and then he learned she was not a woman who cheated herself when she laughed. "Not much. He's dead."

Luke was drawn to her if for no other reason than her crooked smile and those clear blue eyes. "I'm sorry." He nodded toward her hand. "Why the ring?"

With a chuckle, she glanced at James. "It keeps the honest men at bay and the riff-raff from pestering me all the time...except reporters."

Maybe she was older than he thought, and he hoped she didn't take offense at his staring.

"And you?" She stood hipshot, balancing the large pot on one hip. "I don't see a ring on your hand, and you're old enough to have been chased. Are you promised? Looking? Running away from an angry wife?"

He was lost in her gaze, liking that she was not subtle. A man would always know where he stood with this woman.

She looked close to laughing again. "You seem tongue-tied. Do you have a name?" Waiting expectantly, she broke the awkward silence. "Well?"

He felt like he was blushing and couldn't remember ever doing that. Starting to get up to introduce himself, he felt her hand grip his shoulder and push him back down.

"Please." The hand lingered for a moment.

"I'm Luke Randall. Deputy US Marshal out of Fort Smith."

"Well, then. Pleased to meet you." The corners of her mouth turned up. "So, the question?"

He grinned at her. "Which question? Am I promised? No. Running? No, again. Never had a wife to make angry. And I'm always looking."

Holding her gaze, he continued. "As for why I'm a marshal? I suppose the right reason to quit hasn't come along." He shook his head. "It's hard to explain. There's a marshal named Rawlings who said it best. Serving justice gets to be an addiction. It's the rush of taking the next job, like taking opium or laudanum. It's a love-hate relationship. And often deadly for both sides."

"So, did this Rawlings ever quit?"

"Yeah, but it took the death of his wife to do it. It seems part of him died too. Last I heard, he was riding around the country looking for a reason to live."

"Well, I hope you find your anchor. Everyone needs that—that reason to go on."

He was staring at her when James broke into the

conversation again. "So, I'll ask again. Why are you here?"

"I think you've asked enough questions." He stood abruptly, startling the man.

Several laughing children ran by the window, chased by a scruffy, barking dog. He smiled, remembering the squalor he'd seen coming into town. Maybe there were real families here, doing normal things. Not starving. That was something he always wanted. A family.

He glanced at Sarah as she squeezed his arm and nodded at him. He understood. It was a busy time for her, and he had things to do. She walked briskly toward the kitchen with his empty coffee pot.

He could hunt for the outlaw for days in this city. The best way to get Johnny was for the outlaw to come to him. What better way to announce his presence than by using James as the town crier.

"Johnny Ruskin. I've a warrant for his arrest. He robbed a sutlery and killed a couple of men down in the Nation. Know him?"

The reporter looked up at him and squirmed in his seat. "Yeah, but not personally. I've heard he's a real dandy and runs with a whore named Molly down on Virginia Street."

"I thought they were all named Molly."

The reporter laughed. "There does seem to be a lot of them."

As they started to leave, Sarah came out of the kitchen and called to him. "You come back soon, ya hear?"

He waved to her as they both stared at the other. "Count on it."

James spoke as he looked back at her. "I've been trying to get her interested in me for months and not a peep out of her." He glanced at Luke. "I think I hate you."

Luke looked back, and she still watched with a small smile. She was probably responsible for the added spring to his step.

They strolled back to Main Street, toward the town marshal's office. Luke gestured toward the saloon. "Tell me about Jack's Palace. Is that the owner's name?"

"No. I'm not sure if anyone knows who actually owns it—maybe several people. The main source of income in this town used to be lead. Now it's zinc, and the nickname for that is jack. Hence the name. I guess."

Luke glanced at him. "You guess? So much for factual reporting."

"Well, I do know the first floor is for our more genteel folks and their wives. You'd meet a lot of mine owners and bankers in there. It has a bar and a nice restaurant. Vulgarity, coarseness, and violence are not tolerated on the first floor." He smiled. "Those rules are enforced by very large violent men with clubs. I think there's a certain irony in that. Later, the men can migrate to the second floor. That's the gambling hall. I think they have every device known to man that separates you from your money. However, the oldest device is on the third floor. That's the brothel, mostly high-class. By the time you make it out of there, any money you have left will be gone."

As if on cue, they heard whistling and laughter from across the street. They looked at the balcony on the third floor of Jack's. Several women leaned over the rail or stood close to it. Most were scantily dressed at best, others were naked from the waist up, waving at passersby. One woman wore a huge, flowered hat under a pink parasol and nothing else. He didn't think sunburn was going to be a problem for her. They looked inviting from a distance, but closer inspection might find them worn and empty. That they could show their wares in front of the marshal's office told a lot about how the town was run.

Several men were leading women off the street, like they'd be tainted by seeing such a spectacle. In some cases, the women pulled the men away. It was amazing how they tried to wall themselves away from parts of the world they didn't agree with. He wondered how Sarah would react to this. He'd lay a bet that she'd laugh.

James waved back to the women. "Oh, the broken flowers from the primrose path, sending forth their siren call. There's some pretty ladies on that balcony."

Luke chuckled. "You're quite the poet, but I think the term lady might be a stretch."

"Well, for one, I am a writer. As for the ladies? You'd be surprised, Mr. Randall. You just might."

It was quiet, so they went inside the marshal's office. The man sitting behind the desk looked like a banker. His eyes slid from Luke to the reporter. "Who's this?"

Before he could reply, James broke in. "LC, this is Deputy Marshal Luke Randall. You've probably heard of him. Luke, meet LC Hamilton."

"A deputy marshal, you say? As a matter of fact, I have heard of you. You work down in the Nation. I've heard you're one of Fort Smith's hired killers who doesn't give the law much thought."

Luke stared at the man longer than was polite. "You're entitled to your opinion. This is a courtesy stop, Hamilton. I'm looking for a man in your town. Once I get him locked up and arrangements are made to take him to Fort Smith, I'll be on my way."

The man seemed to think for a moment and then

gave a fake politician's smile that didn't extend to his eyes. "I appreciate the thought, and call me LC. I'll help you if I can, but first, there's a job you have to do for me."

Luke took off his hat, rubbed the sweatband for a moment, then re-positioned it on his head. "I wasn't aware you were in my chain of command, Hamilton."

The man turned an interesting shade of red but brought it under control. "Here's the thing. If you help me, I'll help you. Otherwise, you may have a hard time operating in my town. That damned Wyatt left before he could do the job he was supposed to do."

The reporter broke into the conversation with his pad and pencil ready. "Why'd he leave in such a hurry?"

"He got a telegram that Ed Masterson was killed up in Dodge. Left out of here in a big hurry. He has ties with that family—think they used to buffalo hunt together. You can bet there will be some lead flying over that."

Luke turned away, and the marshal's voice stopped him. "Don't rush off. I have the same deal for you. It should be easy for a man of your talents. There's a gambler over at Jack's who's been swindling players. I need him arrested. His fine will be substantial, and you could share in that."

He stared at the man for a moment. The marshal sported a huge handlebar mustache, dark eyes peering at him from under a short-brimmed hat, and a face gone soft with easy living. "So, take your men and arrest him. Several deputies with shotguns should get his attention."

"We could. But I'm no gunfighter, and neither are my men. That's not how we run this town. I figure a famous name like yours would keep him from trying anything crazy. You won't scare him like Wyatt would, but I figure it's worth a chance."

Luke shook his head. "Your reluctance borders on cowardice. Who is this dangerous miscreant that has you buffaloed?" He insulted him on purpose, to see how he'd react. The scary thing was he didn't react at all.

"Otto Shilling."

He nodded. "You're right. Otto won't be impressed with me or anyone else. Whoever accused him of cheating is a liar. He's good enough at cards, he doesn't need to cheat. Wyatt would have known that, too."

The marshal's voice was mild. "You're calling the mayor a liar."

"Being a politician, I doubt he'll be insulted any more than you were at being called a coward." He thought a moment, not wanting to get into their political games. "Let's call it misinformed. Whatever your game is, I won't be part of it."

Luke held up his hand as the man started to protest. "What I will do is go over and talk to him. He doesn't stay long in one place. Maybe he's ready to leave. If he does, that should solve your problem." He tipped his hat to them. "I need to look the place over anyway. Good day, gentlemen."

Taking his horse by the reins, he led him to the barn on the other side of the bank. The sign read Teasdale's Livery, and there were several buggies and horses tied in front. Leading the horse into the shaded entry, he was met by a bow-legged older man who looked better suited to riding than walking. A missing thumb on his left hand made Luke think the man was a retired cowhand. Many a rider lost a finger from a loose dally around their saddle horn when a thousand-pound cow critter hit the other end of the rope.

"How about some feed and water, maybe a rubdown? I may need him back later this evening."

The oldster nodded. "Oats are extra if you want some."

He grinned at the man. "I'll spring for it, but don't spoil him."

"I'll mix it with some molasses. He won't ever want to leave. Not spending the night?"

Luke looked out at the street. "Don't know yet. Not if I can help it."

"That'll be a dollar. In advance. For another dollar, you can leave your money and anything else you hold dear in my safe while you're out and about. It's that kind of town."

Luke gave him a look, wondering if he might have a point. "Don't worry about that. I'm not planning on staying long."

The hostler laughed as he led the horse away. "It doesn't take long, Marshal. Not long at all. This is the fastest town you'll ever see."

"How'd you know I was a marshal?"

"Ya got the look. Seen it before."

———

WEAVING his way across the street and through the horse-drawn traffic, the reporter was obvious in following close behind. Luke started to say something when a commotion broke out farther down the street. The graded road had caved in, leaving a hole at least ten feet deep with a rising plume of dust. He asked a man standing next to him what happened.

"Ah, just another tunnel caving in. Happens when we've had a heavy rain, like last night. They'll fill it up soon."

"That ever happen under a building?"

"It has." The man grinned. "Gets mighty interesting when that happens. We're waiting on the bank to cave in. It'll be a real gold rush."

Luke was surprised at how unconcerned everyone was. "You don't think anyone was in the mine shaft?"

A man with a miner's lamp attached to his leather cap turned to look at him. The candle was still burning against the reflector like he'd just come out of a dark hole. "Well, if there was, it's too late now. People are digging tunnels in too big a hurry around here. There's no safety precautions in most of the mines."

———

ENTERING JACK'S PALACE, Luke paused a moment to let his eyes adjust to the interior. To his right was a dining area next to the windows. Several couples sat at cloth-covered tables. The men and women were dressed in their finest. A partition separated them from the bar on the left. Next to the bar, a fancy, polished staircase made an entrance to the second floor. There were enough plants scattered about to give the place a jungle appearance.

When the bartender, resplendent in a dark suit, bow tie, and immaculate apron, brought him a sarsaparilla, he turned to the reporter. "Why are you following me around?"

Ignoring his question, James pointed at the bottle. "Why are you drinking that?"

He shrugged and made a face as he drank. "In my line of work, it pays not to drink whiskey. The last thing I need is shaky hands. Besides, it feeds my sweet tooth. So...the question?"

The man shrugged and gave his too-bright smile.

"Got nothing else to do until tonight. LC is going to take me with him when he rousts the prostitutes. He just opens the doors and walks on in. That's always a spectacle and worth the entertainment. Besides, I've a feeling you're a newsmaker."

"Is he arresting all the whores in town? Seems ambitious for the size of his jail."

"Whore is such a distasteful word." James laughed. "Besides, he only arrests those that can't pay their fines. Twenty-five dollars a head, every single month. If there's no payment, they have until the next day to get the money or go to jail. It's all business and runs quite fairly."

Luke didn't know what to think of a marshal who would jail women but not confront a gambler. He corrected his thinking. Of course he knew. "Is all that worth his time and trouble?"

"Well, I don't know who does the counting. But it's been said we have more whores than New York City or San Francisco. That's how the city runs. Fines and fees."

He wondered if he should wait for Johnny outside of town, where things were simple and held no distractions. Maybe if the outlaw was alone, he'd be more likely to come peacefully. He'd seen men do crazy things because a crowd was watching, and they didn't want to lose face. There were no easy answers.

"So, where will I find Otto?"

The reporter checked a watch, pulled from his vest by its gold chain. "He usually comes down from the third floor to the gambling hall about this time."

Luke left the empty bottle on the bar and went up the carpeted stairs. He was hoping he didn't trade steady hands for a bellyache. The gambling hall didn't have many players, and already the smoke was a pungent layer trapped against the ceiling. He couldn't imagine what it'd be like later. The open windows had little effect on the room.

The gambler sat in a back corner, alone at a round table. He was huge and resembled an educated bear, with muttonchop whiskers and a bowler hat set at a jaunty angle. His white shirt seemed immaculate, with red garters holding up long sleeves that were buttoned tight to his wrist, so no hint could be made of hiding cards. A pair of reading glasses sat on the end of his nose. The enigma of the man was that Luke knew he had the quickest hands in the business with cards or a gun. His sharp mind made it a useless gesture to cheat—an advantage he didn't need.

He pulled up a chair. "Hello, Otto."

The man glanced at him and then beyond his shoulder. He supposed his new shadow was lingering there.

"Well, if it ain't Luke Randall—purveyor of the law." He held out his hand to be shaken with an old English greeting. "Well met, my friend." The gambler's gaze was curious and intense.

He acknowledged the greeting. "How are the cards treating you?"

The man shrugged, offering a thin smile. "Better than average, I'd say. It ain't how they treat me, but how I treat them. This a social call...or business? I don't remember killing anybody you'd care about...at least not lately."

"A little of both. The esteemed marshal of this town wants me to arrest you for swindling the mayor. I told him the mayor was a liar and that you ran an honest game. Hamilton isn't having a good day. He may have been upset when I left."

Otto snorted. "The mayor? His left eye tics when he's

bluffing, and he bluffs a lot. The man has no feel for the cards."

"Yeah, I figured it was something like that." He shrugged and pinned the gambler with a steady gaze. "Still…it's hard to buck the system in a town like this, and the powers-that-be want you gone."

He was startled when a small hand rested lightly on his shoulder. Not hearing any footsteps approaching on the wooden floor added to the surprise. A high-pitched voice spoke next to his ear. "Otto, who's your handsome friend?"

He glanced around, seeing a short, young-looking girl next to him dressed in a floor-length green gown with white lace cuffs. Her brown eyes stared at him from a face surrounded by blond curls adorned with bright green ribbons. She might have just stepped from a Godey's Ladies book and looked like a child playing dress up.

His first thought escaped before he could rein it in. "How old are you?"

She smirked at him, shaking her curls. "Old enough, handsome. Why don't you come upstairs so I can prove it? Unlike most, I have a private room. You can call me Lilly."

It dawned on him why she looked odd. She wore no makeup and played up the little-girl look. Most women working in a place like this tried to hide their faces behind rouge and lipstick, like a comedy mask in a play. He wondered how the world had come to this point, once again yearning for the open trail and the big, wide open. He understood men, horses, and guns. Not women. And not this.

Standing, he swept his hat off and gave a small bow, playing a game to cover his embarrassment. The situation shouldn't have bothered him, yet he recognized the attraction and felt guilty for it.

"Young lady, it breaks my heart seeing someone your age working here. But I'm sure mine is not the first heart you've stepped on. Let that be trophy enough for you. I'm not interested in what you're offering."

"Oh, you're interested." Her expression was older than her years. "Well, so be it. You will be sorry." Pointing at the door they'd come through, she shrugged. "According to that paper nailed to the door, any girl over twelve years old must pay her fine every month or go to jail. By default, that makes me legal." She looked him in the eye. "And I ain't the youngest here."

The girl reached into her bodice and pulled out a leather pouch. "Of course, I have a protector. I don't have to suffer that embarrassment." Tossing the bag to Otto, she spoke over her shoulder as she moved away. "Pay the good marshal when he comes sniffing around tonight, love. The last time, I couldn't get him out of my room. I need to rest a bit. And please send up some lunch before anyone else visits."

Her heels clicked on the wooden floor as she walked away with a bounce in her bustle, looking over her shoulder at them. Luke turned and stared at Otto. The gambler was a scab that he'd just scratched off and found puss inside.

"Now you run whores?"

The man didn't meet his eyes. "Just the one. Keeps me in poker money. I've had a run of bad luck."

"A man with your skills doesn't need luck." Luke leaned toward him, realizing his experience with the man was all perception and not fact. Before, he'd seen what he expected to see. Now, like lighting a lamp and watching roaches run away, the gambler smelled of old clothes and rotten cigars, his eyes were wide and feverish. His immaculate shirt was dirty gray around the collar, with spots of spilled drink on the front. He wondered if Otto was drinking something stronger than whiskey. On the way to putting his hands on the table, he took the thongs from his pistols.

"I never thought you'd sink this low. I've known you from KC to Dodge and now here. You used to be a good man and ran a clean game. What changed? To my mind, if you'll do this, cheating at cards isn't a big stretch."

He stared at the gambler for a moment, surprised Otto didn't protest his innocence. "Problem is...I already told the marshal you'd never do that. Now it seems the mayor may have been right."

The gambler grunted, his eyes never leaving Luke's face...hand close to his pistol. "No one comes to this city and leaves with their honor intact, not even you. No one. That's just the way it is. The door you came through is still open for your exit. Take your righteous ass out of here."

Luke gave him a cold smile, watching Otto's hand on the pistol. "You have quick hands. But not quick enough. How about we go over to the marshal's office and let him decide? There should be no trouble. Pay your fine and leave this town. Simple as that."

James moved up to the table, flashing his smile. "Gentlemen. Please. This is getting out of hand." He turned to Luke. "Look, there are hundreds of women plying their trade in this city. All have their protectors. Lilly is no different. It's legal...sort of. You can't run them all off." He laughed. "Hell, the miners would lynch you for trying."

"Oh, I know that." Luke held the gambler's gaze. "But I can run this one off. I told the marshal Otto

Shilling was an honest gambler, not one to cheat. It appears he's made me a liar, and I can't abide that."

Someone laughed behind him, glasses clinked as drinks were poured. Business was picking up along with the noise level. His sigh was a long one. "Alright, Otto. You have a choice. I have a warrant to serve on another pillar of society hiding in this town. I'll take care of that first. But you have a decision to make. If I find you here tomorrow, I'll arrest you for whatever charges the town marshal can make up—I'm betting he can be real inventive. Or you can grab that pearl-handled pistol you're tapping with your fingers and take your chances. What'll it be?"

The gambler looked up with flat, dead eyes that spoke of locked rooms no one ever wanted to see. "I'll think on it."

Luke nodded. "See that you do."

Standing outside, he spoke to the reporter. "Can you show me where Johnny hangs out? I've decided not to wait."

James nodded. "You don't waste time, do you?"

He glanced behind him into the gloomy interior of Jack's Palace. His spine tingled, like when he was trailing someone and realized he was being hunted instead. "I want to get out of this place. It's coming nightfall, and that's when the cockroaches come out."

"Then let's go. Molly's place is just down the street."

———

THERE WERE SO many people moving around the boardwalk he almost missed them. Three men stood close together in the middle of the rutted street. How they kept from getting run over was a mystery. Two of the men carried shotguns. He wanted to ask the one in the middle if he was Johnny Ruskin, but the man was grinning like a banshee as his pistol came level.

Luke shoved the reporter to the side as a bullet stung his left arm, slamming through the building behind him and causing a shriek from someone inside. He pulled his belly gun and started shooting. People around him scattered, trying to get through doors or out of the line of fire.

One of the men with a shotgun was down on one knee, holding his belly. The second fired and unloaded his shotgun into a horse racing by. The squealing animal and cursing rider went down in the street, slinging dirt and blood into the air. His shotgun empty, the man tried for his pistol as Luke put a bullet into him.

He was firing his second gun and didn't remember switching. Another bullet punched a hole in the side of his vest as he pointed his gun at the last man.

"Drop it. I figure if you haven't hit me yet, you're not likely to."

"Like hell." The outlaw thumbed the hammer back on his pistol but crumpled when Luke's bullet took him in the chest. He tried to get up and then fell across the legs of one of the other men. Now they could add the smell of blood to all the other city stench.

After all the gunfire, Luke stood trying to catch his breath while re-loading his gun and waiting for the smoke to clear—a difficult task with a wounded arm. He knew people were talking but could hardly hear what was said. Blood dripped from his fingers onto the dusty sidewalk in cadence with a throbbing arm that burned like the fires of hell.

He looked at the reporter throwing up next to the building and called to him. "It's never the same in real life, is it? Write about that, and don't glorify it. There was nothing heroic about this. People died today." His gaze took in everyone around him. "And for what?"

No one spoke as he turned back to the reporter, who was struggling to his feet. "I assume that was Johnny?" James just stared at him, wiping his mouth on his sleeve as he nodded.

He felt someone grab him by his good arm and turned to find the hostler next to him. "Mr. Teasdale, can you point me toward a doctor's office?"

The man snorted. "I could, but he'd likely kill you. Let's get you down to Sarah's."

He looked up and could see her about a block away. Even from the distance, he could see the worry on her face. Once they started her direction, she disappeared toward her restaurant.

"Son, you have to be living on borrowed time. Three men at once? You gotta be crazy."

"It's not like I had much choice." Luke was hunched over and tried to straighten but felt a burning on his side. When he pulled his hand away, it had blood on it. He guessed the bullet punching a hole in his vest was closer than he thought.

When they got to McBride's, the place was cleared of customers. In less than a minute, he found himself in a back room, shucked from his leather vest, and sitting on a chair having his shirt ripped off.

"Hey, that was pretty new."

Sarah wadded the bloody rags and remnants of his shirt and tossed them into a corner, along with his hat. "And which year was that?"

Before he could answer, she turned to the hostler. "Whitey, there are some bandages on the shelf in the kitchen. Bring that and a bottle of whiskey."

He studied her face as she looked at the wound in his side where the bullet grazed a rib. It hurt more than the hole in his upper arm. When Whitey came back with the supplies, Luke was still flinching from her poking and prodding.

His voice was tight with pain. "Mr. Teasdale, would you mind stepping outside?"

"Why would I do that?"

He eyed the whiskey bottle. "I don't want another man to see me cry."

"Nope. I get to stay and hold you down." Grinning, he added. "I'll tell folks all the screeching and hollering was a catamount we found out back."

She shook her head, filling a tin cup with whiskey. "Will you two stop it?" After taking a gulp from the cup, she looked him in the eye with a smile and tossed the contents onto the wound.

———

THEY WERE STILL in the storeroom next to the kitchen as he sat with Sarah, drinking coffee. Whitey had gone for his saddlebags and a new shirt.

"So, I guess I'm staying the night?"

She nodded, sipping coffee and looking out the window. "The scratch across your ribs is more painful than serious. But if you start that arm bleeding again, you could be in trouble."

"And you'll enjoy throwing more whiskey on me?"

Her lips curled at the corners. "It's a good thing you fainted. I had to run a whiskey-soaked rag through the hole in your arm. It'll keep the infection down."

"How'd you learn to be a doctor?"

"Mostly from my mother. We lived on a ranch. The

men were always getting hurt from one thing or another
—snake bites, broken bones, and lost fingers. Whitey
used to work for us."

He flinched, surprised as Whitey dropped his saddlebags on the floor by the stairs—his hearing was starting
to concern him.

The hostler grinned at him. "Never saw a grown man
faint like that. Thought you'd died."

"It was a nap. I was tired."

She interrupted before they could go any further with
their banter. "Whitey. Why don't you go on home? I'll
take it from here."

He frowned and hesitated a moment. "You sure,
Sarah? He can sleep at the stable, or I can bunk him at
my place."

Her eyes were full of speculation. "I'm very sure,
Whitey. My virtue is safe for now. If not, I'll throw
whiskey on him. It'll drop him in his tracks."

"That's a waste of good whiskey." The old man
turned away. "And I wasn't worried about your virtue."
His laugh carried to them as he closed the front door.

She stood and held her hand out to him. "Let's get
you situated upstairs. I used to have boarders, but it
proved too much trouble. I barely keep up with the café.
Anyway, I have rooms to spare."

"You work too hard, Sarah."

"And how do you know that?" Her gaze held his for a
moment. "What do you think, cowboy? Want to take me
away from all this?"

She shook her head. "I don't have a lot of choices. I
must make a living, and cooking is something I can do.
One thing is sure: You'll never find me leaning over that
balcony at Jack's."

His hand moved up and tucked the errant wisp of hair

over her ear. "You're a beautiful woman. Why aren't you married?"

"Too many questions, boy. You're starting to remind me of James."

As they walked toward the stairs, she held his good arm against her, and they leaned against each other. "I can walk, you know. Not that I'm complaining."

"Oh, I know you can. You're a strong man." She chuckled. "Well, mostly."

He stopped again. "I need a bath and haircut. Is there a place close? I can walk there as easily as upstairs."

Pushing him forward, her voice was soft. "I'd agree on the bath. There's a tub in your room. I'll heat water and have some boys bring it up for you." She chuckled again. "They're always close by because I pay them with cookies."

"I like cookies."

She gave him a long look. "I bet you do." Then her voice became stern. "If you get soap in those wounds, they might get infected."

He sighed. "There's always whiskey."

———

LURCHING from sleep a couple of hours later, his thoughts were of swimming in cold limestone spring water. He faced a window turning dark with twilight, soon to be gone. Sitting in the cold water and tub, it took him a moment of staring at the unfamiliar room to remember.

Three boys had trooped in carrying buckets of hot water from the kitchen. After a couple of trips, the tub was filled, so he locked the door, undressed, and sank into the water with a grateful sigh. Wounds be damned.

He needed this. His muscles relaxed, and he leaned his head back...

"I have never..."

He bolted upright in the tub, spilling water over the side, before sinking back down.

"...seen anyone sleep like you."

"Sarah? What the hell?"

Her laugh was musical, and he wanted to turn and look.

"Just stay where you are, boy. Your clothes are on the bed with a couple of towels. Oh, and I cut your hair, so you need to wash that too—if you can find the soap. I didn't go looking for it. And there's a straight razor there with the towels. Don't cut your throat."

"You cut my...? How'd you...? Sarah—" He almost drowned when she laughed and pushed his head underwater.

———

LATER, squeaky clean after shaving and a bath, he was dressed and standing at the window. The room faced the street. Outside, a man walked by on stilts, lighting lamps along the boardwalk. He'd never seen that before. Kids were throwing rocks and sticks in his way, trying to trip him, but the man just laughed at them. When Luke pulled the shade and turned from the window, Sarah was sitting on the lone chair in the room.

"I distinctly remember locking that door."

She waved a key at him. "Really? I didn't notice." Gesturing toward the bed, her voice was soft in the quiet room. "Please sit and tell me about Luke Randall."

He looked at her for a moment and had a sudden vision of her at the ranch, meeting him on the front porch, kissing him hello—kids running about. Her blond hair was still tied in the back, and he figured she didn't have much time for primping during the day. Everything about her looked sensible, from her worn and sturdy shoes to her simple, no-frills dress and steady blue eyes gazing at him. He was thinking she should have blinked by now, but that relentless gaze bore into him. The intensity changed his mind about things. He ran his hand through his hair. There wasn't much time for courting. Hell, they'd just met today—it seemed a lifetime ago. And he wanted out of this town in the worst way. But she was here, and he didn't want to leave without her.

When he tried to speak, he had to clear his throat. "Thank you for everything."

She gave a little head shake and looked startled for a moment. It broke her concentration. "What…?"

It was easy to smile at her now, the spell was broken. For a moment, he'd felt like a mouse in front of a fox. "Thanks for the loan of the razor. For the bath and haircut and taking care of my wounds. Giving me a place to stay. You didn't have to do any of that with me being a stranger."

Her eyes seemed to get bigger. "Stranger? I never felt you were a stranger since the first time I saw you." She gave a little head shake, like she was trying to clear her mind. "I still need to wrap those wounds and put honey on them this time to keep infection away. For the rest of it? Think nothing of it. I enjoyed…uh…" She giggled. "I was glad to do it."

He grinned at her, watching a flush cover her face that matched the one adornment on her dress—an embroidered pink rose.

"My story? I've been a marshal for over ten years.

That's a long time in this line of work. There's age on me that doesn't show...the things I've seen—I haven't always been a good man." He stared at the floor. "You should understand that."

"I didn't see much evidence of age while I cut your hair, and none of us can be good all the time. Sometimes we don't want to be." She chuckled at his discomfort. "So, you've been around a while. I'd call that maturity."

With a curious look, she continued. "Do you like being a lawman? I mean...today was—three men? I don't know how you survived that. When I heard the gunfire..."

He wished his hat was close or something. His hands needed a prop to cover his nervousness. "Those men worked against themselves by standing close together—got in each other's way and were in too big a hurry to kill me. And I was lucky."

"Lucky? You had a host of angels guarding you this day."

Luke shrugged, watching her small foot pat the floor. Was this going too slow for her? "Probably dark angels. But like I said earlier. It's a job until I find something better."

She nodded. "Something better. You said that before. What would that be? Any prospects on that?"

"Some. I've got a little horse ranch west of Springfield. Bought it from a man going to California to look for gold. I told him he was leaving the best thing he'd ever have, and the man laughed at me. It's a place that needs a lot of work. A couple of Kickapoo riders tend it for me when I'm not there. Good men with families." He caught her gaze. "It's lonely."

He was surprised to find her standing in front of him,

moving in close. He was getting that intense stare again and couldn't take his eyes from her lips.

"And why aren't you?" Her voice was so soft, he strained to hear. "There, I mean. You could have been killed today. Why risk that? Shouldn't you be tending your ranch?"

"You really mean, why am I a marshal." He took a deep breath, letting it out in a sigh. "I can't explain it any better than I did this morning."

Her hand was on his shoulder, lightly caressing his arm. He was sure she could feel goosebumps rippling his skin.

"And you've never married?"

When he shook his head, she continued. "You're a man with a ranch that needs a wife and children to make it whole. You're neglecting that. The same thing you told the previous owner applies to you, don't you think?"

He didn't know blushing was contagious, but he'd caught it from somewhere. "I don't understand women. Never met any I'd want to keep around. In my line of work, you don't meet a lot of good people."

"You're looking at it wrong. You only have to understand one woman."

His hands somehow found themselves circling her waist. "I'm not a good man, Sarah. I can see where this is going. Not that I mind, but you can do a lot better than me."

"You said that before, but I don't agree. I've been told by someone I trust that you're a good man—honest to a fault and dependable. I like what I see."

"Now who told you that?"

"Whitey. He seems to know a lot about you."

He pondered that a moment, sure he'd never met the man before today. "How do you know him?"

"Well, like I said, he used to work for us." She sat on his leg, arm around his waist. "I was just sixteen when Jimmy McBride came riding up to our farm. I knew it all back then, oh Lordy, how I knew it. When you're young and in instant love, you don't listen to anybody, especially your parents. The first judge we could find married us.

"It was unfortunate my new husband was a fiddle-foot and gambler, always looking for the next big score—for both of us. There always seemed to be money for hotels and train rides. A couple of years ago, we wound up here in Joplin. He was sitting in a poker game at Jack's when he tried a bottom deal. The man he was playing against shot him in the belly."

He reached up to snag a tear before it coursed down her cheek, and she gave him a grateful look.

"It took him a week to die. It was the worst time of my life. I was alone in a rough town with men offering to take care of me, even before he died—there was no doubt what they wanted. I didn't have money. The other gambler took his winnings, and LC took the rest for fines and fees. I needed a friend, and Whitey helped. He made sure I had things—even set me up to buy this restaurant so I'd have a job. Where he got the money, I have no idea. Well, I suspect he got it from my parents. I was ashamed to ask for their help. Without him, I might have ended up working at Jack's."

She looked at him with that unblinking gaze. "So, you can see I'm not a squeaky-clean candidate for the nunnery, and I've got an impulsive streak. I've got my own bumps in the road. But something I've always wanted was a home. Roots. Are you a roots kind of man? Am I being too forward?"

"I can live with it." He pulled her against his chest. "So, you're experienced. Seasoned."

Her chuckle was a soft breath against him. "Not really. Just god-awful determined not to quit—to not give up."

"Not every woman would have the grit to do that. It's a good thing that you found the strength to go on. A lot of women would have taken the easy way out by working at Jack's or someplace like that. I've seen it too many times when girls are desperate. I'm proud you're the woman you are. You should be too."

She stared at him as he brushed her lips lightly with his fingers and then settled his mouth on hers. Her lips parted with a sigh. She'd chewed some mint leaves, and he hoped his breath was as fresh—and knew it wasn't. After a few moments, he let his hands drift down her curves, and she acquiesced for a time, giving him soft moans of approval. Then she pulled away.

"I said seasoned, not easy." She squirmed in his lap. "Maybe you need to jump in that cold bath water again."

He took a deep breath and tightened his grip on her. "Look. You've nothing holding you here except this café. Why don't you come with me when I leave? I don't think you'd regret it. If things don't work out, I'll get you started somewhere else. You deserve a good life, Sarah."

"So do you." She stared at him for a moment before she stood. "We've got some talking to do, so don't run off tomorrow. This is sudden, and I need to think. Whitey wants me settled somewhere so he can go rambling again."

"Do it for you, not Whitey."

After she bandaged his arm and ribs, she leaned forward and kissed him again. "I can't seem to get enough of that." With a schoolgirl's giggle, she went out the door.

He gazed at the closed door a moment, knowing he'd just been cut out of the herd, hog-tied, and roped down. The branding would come later, and he wasn't sure how he felt about that. The biggest mystery was why he couldn't get the smile off his face.

———

BREAKFAST the next morning was a crowded affair. He came down in his new shirt and mended vest into a maelstrom of activity. Standing for a moment, not seeing any open tables, he felt a tug at his arm. An older woman with white hair and a flushed face led him to a table by the back door.

As he pulled out a chair, Sarah came bustling in and kissed him on the cheek. "Big breakfast?"

He thought of what the morning might bring. "I'd better not. Some of your coffee would be good."

She stood staring at him, and he wondered how she got to know him so well in such a short amount of time. Her head was slowly shaking, but her gaze never left his. "No. Please, no."

Luke nodded. "I'm sorry. I've one more thing to do. I'll try to avoid it, you've got my word on that. But I might not be able to."

Stepping closer to avoid all the noise and clatter, her eyes belied her calm voice. "You're my man, whether you want me or not. I decided that last night. Do what you must, but, dammit—stay alive. You hear me?" Her hand clutched his arm. "I didn't give you much chance to talk last night, but I have to know. Will you have me as your woman?"

He held his gaze steady on hers. Her eyes filled with tears when he didn't speak right away. "I'm tired, Sarah." When she started to speak, he held up his hand. "I'm tired of being alone and hunting people that want to kill me. I'm tired of waiting for that one bullet that ends it all. More than anything, I want to wake up with a good woman and take her to bed every night. Is that plain enough for you? I want you to come with me when I leave—the long courtship can come later."

Her sigh was so long, he was afraid she'd never take a breath. "If that wasn't a proposal, it was damn close enough. My answer is yes. I'll make sure you'll never regret it."

She didn't leave his side until he finished his coffee and left. A glance over his shoulder found her still staring at him with her hand over her mouth, the other clutching her belly.

When he walked into the marshal's office, Hamilton was behind his desk, pouring a glass of whiskey.

"Kind of early for that, isn't it? Rough night?"

The man stared at him with red eyes. "It could have been better. What can I do for you, Luke?"

He plucked the badge from his pocket and dropped it on the desk. "If you'll wire the office in Fort Smith, they might give you a reward for Johnny Ruskin. Tell them I said to do it. You can also tell them I quit. You'll have to take care of your own damned problems."

The marshal picked up the badge, fingering it for a moment. "I always have, one way or another."

Neither cared much for the other, and that was fine with Luke. When he walked out the door, he felt weight lifting off his shoulders. His mind was on seeing Sarah and a large lunch when a voice brought him to a halt.

Otto Shilling was standing in the street with his

pistol leveled at Luke.

"I thought it over, Luke. I'm staying in town."

Nausea came and went in the blink of an eye, along with a sudden chill—he could not win this one. He was going to take the lead. Like all good gamblers, Otto wasn't taking any chances.

"I turned in my badge, Otto. I don't care if you stay or go. It's none of my concern. Not anymore."

The gambler waved his gun side to side. "It doesn't work that way. You called me out. People heard you."

"Since when do you care about what people think?" He saw James writing furiously on his notepad, partly hidden in the gathering crowd. "It wouldn't be that a certain reporter put you up to this? Talked you into it? Another gunfight he can write about? It wouldn't be the first time the news reporters made a problem worse just so they could write about it."

Otto's eyes flickered for a moment, and then he smiled and shrugged. "Don't matter. You'll be dead anyway."

Luke had heard of men beating a drawn gun but didn't believe it. He was fast. It was a gift no amount of practice can make better. But no one was that fast, and Otto's gun was coming level again.

"Is she your daughter?"

Those dead eyes blinked in confusion.

"That baby girl you pimp over at Jack's. She's still a child. Is she your daughter?"

The gambler was stunned and looked embarrassed, quickly glancing at people around them. Public opinion mattered. You can't make a living if none of the suckers come to your table.

"Are you crazy? No, she's not—"

Luke drew, the gunshot loud in the still morning air.

Surprise marking his face, Otto backed up a step, blood leaking over his vest. But he was a bull of a man with no quit in him. Luke kept thumbing the hammer and firing until the man finally fell into the dusty street.

Gunshots were still echoing between the buildings when Lilly came out of the crowd and stared at Luke for a moment. Rolling the gambler's body over onto his back, she reached into a pocket and pulled out a fist full of money. She looked at him again with a raised brow.

He shook his head and waved her over to him. Some of the money was bloody, and she wiped it on her dress. "Looks like you've got a stake."

"No more than I worked for. The bastard took most of it." She was busy stuffing money into a hidden pocket of her dress.

Considering her hard eyes, he wondered if there was anything to save. "You have a chance if you'll take it. Use some of that money and hop the KATY railroad up to Kansas City. Anyone can tell you where to find Pastor Bennett. He runs a church and rescue mission for those who want it. Tell him I sent you, and he'll take care of you. Hell, he'd do it anyway, but he's a friend, and I like to let him know I'm alive on occasion." He wondered if he'd gotten past that hard protective shell she put around herself.

"Why should I do that?" She patted her pocket. "I have enough money to last a while."

He felt lightheaded and wondered if the bandage on his wounded arm had broken loose. The pain was worse when he tried to move it. "Look around you, girl. Think about what you're doing. Is this how you want things to be? It may seem like an exciting life, but you can do better."

She looked at the blood dripping from his hand.

"Same might be said for you, Marshal."

She went back into the building, and he hoped she'd grab her belongings and go right out the back door—he didn't have much faith in it.

When Hamilton finally ventured out of his office, Luke handed him the warrant on Johnny. "Here, I forgot to give you this. Tell the mayor he can thank me some other time."

He turned and was surprised when he staggered into an awning post, seeing a familiar face. "Did all the noise wake you from your nap, Whitey?"

"Nope. Old as I am, I'm afraid to sleep—I might not wake up."

"Well, sorry for the commotion. I didn't want it that way." He glanced over his shoulder at Otto's body, surrounded by people. Why weren't they at work?

"I'm damned lucky to be alive. Or just damned. Sometimes it's hard to tell." He looked away a moment and then back at Whitey. "I never thought I could beat him. He had a pat hand."

The old man snorted. "Way I saw it, luck didn't have much to do with it. He was a poor shot, and you weren't. Besides, this ain't nothing. Killing someone doesn't mean anything around here. People don't care about that. It happens every day. Now, if you robbed the bank, they'd boil you in oil and hang your body up for all to see while the crows pecked your eyes out. Or put you in jail for a hundred years. Messing with the flow of money is the only real crime around here."

The hostler pointed at Luke's shoulder. "Is that new? You're bleeding bad from that shoulder. We better get you to..."

Luke felt someone grab his arm as he looked around the crowd again. "Where's Sarah? I thought she was here." He wondered how the boardwalk got so close to his face. Whitey was bent over him, shaking his head, and then the image faded away.

———

LUKE WOKE to a dull ache in his shoulder. He was being jostled and rolled on a pallet of blankets, and his groan was cut off by a gasp when another bump came. He knew he was in a wagon because one of the wheels needed grease, and if there were supposed to be springs underneath, someone had stolen them. He opened his eyes to see out the back of the buckboard, but the end gate was up. All he could see was blue sky, dotted with puff-ball clouds.

Propping himself up on his elbows, he could see better, although his shoulder didn't like it much. Two horses were tied behind the wagon. Sitting on a high seat, Whitey grinned at him from another wagon piled high with furniture and boxes, following behind the horses.

A sharp whistle hurt his ears, and his wagon stopped. He was attacked by a kissing and crying female as she checked his bandages.

"What's going on, Sarah? Where are we?"

She helped him sit all the way up, and Whitey grinned at him, hanging over the back of the wagon.

He shook his head and was pleased it didn't hurt. "So, talk to me."

"Well, after you fainted—" She was startled when he interrupted.

"I never faint."

Smiling, she shook her head. "Anyway, after you proposed to me—"

He reached for her. "I don't remember that."

Whitey laughed at that one. "You did, Boss. I'm a witness."

Sarah was speaking again. "And then after we chased that little trollop away, she came back and wanted to go through your pockets—said you owed her money."

He glanced at her. "You don't believe that for a minute. Besides, Lilly's going to turn her life around."

That produced a very unladylike snort. "Oh, please."

Her hand was caressing his face. He could get used to it. "So why are you trying to bounce me to death in this wagon?"

She glanced at Whitey. "Well, we waited a week for you to mend some."

"I've been out a week?"

The hostler's voice was serious. "You fainted a long time."

"Did not."

Watching him, she continued. "Anyway, once your fever broke, we decided to go ranching."

He stared at Whitey for a moment. "Why is he here?"

She shrugged. "I needed help, and you need a foreman. It's been a busy week with selling the boarding house, his livery, and all."

"What do you mean, all? There's more?"

Her expression sobered but didn't waver. "We got married. I'm not going to shack up with some out-of-work marshal living in sin."

"We—"

Whitey's smile was so wide he was showing where he'd lost a couple of teeth, way back inside. "Yep. I witnessed it after we signed it for you. The parson was most understanding. We told him how you were setting everything up before you got ambushed. When we got through with the paperwork, I never seen a man laugh like that."

A deep breath settled his nerves—mostly. "Well, now. It seems I got a lot accomplished while I was resting."

Shaking his head, Whitey chuckled. "You fainted again."

"Did not."

He looked at Sarah, and her eyes were soft and pleading. She looked about ready to cry before he drew her in close with a whisper.

"I accept." He thought for a moment. "Say, did we have a honeymoon during this week that I can't remember?"

Her face went from pink to red. "No. We did not. And if you don't behave yourself, it won't be anytime soon."

"Good. I'm thinking I'd want to remember that." Glancing at the grinning man hanging on the tailgate of the wagon, he spoke in a stage whisper. "So, in addition to a new wife, I've got a foreman now?"

She nodded, a wary look in her eyes. "You do."

"Well, I already have two riders. I figure any foreman worth his salt will have to do the plowing. We've got crops to put in. I want to raise corn for silage."

"Now, wait just a minute…"

He gave the man a stern look. At least the best he could manage. "You've been grinning at me since I woke up. Where are those pearly whites now? Huh?"

She kissed Luke again and smiled through tears. "I need to quit doing this or we'll never find a campsite. I'll let you two hash this out."

Whitey dropped from sight and then clambered back onto his wagon. They had to yell at each other over the noise of the two wagons. "Ain't nothing to hash out. I ain't plowing."

Luke tried to ease his position, leaning against the front of the wagon. "You expect to eat?"

He heard a big sigh from his wife. "This may have been a mistake…"

———

HISTORICAL NOTES ON JOPLIN, MISSOURI

Jack's is loosely patterned after the House of Lords, whose orgies at New Year's were known worldwide. The exact time this establishment opened is hazy at best, as was the ownership.

In April 1878, Wyatt Earp was in Joplin looking for train robbers when he heard of Ed Masterson's death in Dodge City and left immediately. Ed and Bat Masterson were buffalo hunters before taking up the law.

The Marshal of Joplin in 1878 was L. Cass—LC—Hamilton. Common street walkers were confined to 3rd Street, so they didn't interfere with the bordellos in the finer houses.

Molly Tate ran a bawdy house on Broadway. Lillie Wiggins's place was on Virginia Ave.

Lead was discovered before the Civil War, but in 1870, it was Zinc—Jack—that made people rich. It was used in paint and as an alloy to galvanize metal and copper.

The newspaper at the time in Joplin was the Daily Herald. Their reporter was James Donnally.

And yes, old mine tunnels still cave in today after heavy rains. They're called sinkholes now.

Source: Joplin News Herald, Joplin Globe, and Joplin Ordinances.

BENNETT'S COUNTY

The front door of the sheriff's office banged open, and a massive form called Emma blocked out the sun. A screeching grunt and fumbling commotion made me turn, and I caught sight of my deputy fleeing out the back door, his overturned chair left spinning on the hardwood floor. Damned coward. I thought the back door was stuck. It didn't take him long to fix it.

Emma's strident voice brought my attention back. I'd just received a slat-backed office chair and was trying it out. I found it in a catalog over at the mercantile, and the stage brought it late yesterday evening, along with several hand-delivered ribald and unsavory comments. The chair was made special with wheels on its legs, and I liked the hell out of it. Took me two months to get it. I figured to charge two-bits a ride, kids were free for a once-around. It even had arms on it, so you wouldn't get thrown.

The only trouble with it so far? The old building housing my office didn't have a square corner in it, and when they put in the wooden floor—well, level wasn't a real concern. I kept drifting, one way or another. The heaviest thing in the room, not counting Emma, was the pot-bellied stove. The way it made the floor sag, I'd have to be careful in the winter.

The woman seemed to have no thought for my chair-riding ability and didn't waste time. "Sheriff Bennett. I'm glad you're finally in your office. It would be easier to find you if you'd stay put occasionally and keep regular hours."

I'm not easily startled, but that took the cake. She'd found me every day for a week. And as county sheriff, my job would be defined as being out of the office. That's where all the miscreants and ne'er-do-wells are. Out there. Hiding in the bushes.

Holding up a placating hand, I tried reason. "Mrs. Arnold, you called me Billy every day last week. You might as well keep using my first name. Now what's your new problem today?"

She pulled a small man around from behind her, and I wondered who else she was hiding. I started to roll my chair to get a better angle when she spoke.

"Tell him, Samuel."

Samuel was about half the size of his wife, a phenomenon I'd seen before. I always looked closely for bruises, but I never found any on him. I shouldn't be suspicious. I'm sure she's the sweetest thing on earth.

He sure was jumpy. If you came up behind him and poked him in the ribs, he'd jump about two feet in the air. Some of the boys had taken to coming up behind him on the street and setting off firecrackers. Jumpy. I needed to catch those boys because the noise was hard on the horses. We had a couple run off. One had Samuel on it.

He took his hat off and worried the brim a little. "Well, Sheriff, Emma thinks that witch is at it again."

It was a morning for contemplation. The most wondrous thing is how ideas get started—good and bad. Most folks hold their opinions to themselves. Seems the ones we don't want to hear are always proclaimed the loudest. The dangerous thing disturbing my contemplation is that these people were serious, and that was disturbing. There's no amount of trouble that can come from people who convince themselves of their own stupidity and follow their newfound belief in righteous indignation. I studied them close, as I practiced my reply. My lips may have moved some.

"Which witch?"

Emma gasped. "There's more than one?"

In a practiced move, both turned to the side and spat between their fingers. Hers landed first, but she's a lot bigger—more power.

She turned back to me with a triumphant stare. "I knew it. We have an infestation."

Visions of broom-handled harridans in black hats flooding into town flashed across my mind. Maybe it was time I took up drinking. Moments passed before I could speak. Flummoxed is a big word, but it was adequate for the moment.

"Did you spit on my floor? You can't run around here spitting willy-nilly. Are you possessed or just addled?"

They both shrugged in unison, although Samuel was edging around to stand behind her again. "It's to keep from being hexed."

"Hexed?" I tried a calming, deep breath—it didn't work. "You just spat on my floor. I'm the county sheriff, and you just spat on my floor. That kind of disrespect cannot be tolerated. I could arrest and jail you for that, and I don't have keys."

She leaned to the side, trying to catch a glimpse of the jail. "You don't have locks on the cells?"

"Oh, I have locks—just no keys." The building's architect, along with an aversion to square and level, must have had a strange sense of humor—or forgot to order keys. The only locksmith around was a tinker who roamed the hills fixing watches or about anything that needed fixing. So far, he hadn't been around.

Emma gave me a look she must reserve for recalcitrant children and husbands. "We should spit more. It'll help soak up the dust."

Conceding the point, I settled back into my chair, steepling my fingers as I stared at them. I anchored one leg to keep from drifting away. "Listen to me. I don't know what you're trying to accomplish, but there are no witches around here. There are no witches anywhere. No witches. None. Period."

It looked like neither would accept my proclamation. I expelled air in the sigh of the eternally oppressed, shaking my head. I was starting to get a headache.

"Alright. I'm going to hate myself for this, but why do you think there's a witch working in my county?"

Emma puffed herself up and started to speak until I held up my hand. "You tell me, Samuel."

He stood straight, about shoulder-high to his wife. His oversized hat stuffed full of paper covered his ears. A drooping mustache made him look like a miniature Mexican bandit, at least like the dime novels described them. He wore an old dragoon horse pistol that Emma would have to help him draw from his holster. I don't know how he pulled the hammer back. Maybe it was just for show.

His thin voice was indignant. "Our milk cow is dry again. And we can't find a couple of our pigs."

My face twitched. When I tried to stop, it got worse. My left eye started to leak water. "Your cow went dry?"

I sounded like the village idiot to my own ears. I'm not sure I could fix that. Or convince myself that I wasn't. It was too bad the deputy ran away. At least he'd have been a witness to this conversation.

"Do I have to explain this to a farmer? Cows stop giving milk after a certain length of time, and then they need to get cozy with their favorite bull again. It's the way life is, unless you're a lizard." I paused a moment. "By the way...where is your bull, Samuel? I know you have one."

His hat was not going to survive this encounter, and some of the paper stuffing fell out. "Uh, he ran off."

"Well, I'll be damned. You mean that falling-down joke of a split-rail fence you keep working on didn't keep in a two-thousand-pound bull? I find that hard to believe. You do know that Jerseys are skittish and head-strong—the bulls doubly so? You can't tell what they're going to do from one moment to the next, and they're dangerous because of it. The only way you can keep him close is with a rope and a nose ring. You should know that."

I was raised in these hills and knew it was an unfortunate fact that superstition always trumped logic, so the next comment didn't disappoint me.

"We're thinking that witch ran him off. It's what they do."

"How do you know that? Are you the town expert on witches?" If there was a book on witchery, I needed to get it and study hard. I could be missing something. "You're thinking a witch, who probably spent years in training, would waste their valuable time running your livestock around? You don't think there are more important things they could do?"

I shook my head at them. "For your information, your bull is visiting over at Fred Hansen's place, taking care of his cows. Fred appreciates the loan and told me you can come and get your bull anytime next week—the week after, at the latest. He should be finished visiting Fred's herd by then. And before you ask...I have no idea where your pigs are. There are plenty of those razorbacks out in the hills, go grab some new ones."

Both were silent long enough for me to stand up and look official. Maybe this encounter was over. I moved my pistol belt to a more comfortable position. Some days, you feel like you gotta shoot something just to watch it blow up.

"Is there anything else?" I should have left with the deputy. Predictably, there is always something else.

"Well." Emma put her hand on Sam's shoulder for support. "Tall Johnson, you know—lives over on Bitter Creek? Something keeps turning his horseshoe over. He keeps it nailed over his door, pointed up so his luck doesn't run out. That leads to some dire problems. He's feeling poorly, and his crops ain't doing so good."

"Dire?" I nodded. It looked like an easy day for problem-solving. "I know old Tall and don't doubt your word on that for one minute. He couldn't find luck in a field of four-leaf clovers. But he has two problems, other than being the worst farmer I've ever heard of.

"The first problem, he hardly ever leaves the tavern. He feels bad because he's always drunk or hungover. His wife does all the work around the farm. And Emily is no bigger than a pound of soap, so she can't do the heavy stuff. But she's a worker and tries real hard.

"The second thing? He's trying to grow crops in the shade on rocky ground. If he wants to raise corn, he needs to find some land with sunshine on it and dirt you can't use for cannon balls. He can't raise enough corn to feed the raccoons. Is that it? Anything else?"

Emma examined every wall except the one behind me. The spiders were already hiding out in the corners, except for the ones running up and down my spine. She interrupted my yearning glance toward the back door.

"There is one other thing, but it's embarrassing for a lady to speak of."

I flinched at that obvious misconception. My fingers drummed on the walnut grip of my pistol, and I sat down before I did something foolish.

"I'll try and control myself. If it gets too delicate, I'll hold my ears. So, please. Trot it out." I was curious how such a large person could have such tiny eyes that never settled on anyone. Except now. Her gaze pinned me with a level stare.

Taking a deep breath, she continued. "There's dancing going on."

My face twitched again. "Oh, no."

Words broke uninvited from my mouth, and I guess my tone gave me away. "You mean like with instruments, singing, and such?"

"You don't believe me?" Her eyes bulged, and her voice screeched. "Someone saw women dancing in the woods yesterday evening. They said those women didn't have enough clothes on to wad a shotgun. It was awful."

My feet slammed to the floor from their lofty perch on my desk. "Who was it? Where did this happen?"

Samuel got caught up in the excitement. "They weren't rightly sure. It was getting on dark, and I guess they didn't notice any faces."

"So, you have witnesses that don't know their own names, or those of the dancers? And they couldn't remember where it happened? Sounds like they lost their minds."

I thought for a moment. "Wait. Is Wiley Odoms spreading his corn squeezins around again? He's got to start aging it more than a couple of days. A man I know swears on a stack of bibles he drank a jar of that and woke up in the woods holding a half-eaten bear leg—hair and all. Did you know the blacksmith uses that stuff to start up his fire?"

But naked dancing? In my county? Finally, something I could investigate. And I do love a good mystery. I stood and offered to shake their hands.

"As upstanding citizens, I appreciate you letting me know about this. I'll get right on it, folks. You have my word as the Bennett County Sheriff."

The looks they gave me were not encouraging. After they slammed the front door, Deputy Jones came slinking in through the back. He gave up trying to close the warped door and left it to swing open.

My new chair was developing a squeak. "Jones, have you been messing with Tall's horseshoe again?"

His feet scuffed the floor, but I could see him smiling. "Aw, come on, Billy. It's so easy. He only has one nail in it. We kind of use it for a signal. When the horseshoe is pointing up, I know he's home."

"And when it's down, he knows someone's been there." I shook my head. "Well, stop it. He's going to figure it out someday and shoot your ass for trespassing and sneaking around his place. You'll cause a scandal, or something."

Jones grinned at me. "Emily thinks it's kind of funny."

"And that's the other reason you need to stay away. In case you forgot, Emily is his wife. Now, I understand Tall is a drunk and hardly ever home to work his land proper —I know that. But I figure he's the one who should be plowing his fields, and he still knows how to make a gelding out of a stallion. And no one would blame him. Are you hearing me?"

"Sure." He shrugged. "You'll need some help investigating those dancers. I'll be glad to help."

I tried to keep my gaze stern. "Nope. That's something I'll have to do. It's my job, you know."

Sometimes it's hard to keep the peace. And I'll admit my idea of peace isn't always the same as other folks. I don't believe in meddling with people's business unless they're harming someone else. Most people know me, and some might call me a traitor. But not to my face. I had a reputation for being a pretty good scrapper before I left home, and folks remembered that. Some had to be re-educated.

I fought with the Third Arkansas Cavalry Regiment, which was about the dumbest thing I've ever done. I vowed early on not to shoot at anyone I knew, but it's hard to ignore Minie balls coming at you like a cloud of hornets. About the only thing that misadventure got me was a shoulder wound picked up at Jenkin's Ferry that hurts when it rains, and a job as the county sheriff. If I'd fought for the secession, no job would be available, and the federal government would steal any land I had— which I didn't.

I applied for the job when we mustered out of the army. Me being a Union soldier went along with their idea of reconstruction and occupation, so that greased the wheels—along with no one else wanting the job. It didn't hurt that the county already had my name. It was a small county, mostly uphill and down, with one settlement straddling a notch between the highest peaks. Since most travel funneled through the pass, the town prospered.

When my appointment came from Fort Smith, the first thing I did was send the Federal soldiers high-tailing it out of there. They grumbled and cussed, but they went. You might put it down to how mean I am, but you'd be wrong. I just reminded them our county was small and poor. There were easier pickings, other places.

There was wealth in Bennett's Pass, but it was hard to find for an outsider. And it's been my observation that mountain folk are obstinate. They're full of life and love. But if there's a scab—don't pick at it. Outside folks don't recover from meddling in mountain affairs.

Riding a rolling chair on a sloping floor is hard work, and my belly was grumbling, so, leaving my deputy in charge of the office, I stepped outside, thinking about lunch. Our town is small enough to survey the street with a couple of glances. But a glance could never harness the intrigue an observant man could see.

One end of the street sported the Mountain Goat Saloon and Billiard Parlor. I asked once about the goat part but didn't receive a satisfactory answer—in fact, no answer at all, just a stare. And it's a blank stare. They think I don't know. A local group from deep in the hills calls themselves Mountain Goats. They sell their product to the saloon—unrefined and fresh. One drink, and you know why they call it a skullbuster. Or block and tackle whiskey. Take one drink, and you'll walk a block and tackle anything. But I keep watch on them. Most of the trouble hereabouts walked through their doors on a regular basis. Walking in. Staggering out.

A mercantile selling everything from bullets to

shovels was across the street, along with a dressmaker and clothing store. And they make hats. We have fine hats in our town. If they sell it to you, they'll clean and re-shape it for you after it's been sat on, run over, stomped on, or caught in a turkey stampede. They even repair bullet holes. And free of charge. Everyone bought at least one of their hats because that hatmaker is talking about moving to Texas. Why worry about hats? It's a town badge, a rite of passage. Dirty, beat-up hats spelled stranger and usually trouble.

My side of the street had the sheriff's office, a barber shop, and the Rest in Peace bathhouse. A husband-and-wife team ran that establishment. They'd alternate depending on what clientele came through their doors. The building sat atop a warm spring that bubbled up and then ran off down the valley. Using an aqueduct system invented by the ancient Romans, I took Herbert's word on that one, they had hot water for private rooms. The first part of the week was reserved for men, and the women used it the rest of the time. There was a soapy runoff going down the valley, but it didn't seem to hurt anything. We may be poor, but we're clean.

That the apothecary in the building next to the bathhouse dispensed medicinal concoctions probably didn't have anything to do with resting in peace and comfort. Probably. But they always had a cure for what ails you. They may have been closely related to the Mountain Goats. Their medicine didn't cure your malady, you just forgot you had it.

Seeing no excitement on the street, except for a buzzard keeping a lonely vigil on a hitching post, I walked down to Etta Mae's place. Before entering, I glanced back at that buzzard. It seemed to be waiting.

Evil portent? Lost and tired? Dunno. Don't know who to ask.

Etta Mae was a single woman who put on a simple fare for folks passing through and townsfolk who didn't want to go home and cook. After a meal of fried chicken with the fixings and a slice of dried apple pie covered in cream, I sat back in my chair, thinking about life in general and naked dancers. My assumption was that they were all female—I refused to think of any alternative.

And skeeters. And chiggers. I should look for women with enough bites on them to look like they had the pox. Mountain country is one of the reasons clothes were invented—it was scratchy country. Or I could look for missing women. Some of our skeeters are large enough to carry off a small woman or child.

Maybe I needed some help. I sure didn't want to waste valuable time. This needed to be solved quickly so it didn't get out of hand. The only drawback? All the clues I needed to see would be covered by clothing.

Etta Mae was a good-looking woman, unencumbered with menfolk. Maybe that was why. We had several ladies around town in that circumstance, but the war did that to us. Many of the local men didn't come home for one reason or another. Some died, some left for parts unknown. I can't figure what they'd find in other places that would be better, but some cannot ignore the quest for adventure.

She was as big an attraction as her cooking. With hair so lightly colored it was almost white, soft brown eyes, and nearly flawless skin, some came to drink coffee and watch her. She didn't seem to mind if they were a paying customer. I could tell she knew I wanted to speak with her because she kept watching me—kind of like I'd watch a hothead and troublemaker in the saloon.

The room had emptied out of customers when Etta Mae ambled over to my table with a coffee pot and an extra cup. She sat down and poured herself a cup, staring at me the whole time while hitting the cup dead center. I couldn't do that on my best day.

When I returned from the war, I'd made some eyes at her, thinking I should settle down with a good woman. After she asked if I had some sort of affliction, I quit doing that. She seemed to appreciate it. Upshot is, we became good friends. I don't know why she's unattached, and she hasn't enlightened me on that subject. Some things you don't ask if you want to keep your head attached to your shoulders.

Her voice was buttery smooth and made the hair on my neck stand up and wave. "What's going on with you, Billy? You seem to be mulling over some weighty problem."

I saw no reason to delay my investigation. And there was no way to sugarcoat this. "You are friends with most of the womenfolk around, aren't you?"

She nodded, getting a wary look about her. "Most, not all."

"You know Emma Arnold? She's reporting some witchy things going on. You heard about any of that?" I watched her real close and noticed a tightening around her eyes.

Etta Mae snorted into her coffee cup and then used her apron to wipe her face. "Pot calling the kettle black, don't you think? That woman's a witch in the oldest sense of the word."

I couldn't argue with that. "There's also a report of women dancing naked in the forest." I grinned at her. "You do understand it's my sworn duty to investigate that."

We always seemed to be comfortable together. Her gaze was taunting as she grinned right back at me, the afternoon sun highlighting little blond curls escaping the white cap she wore while cooking and making shadows in the dimples of her cheeks. You might call her fetching. Pretty wouldn't do her justice with those brown eyes staring at me. Be nice if she would blink, though. At least occasionally.

We took another sip of the black liquor called coffee.

"Why, Billy Bennett, it must be awful having to investigate something like that. I don't know how you stand it." She slipped into a southern accent, bringing visions of antebellum homes set amid trees adorned with Spanish moss. And yes, I'd seen them. "I just cannot imagine the trials and tribulations you face being the county sheriff. But then, you were always strong. Are you getting anywhere with your quest?"

"Nope. I just heard about it today." I wanted to roll my eyes, but it would have ruined the stern look I projected as I shook my head. She didn't seem impressed. "Look. We can have some fun talking about this, but you know the people around here as well as me. This could have a serious side. There's some...well, peculiar folks about."

"Peculiar?" She gave a quick look around and, seeing the café was empty, she relaxed in her chair. "Look at it this way. It's the middle of summer. You know it gets so hot in here sometimes it's hard to breathe. The only breeze we can get is if I hold a chicken in the air and let it try to fly away. I can fry an egg on a flat rock if it's out in the sun. All those old sayings apply here because they're true. Just think about how nice it would be, say after a nice swim in some cool limestone spring, to just dance and enjoy the sunshine until you're dry all over. You can stand and breathe in the smell of jasmine and honeysuckle. Pine trees release their scent at sunset, do you remember? Of course you do. It smells so clean and fresh. You ever think about that?"

"I'm starting to get my mind around it." I felt an urge to loosen my shirt collar and hoped she didn't think I had a fever. "To be honest, I doubt if I will think of anything else for a good, long while."

"You're always honest. It's one of the things I like about you." She looked pointedly at me as she scratched at her side. "Well, there's no harm done by it. Not a bit. Is there?" She smiled at me again, bigger this time. "Not that I'd know anything about that kind of goings-on."

It took me a moment to figure out how to answer that, distracted by her scratching, and I don't know if I got it right. We were having fun with this, but it could be a serious matter. If a dozen people look at any one occurrence, there will be a dozen opinions on what went on. Some could be harmful.

"I wouldn't want anyone to get hurt, Etta Mae. For whatever reason, some might not understand it. There are folks in these hills that haven't been twenty miles from home. Ever. Some of their opinions haven't changed in a hundred years."

A thought occurred to me. "My god, woman. There are Baptists around here. Look, you need to gather your...friends and spread a word of caution." I stopped and smiled at her. "Not that you would know anything about it, of course."

"Wait. I'll help with your investigation." Etta Mae put her hand on my arm to stop me as I got up to leave. "Here's what you should do. There's a nice little spread a couple of miles north of here—down in Cold Hollow. A widow and her sister live there. She might know something."

My sleuthing was getting somewhere. Etta Mae probably felt the heat from my probing questions and was deflecting to someone else. "Does this widow have a name?"

"Sarah Bray. She bought the old Bronson place early this spring to raise a few horses." She stopped me again. "And, Billy, she really is a nice lady. And a friend. But you be careful."

That set me back. "Now, why would I have to be careful?"

"You're ripe for the picking, Billy." Her expression turned serious. "You're an easy-going man, and don't take yourself too seriously. I appreciate that and your friendship. But you want more than I can give. I'm thinking you have a lot more experience dealing with men than women. You've been sidling up to me for a while, so I know you're looking for something more permanent. But Sarah has a way about her, and she's looking for someone too. You might say she's waiting for the right man to come calling. So, I wouldn't want you to go there unless you want to be caught."

I gave her the saddest look I could come up with. "No chance for us? Not even a little bit?" I wasn't sure what I'd do if she changed her mind, but thought I'd ask. It was the polite thing to do.

She shook her head, meeting my gaze. "You wouldn't understand, but no."

An easy-going man? Maybe. I do believe it's easier to walk the valleys than trudge the peaks. So, the widow Bray? Caught? Well now. I have some wiles of my own. I said my goodbyes, wondering why Etta Mae would be so shy about commitment. And wondering how my lighthearted quest had turned serious. It wasn't how I thought my day would go.

———————

I LEFT a note at the office telling Jones to hold down the fort and that I'd be gone all day. He should be fixing the back door, but I suspect he's helping Emily Johnson inspect horseshoes.

No one calls my deputy by his first name. Why any sane parent would name a boy-child Herkle I'd never know. For all that, he was a good enough man and passable deputy if his practical jokes didn't get him killed. I gave it even money.

I'd never been to the old Bronson place that the widow bought. All I knew was a general location—north of town and a little west. But that was enough for someone raised in hill country. After a mile or so, the trail jogged to the right, and I went left, following a trace through the hills. It was just wide enough to hold wagon tracks. Any sign of recent travel was lost in the spongy leaf-covered forest floor.

The morning was glorious, and it was days like this that I knew why I'd come home after the war. Dappled sunlight painted the ghost of a trail that I traveled. Leaves from seasons past muffled our progress, and I could hear a mockingbird in the distance trying out some new notes. I wished he'd get it right, he was off-key on most of them. If I had a flock of them singing at once, I could get any criminal to confess—even if they were innocent. It was such a beautiful day I felt like whistling just to mess with him.

Trying to figure out that bird's tune, which switched from imitating tree frogs to a strangled crow, I didn't pay as much attention as I should on the trail and got surprised. Rounding a limestone outcropping, I stumbled on a curious sight. It would have been funny—if not so serious.

A woman stood in the back of a buckboard. Her black hair shining in the sun had a life of its own. Bright, blue eyes settled on me as I rounded the rock. The sun picked this spot to shine through the canopy of leaves overhead, holding the woman in a golden halo. The only discordant note was the rope around her neck and hands tied behind her back.

"You!" Her voice was soft but carried well. A surprised expression gave way to pleasure, and then she smiled at me. Only at me. For a moment, it seemed the two of us were alone in that clearing. I'd heard poets, or those who claimed to be, talk of that but never experienced it. Around lonely campfires in the deep woods late at night, whether listening to the hounds give voice to their chase or wounded soldiers wailing in despair, everyone is a poet. I could never get it right.

I took a sudden, deep breath, trying to get rid of a spidery feeling making my hair stand up. I'd never seen a woman this beautiful. Fond memories of Etta Mae slunk away without a whimper, as well as the warning she gave. I could imagine her smirking at me, shaking her head.

At the woman's one spoken word, the people surrounding the buckboard flinched so hard the horses hitched to that wagon got skittish. She was calmer than I would be in that circumstance. Jumping my horse forward, I grabbed a bridle and settled them down. Looking around, I wasn't surprised at the members of the small lynching party.

I centered my gaze on Emma. "I thought you were supposed to burn them."

She slapped her thigh, startling the impossibly small horse she rode with a triumphant yell. I had to grab those horses again. "That's what I said. But these girly men don't have it in them to do it."

Besides the Arnolds, there were four men. One was Tall Johnson, and I didn't know the other three. My head shook once as I sighed. How they pulled Tall out of the saloon for this misadventure was a mystery for another day. I backed my horse so I could keep all the parties in view.

"Mr. Arnold, it would be a kindness to me if you'd untie the rope from the tree and then let that woman go. We don't want any accidents here." When he didn't move, I pinned him with a level gaze. "Consider that an order."

Emma raised her hand, intending to lay a quirt on the horses pulling the buckboard.

When you travel around the hills of Arkansas, you'd better go armed. There's no end to the kinds of critters you can run into. Bears and big cats being the friendliest. Some of the hill folk are cranky. Being prepared, I already had the hammers of my double-barreled coach gun pulled back, and we were into can't miss if you try territory.

"I'd hate to shoot a woman, but I could manage it—if I had to. The upside is...it might solve some problems for the community in the future if you go ahead and try. It's up to you."

"We'd just shoot you, Sheriff." I noted the man who spoke, a stranger to me, but a face I'd remember. He didn't have a gun drawn.

"That's all right. I've been shot before. You just do what you gotta do." I looked back at Samuel and wondered why he was hesitating. Maybe he figured to get rid of two bothersome problems at once? Not that I'd blame him.

"Samuel, right now would be a good time to move."

He gave me a look that made me think he might be as mean as Emma but finally did as I asked, even untying her hands.

I glanced at the woman standing in the wagon and asked something I already suspected. "What's your name?"

"Sarah." Giving Emma a look that turned the woman pale, she stood, rubbing some circulation back into her wrists. "I'm honored to meet you and pleased you've been sent to me."

Well, that was formal. And how would she know that? I hadn't heard the thrumming of a carrier pigeon to bring her a message. She said it like a pronouncement, which made me curious, but I was too busy to follow up on it. I couldn't spare her a glance. The three strangers were getting antsy.

As I turned to face the three men, I spoke to her again. "You haven't been harmed in any way, Sarah?"

She was moving around, but I still couldn't give her another glance. "No, sir. I have not...thanks to you. The only harm was in their intentions, but you stopped them."

I turned my full attention to the others. "You folks go on home. I don't want to hear any more of this foolishness. I could press attempted murder charges and hold you until the judge comes around, if he ever does, but I'll let it go...just this once. Now git."

Tall's voice was plaintive. "You can't let her go, Sheriff. She told me I was going to get a boil on my face and die from it. If we hang her, the curse goes away."

Emma squirmed like she had a saddle sore in an embarrassing spot while Sarah gave her a little smile.

"Tall, if you kill her, you'll die anyway, and I'll use the noose you've already made to hang you." If I ever wondered how whiskey could pickle a brain, the evidence called Tall Johnson straddled a horse in front of me. "Now, if she really did lay a curse on you, which I doubt, why would she do something like that?"

A very unladylike snort came from the wagon. "I can answer that question. When he tied my hands, he had his hand up my dress. Way up."

I shook my head again. I'd noticed him rubbing his face when I rode up on them. "Tall, if you ever get sober, you'd know that's plumb foolishness. However, I'm betting you *could* rub a hole in your face if you don't quit. If it gets infected, that could be a problem. But that's on you, not her."

Wheeling her horse in the small clearing, Emma had a parting shot. "Don't let her look directly at you, Sheriff. You'll be hexed if you ain't been already. It's what they do."

The Arnolds and Tall Johnson rode away, slinging righteous dirt-clods from their horses' hooves, but I stopped the three strangers from leaving. They had a nervous look about them.

"Where are you boys from?"

I still had the hammers on that Greener cocked, and they didn't quite know what to do about it. It didn't need to be aimed, just pointed in their general direction. "Just so there aren't any misunderstandings, did you notice how the ends of the barrels on this shotgun are kinda flattened? It was made for riot control in prisons. The barrels spread the pellets out sideways in a big hurry, and the load is double-ought buckshot. It ain't for hunting birds."

One man finally found his voice. "We're from up in Missouri. Just friendly folk looking about for a place to light for a while."

Their clothes were dusty, and the tired-looking horses were crusted in sweat. Bedrolls and slickers hid heavy saddlebags. Looked like they were on the move. I nodded to them.

"You know, I've heard fairy tales since I was knee high to a short frog. And I think I just heard another one. How'd you happen to be here, helping the Arnolds on their witch hunt? Did you just happen by?"

Their spokesman was the man who'd threatened me. "That's right. We just rode up on them, same as you. Hadn't quite decided on what to do about it when you showed up."

"It didn't look like you were objecting much." I contemplated them for a moment. The sound of the woman climbing over the seat of her wagon came to me, but I kept my attention on these men. They'd done nothing wrong that I knew of. I just didn't like their looks. There was another kind of spidery feeling running up and down my spine—far different than that caused by Sarah.

"All right. Here's how we'll play this. About a short day's ride in any direction will get you out of my county. I'd take it as a personal favor if you'd see how quick you can make that trip. And you get to pick the direction."

The man tried to bluster. "We done nothing wrong—"

I held my hand up to stop him. "Oh, I'm sure you'll remedy that given enough time, you've got the look— just not in my county. You can take your mischief elsewhere."

An explosion echoed through the valley, rustling the leaves around us, seeming to come from up the mountain.

"What was that?"

Head shaking, I didn't take my gaze from them. "Probably the Mountain Goats. I told them they shouldn't put black powder in their skullbuster. The strychnine gives it enough kick for anyone. They never listen."

After giving me the stinky stare, they ran out of reasons to stay, and I was glad to see them turn their horses and ride away. Armed with rifles and handguns—a lot of handguns, as most border guerrillas carried them during the war—they still didn't want to argue with that double-barrel shotgun at short range. That was wise on their part. It would take saints and sinners alike, and I'm sure their horses were grateful. I didn't know those men, but I knew their type. I'd stay wary of an ambush for a while.

"It might have been better to shoot them."

Her soft voice was tight and angry. I decided right then not to low-rate this woman. She looked gentle, but I had an idea I didn't want to see the other side of her disposition.

The last thing I wanted on my mind was fabric and color, but dressed in a blue cotton blouse and gray pleated skirt, she looked like a beautiful painting perched on the seat of that wagon. Reaching beneath her, she brought out a long-hooded bonnet, put it on her head, and tied the strings under her chin.

Somewhere I'd lost control of my mouth—maybe my senses. "Seems a shame, covering up that hair."

She glanced at me, startled and curious. Her look

softened, and it took but a moment for that bonnet to come off. "Whatever you wish, Billy."

Well, that sounded...I shook my head. How the hell did she know my name? "How did all this come about, Sarah? What brought you and the Arnolds together?"

Her shrug was expressive and slow. "I was going to Tall's place to talk with Emily. We're thinking of having a party in a week or so. I didn't get very far, did I? I can't believe Tall treated me like he did. He's never shown me disrespect before."

Her attention seemed to wander a moment before she turned to me. "You know anyone who plays the fiddle? Or a guitar?"

I hesitated a moment at the abrupt shift. "There's a few around. I'd bet there's a fiddle stashed under the bed in almost every cabin in these hills. Etta Mae would know of them." I glanced at her. "I've been playing second fiddle most of my life."

It disturbed me that she could follow my train of thought when I never knew its intent before it left my mouth.

"Not anymore, Billy. Not anymore."

She didn't seem to mind me watching her, holding a little smile on her face as she met my gaze. This was a rarely beautiful woman. Far too pretty for the likes of me. To be honest, she gave me an unbalanced feeling, like I couldn't quite find steady ground. I'd felt like that once before in the Louisiana swamps, where the hummocks of earth seemed to be floating on water. People that lived there called them quakies, and horses would stand spraddle-legged until someone led them off.

"You should carry a weapon." I took off my hat and wiped the headband with a handkerchief. "There are bad people out in these hills on occasion. I'm thinking we just met three of them."

Her laugh was soft. "Just three? I wouldn't put a chance on any of the six."

I enjoyed watching her another moment. It could get to be a habit. "I'm curious. When I rode up, you seemed surprised it was me. Were you expecting someone else?"

She shrugged. "I knew someone would come. That's the only reason I let them treat me the way they did. We'll be equally yoked the rest of our lives. That it was you surprised and pleased me. Etta Mae said you gave up on women when she turned you down."

Sarah laughed. "She's always thought well of herself, and I think she's wrong. You're a handsome man, Billy Bennett."

Well, this was a bit sudden. Equally yoked? That phrase she threw in surprised me. I'd read my Bible too. That it came from someone suspected of being a witch was unsettling. I didn't think they were big on the Bible. Then again, I could be wrong.

"Well, I did give up on romancing Etta Mae. Let's say I did some retreating and contemplating. But we're still good friends. Who told you someone would come?"

Evasion wasn't a good look for her, but she surely dodged the question. "I just knew."

We sat in the near silence of the forest, looking at each other. I'd seen other people do that, but they'd been married for a lot of years. It's hard to lock gazes with someone for any length of time without some sort of embarrassment setting in—the gaze darts away, only to come back after losing the staring contest. There was none of that. It was more searching, curious about a newfound interest.

That same off-key mockingbird had followed me

around, and a squirrel barked nearby—could have been the bird. Wind moaned through nearby pine trees, bringing the smell of far-off rain.

I sat relaxed as a cat in sunshine. And if I were a cat, I'd have run out of lives a long time ago. Curiosity seems to be a curse, but I wasn't ready to let it go. There seemed to be much at stake, and I wanted to know why.

"Are you one of those fortune tellers? Can you tell the future? I'm only asking, mind you, because I'm short of cash and don't know whether to start gambling or rob a bank."

Her laugh was a beautiful sound and unrestrained. "This is going to be fun. No, you don't need to do any of that. Not that you would—you're too good of a man."

I watched the trail the three men took, wishing we were under cover. And a good man? Right then, I knew she was lacking education. "Maybe you haven't talked to the right folks. Some would disagree with you."

"Maybe." She gave her raven hair a slow shake, using her fingers to comb it from her eyes. "That damned war robbed us of a lot. You of your innocence—me of a husband. It left many of us broken and searching for our proper way in life. But we can recover from our hardship. I believe that."

I'd been staring into her eyes a long time. Too long? Maybe Emma Arnold was right. "Are you putting a spell on me?"

She laughed again. "That's obvious, don't you think? You are a little slow about some things."

Can't argue that. I like things spelled out. "Why? You don't know me. I told you I'm not a good man, at least not one any decent woman would want. You're wasting your time. Perhaps I'm just a distraction? Something to spice up a dull day? A dalliance?"

"Nonsense." She fluffed out her hair and then fingered errant curls away from her eyes again. I was detecting a habit. "You're an old soul, Billy. You have no idea what you are or can do. It's important to have someone at your side for guidance."

Now I was confused and a little scared. Did I need a keeper? "I'm not really good at being guided. Got a stubborn streak a mile long. Even if I knew what you were talking about, which I don't—how could you know something like that?"

She shrugged, looking away. That halo of hair seemed to sparkle. "That's not important right now. I just do. The what is always more important than the why."

I settled in the saddle, hooking my knee around the saddle horn. "Well, it's important to me. I have decisions to make. Why things happen helps."

"Decisions?" She studied me for a moment and the little smile came back. "Well, that's different."

Settling herself comfortably on the seat of the wagon, she picked up and began untying the knotted rope that had graced her neck. Then her direct gaze held my eyes. Her voice changed into an accent I'd only heard once.

"What do you know of England?"

I was startled enough at the change to back my horse a step. "I once served with a man from England, from London, to be exact. He was a fine man and a crack shot with any weapon."

She nodded, coiling the rope and tossing it into the back of the wagon. Continuing, she used another accent that I knew well.

"And what do you know of Wales?"

I had to chuckle at that, thinking of a livid face and a cursing soldier. "A place that Englishmen didn't like. We didn't get along much once he learned my momma was Welsh."

She seemed to mull that over for a minute, slowly rocking on the seat as she studied me. "And your father?"

I'd had a good time being raised in these hills. Poor, but everyone was. My wave took in the surrounding forest. "He was homegrown—right here, as am I."

"Are you sure?"

"Well, we're all from somewhere else if you go back far enough. Even the Indians took this land from somebody. They didn't just spring up like a rock."

She watched me—more like inspected me. I began to wish I'd shaved and spruced up a little. "Are they still alive?"

Well, that was a sore subject. "Yes, ma'am. At least, as far as I know. When I went north to join up, they went south to Texas. I got a letter from them once. They are living on the coast, fishing every day, and living the good life—providing you like fish."

"I must meet your mother. I'm from Wales, too. We'd have many things to talk about. Especially about her boy-child."

She stiffened, and her gaze met mine. "You need to take me home."

"Why? You got all the way here by yourself." I thought my quip was disarming...friendly. And I had every intention of taking her home.

Those blue eyes pinned me to my saddle, and I swear the temperature changed. My horse rolled his eyes at me and quivered. Probably had a fly in its ear.

"I can see why you've never married. Do you ken the word peckish?"

I sobered some at that, my gaze narrowing as I stared

at her. "Well, folks around here would call me nettle-some." The horse shuddered again and looked at me. He had that wanting-to-get-gone look to him.

She shook her head and then smiled at me. It was a big smile. "You're educated. Good. It will make conversation easier for us. But for now, it seems those men you ran off are headed toward my ranch."

Glad I was educated? One thing I remembered of my father. After an argument with my mother, he told me an educated man is more easily led down a path to destruction. Did he mean persuaded?

I was starting to get an inkling.

———

SHE LED THE WAY, driving the buckboard with a single-minded purpose. The trace was narrow, so I lagged. Being away from her allowed me to ponder, although it seemed her thoughts touched me occasionally. Surely, I imagined that.

Being close to her was a distraction. It might take some getting used to. She smelled too good and looked too good. When she talked, it seemed every word was so important, I had to drop everything and listen. With few words, she seemed to offer something, but I wasn't prepared to go there on an hour's notice. Although some might bring up the adage of not looking a gift horse in the mouth.

I don't believe in witches. I do not. But then, every woman will practice witchcraft in her own way at times and for many reasons. And I suspect some are better at it than others. I'd tried the same thing with Etta Mae with disastrous results. It didn't take much imagination to hear her laughing over that incident.

Most folks wouldn't call me educated because we didn't have schools around. But momma was, and she taught me all she could. Although she seemed to think there were some things my head wasn't ready for. Our home was filled with books and my mind with stories she told. Papa helped with stories too, always told to make a point, but mostly, he farmed and hunted. We never had much, but it was a good life for a boy growing up.

The hills around us had as many girls as boys, so I'd been educated a few times that way. It seemed to be a mutual quest at the time. And what that circuit-riding preacher didn't know wouldn't get him all riled up to preachify our sins away. Seems about all the hillfolk could raise on poor ground with any consistency were children.

What food we had was fetched by hunting and fishing or gathering greens. Anyone starving was too lazy to go find food. It was all around us. Of course, an occasional chicken from a neighbor's roost wasn't out of bounds— as long as we just took one.

I do have a problem, and I've acknowledged it from time to time. Some call it a mean streak. I'd call it being perverse. Peckish? I don't like to be led. And if I am to do something, I want it to be my choice. I have heard the phrase *stubborn as a mule* applied to me more than I thought proper.

When my folks went south, it wasn't a peaceful thing. Papa was mad at me for siding with the Union. I couldn't help it. And it was my parents' fault. They'd taught me to look at problems in a straightforward manner and take that knowledge to a logical conclusion.

Thinking of the war, I felt the southern states were in the right. The states had every right to secede from the

Union by a vote of the people. But they were going to lose the war. For the same reason, the Indians would lose their war. It was a game of numbers. The Confederacy would run out of resources while fighting long before the Federals. If every man-jack in the South went off to fight for the states' rights, who was tending the farm? Taking care of family? Raising cattle? Growing food? Fishing?

Men in the northern army thought all southerners owned slaves to tend the farms. I'd never seen one, didn't know anyone who had slaves—I didn't hold with it anyway. That wasn't what the fight was about, but most weren't told that. Toward the end of the war, a Union officer asked a Confederate why he was still fighting. The reply was simple. *Because this is our land…and you're on it.*

———

SARAH STOPPED the wagon and brought me out of my reverie. My mind had gone off on a rabbit trail instead of tending to business. Maybe that was my problem. I was being led, and it sure looked inviting. Was it somewhere I wanted to go? I'd known her a mere hour, but it seemed like an important decision. I couldn't see a downside. Most men I know want hearth and home, or some version of it. She seemed to be offering that in a beautiful package, all tied up with a bow. Why?

Before us lay a small valley. The house and barn were nestled up against a bluff that would make a good windbreak in the winter. A few horses swatted their tails at flies as they grazed in a meadow of belly-high grass. The hills around made a natural fence that only the most adventurous horse or cow would try to navigate. Most wouldn't leave available food and water unless driven. It was a beautiful place.

She spoke quietly, indicating the valley with a nod of her head. "How do you like it, Billy?"

When I replied, I was looking at her. "It's beautiful. Peaceful. Dangerous."

Her head whipped around. "I'm not, you know. Especially not to those I hold dear. And never to you."

She continued. "What about those men down there? If we go down, they'll want me. I doubt if they'd have let me hang, although that would be preferable to what they had in mind. And we can't run, they may follow. I keep wondering why you're a sheriff. Etta Mae says you're a gentleman with a fine mind, not given to violence. I'll not have you killed. Let my sister and I take care of this. We have our ways."

Well now. Was this our first disagreement in our short history? "Etta Mae should have gotten to know me better. I'll be going down there to have a word with them."

"A word?"

That hair got messed up again, covering one of her eyes. Guess I knew why she wore a bonnet. "You know. Teach them the error of their ways. Instruct them in proper behavior. Maybe smite them hip and thigh."

"Are you sure you can...Etta Mae said you always tried to avoid any kind of...never mind. I'm babbling like a little girl. So, we're going down there? Are you sure you're alright? You're looking a little pale."

Fright? Common sense? Maybe some of both. "Yes, ma'am. I surely am going. It might be better if you stay here. You don't have to go."

"Oh, yes. Yes, I do. I left my sister down there." She grinned at me, and her expression was something I'd have to ponder about, given that she should be scared. I'd seen cats with that expression—not necessarily predatory, just watching. If she had a tail to twitch... "I don't know what you're after, exactly. But she might be the witch you're looking for."

It took a moment to find my voice. "I hope the games you ladies are playing don't get someone hurt."

"Games? You think...?" Her hand came to cover her mouth for a moment. "Oh, Billy."

I pointed my horse down the trail toward that house, and she followed close behind. It seemed the temperature dropped, and I shivered. No wonder they called it Cold Hollow. I finally remembered what I'd been told about this place.

There were several springs surrounding the valley. Those springs and pools were so cold you could hardly swim in them, even in the summer. Turtles and frogs were smart enough to stay away. Cold air stays close to the ground, and there wasn't much sunlight on the road to warm it.

She'd seen me shiver and misunderstood. "You should not worry. You need to stay strong and know you're protected."

"Protected?" I was already watching the windows for any sign of life in that house. I held the Greener across my saddle and took the loop off the hammer of my pistol. "You know what I've learned in my short time on this earth?"

"What?" She raised her voice over the rattle of the wagon and her horses.

"Change is a constant, and we can never understand everything we see. Says that in the Book."

A cattle stampede couldn't be noisier than that wagon. I saw a curtain move, and my Greener covered that window. We stopped by the front porch. No sound came from inside the house. I started to dismount, but before I could say anything, Sarah breezed through the door.

One thing I noticed on the way in was one of the bags hanging over a saddle had Bank of Big Springs printed on it. A large withdrawal of legitimate funds? Doubtful. Maybe they thought we couldn't read or just didn't care who knew? And if they didn't care...?

When I walked quiet-like into that cabin, all eyes were on Sarah, and the men looked plumb delighted. They grinned like Santa had just delivered another present for them. The women favored each other enough to be twins, except one was tied to a chair. Guess the men were agnostic toward witches. Their guns were drawn but not pointed anywhere in particular. I wondered about that. Seemed careless. Whoever peeked out that window must have only had eyes for Sarah. They didn't seem to know I was there. And that was more curious. Strange, in fact.

I spoke from the door. "You boys drop those pistols."

My words seemed to get their attention and brought action. To say they were startled would be an understatement. The man nearest me flinched, bleated in surprise, and shot into the floor. By the time I said "pistol," the other two were turning their guns toward me, so I aimed between them and cut loose with the shotgun, thankful the ladies weren't in the way. One man moved just as I shot, and the other turned and dove through a window, glass, casing, and all. I don't know what he hit going through, but one of his legs remained hung up on the windowsill and didn't quiver. The man who moved first took the full charge and wasn't going anywhere.

The third man was little more than a boy. As he

cocked his pistol again, he dropped it, and the gun went off, the bullet slicing me on top of the shoulder before burying itself in the wall behind me. I reached out and tapped him with the barrel of my pistol. He dropped like a sack of potatoes and didn't move an inch.

The boot hung up in the window was starting to move, so I reached through and grabbed the shirt collar of that man and dragged him inside. I guess he found out a window ain't that easy to dive through, especially one as well built as this one. His eyes wouldn't focus on anything, and his hat wasn't going to fit because of the knot on his head.

Helping both men outside, I roped them to the hitching post. When I went back inside, Sarah had untied her sister, and both stood staring at me—hands folded in front and alike as peas in a pod. With the window broken out and the door open, the powder smoke was almost gone.

The sister spoke first. "Is this the one? He looks kind of...scruffy."

Sarah spoke after nodding to her sister. "He seems a little sudden, but I do like him." One eyebrow rose as she studied me. "The violence does surprise me."

The twin spoke to me as she rubbed the rope burns on her wrists. This was going to be a real problem because they had the same voice. "You needn't have done any of that. I had them spelled. When you came in, didn't you see they weren't moving at all?"

My shoulder was starting to hurt, and I was leaking blood on their floor. "Yes, ma'am. I should have seen you had them under control, guess I missed that. What I did notice is they had you trussed up like a Christmas turkey on that chair. Did you get a late start with casting your spell?"

Sarah looked at her sister and shrugged. "He's peckish."

By the time I pulled the dead man out and off the porch, I was feeling kind of weak and breathing heavy, sweating more than the work required. I felt bad for messing up their floor with that dead man. Of course, he didn't feel it none.

I amazed myself when I offered to replace their wooden floor, given my inability to join two boards together, but my words kind of slurred, and I don't think they understood. Confused, I slumped down into a chair on the porch to rest. I wondered if there were some left-over spells hanging around in the air, and I'd caught one. I'd have to learn how to avoid such things.

About that time, Sarah noticed my wound. With a screech, she pulled me up from the chair and walked me inside. She threw me on a bed, at least it felt like it, and ripped my shirt apart. That was a good shirt, too. It was good for at least four, maybe five more washings. I started to argue about that, but somewhere in the discussion, I just faded away.

———

WHEN I AWOKE, I could smell chicken frying and see the two women bustling about the cooking area. I must have made some noise because Sarah came over, putting her hand on my forehead.

"Good, the fever is gone."

"What fever?" I moved my shoulder, and it didn't feel too bad. I'd been notched before. "How long have I been here?"

"Going on three days. You caught a fever. I figure you must have been coming down with something before you were shot. I never heard of a fever coming on that quickly from a wound. And it's not infected. We took care of that."

Holding thoughts together wasn't something I was doing very well. "How could I have been sick? Don't you have potions or something to give me?"

At her irritated expression, my addled brain finally came to its senses, and I changed the subject. "What about those men I tied up? You didn't let them go, did you?"

She smiled, and I was glad to see it. I was going to take a personal interest in not making her mad.

"We got hold of Mr. Jones, and he came out to get them. Seems they were wanted for a bank robbery in Missouri."

I snorted, thinking of the printing on the bags, and it hurt my shoulder. "Yeah, I'm guessing Big Springs. Jones figure all that out by himself?"

"Well, we had to prod him a little. Emily was here too, so she kind of helped. He gets awfully distracted with her around."

"No wonder Tall stays drunk all the time. That girl has a wandering eye." I looked at the twin. "What's your name?"

"I'm Kate, and I'm most pleased to meet you. Thank you for rescuing me."

Heaving myself up from that bed, I felt a breeze. "Uh, Sarah, where's my pants?"

Huddled with a blanket over my lap, I watched as she crossed to a chair and picked up my store-boughts. She handed them to me and stood watching. I stayed right there, waiting her out.

Finally, she smiled. "Modest? Now? How do you think you lost your pants?"

I didn't budge.

With a smirk, she turned her back. Dressing wasn't easy. I was still dizzy, but got it done. With Sarah's help, I wobbled barefoot to the table, buttoning a new red shirt I didn't remember I owned. Maybe Jones delivered it.

It was never a good practice to put off something you didn't want to do. But duty called. "Well, Kate. I'm glad everything turned out good for you, but we need to have some words."

"All right." Her smile was like Sarah's. It was a cat watching a mouse kind of smile. "Spit them out, and I'll try to make sense of them."

She was stirring something in a black kettle hanging from a rod in the oversized fireplace. I contemplated that a moment, thinking of frogs and newt's eyes—the exact witchy recipe eluded me, and I had no idea what a newt was. At least she wasn't wearing one of those pointy hats like some drawings I'd seen. No cats, either. Problem was, I didn't smell beans or roast from that funny-smelling pot. Fighting back a chill, I shuddered and continued.

"Kate, I'm sworn to protect the folks in this county. Now, some are getting a mite skittish about certain things. Sarah probably told you. They're afraid of spells, potions, and other witchy things going on around them."

Her eyebrows rose to an impossible height before she smiled. "Witchy things?" She glanced at her sister before laughing.

Sarah came over and put a plate of biscuits with milk gravy poured over them right in front of me. My stomach grumbled, and I nearly fainted from the smell. How could they know this was part of my favorite meal? I tried to take my eyes from the plate in front of me.

"They also don't like women dancing naked in the woods, thinking there is some kind of pagan ritual going on to call in the devil's minions—or something."

Kate looked over her shoulder at me. "I didn't think anyone cared. There were at the least ten, maybe twelve, people watching. They didn't seem to mind. Never complained a bit."

I closed my eyes for a moment and sighed. I hadn't heard that—except the part about not seeing faces. Which was understandable, I suppose, depending on whether men or women were watching.

"Well, it's got to stop."

Sarah came over and leaned against my good shoulder while she put a couple pieces of fried chicken on my plate. Damn, I like fried drumsticks. And added to biscuits and gravy? Oh, my.

She spoke softly while Kate stared cat-eyed at us. "Is there anything else concerning you, Billy? Anything at all? Can I cut this up for you?"

Well, I looked around that room a minute. My mind seemed to be jumping all over, searching for a way out and finding none. They'd breached the ramparts and damned well knew it—I could tell by their knowing smiles. I hadn't gotten a shot off defending my castle—well, not at them.

"There is one more thing."

Both looked at me expectantly. Sarah had another piece of chicken speared on a fork. I sighed. Again.

"I see some molasses in that jar. Would there be some hot bread to go with that?"

There was.

———

I AWOKE that evening when a piece of green wood popped in the fireplace. My dreams came rushing back—the gun battle and fever, an excellent meal served up by sisters who could be twins.

The tick-tock of a mantle clock kept syncopated cadence, with a raven pecking around outside, perched on the windowsill. I flinched when it stopped and looked at me before returning to its quest. My foolish thoughts were thrown back into the well of superstition. I have enough problems without inventing more.

Unless the ladies were outside, I was alone. One thing about fried chicken and all the fixins. It'll put a serious nap on you. Fully dressed, I was stomping into my boots when I saw the note lying on the table.

Gone to town. Etta Mae in trouble.

I pondered that a moment and felt no urgency. What kind of trouble could a purveyor of eateries get into? Most people I knew would ride miles to sit at one of her tables. Someone doing her harm could expect serious consequences.

But still…I'd woken in a restless mood, so I saddled my horse and headed into town. It was nearly dark when I arrived. The street seemed deserted except for several horses tied up in front of the Mountain Goat. Lanterns were being lit, showing yellow through windows and doors. Someone had baked a pie, and I nearly turned into the wind to go find it. I imagined it sitting on a windowsill to cool, waiting…

Tying my horse in front of the jail, I left a dusty trail through the dying sunlight as I crossed to the saloon. Laughter carried through the open windows, overshadowed by someone playing the piano like a blacksmith beating hot iron.

As I stepped through the doorway, conversation died.

Tables and chairs were full, along with several men leaning on the bar. The scuffed brass footrail shone in the flickering light from the oil lamps and chandelier.

We have a small community, and I knew everyone in the building, if not personally, then by sight or reputation. Some nodded hello, but most ignored me—not from acrimony but because I was a common fixture around town. Body language is something every lawman learns. Men gazed at me and then gave a furtive glance toward the one man in the room I did not know.

He was dark of visage, like a weathered seafarer I'd met once, with a gold ring in his left ear. If there were pictures of pirates, he'd be on the poster. He dressed all in black, with a silver hatband and studded pistol belt. Ivory handles shone from the tied-down holsters. A dandy of the finest order. I wondered if the mercantile would have an ostrich feather for his hat. He seemed to want to give the impression that he was a gunfighter—a bad man. I wondered if it was all show. There was only one way to find out.

I could see him watching me in the mirror fronting the bar as I stepped up beside him and motioned to Wilhelm, the bartender. The mirror was a painting in reverse, showing the two of us at a hastily cleared counter, the local denizens all staring at our backs. It wasn't odd that the women were present. Wilhelm didn't allow working girls in his establishment, and ladies were welcome to come in and enjoy a sarsaparilla or fine wine, sometimes whiskey. They could even sneak in a cigarillo if they thought no one was looking. It was noteworthy that they huddled in a corner like three damsels in distress.

"Wilhelm, that bottle we keep for special occasions. A shot of the house finest for this gentleman, please."

The dandy turned to me as the two glasses arrived, gaze lingering on the badge pinned to my vest. Though he tried hard, he couldn't keep his distaste from showing. "Do I know you?"

I held my glass up, admiring the amber liquid a moment before drinking it. "Nope. I'm Billy Bennett, sheriff of this county. What's the name you're using today?"

He gave me a flat stare. How could he not like me? We'd just met. "Bane Wolfe. With an 'e.'"

"On the Bane or the Wolfe?"

It seemed a fair question, but he didn't reply. The man seemed edgy, like his plumb bob would never center over the mark. One hand or the other always seemed to be caressing a pistol butt. He had two, and they were very pretty.

"Well, Mr. Wolfe. I always buy strangers a drink as they're passing through our town. Kind of a tradition."

Pausing a moment, my gaze met his. "You are passing through, aren't you? The trails are easy, even at night."

He gave me a cold smile as he held the drink up to his nose. "What is this? It smells funny."

I didn't answer right away. Glancing toward the women, my attention was on the violent shaking of Sarah's curls. A warning? The other two women were drawing strange figures in the air with their hands. To be honest, they looked a bit addled. If she was trying to pass a message, I was too dense to get it.

Moving my attention away from the ladies, I nodded to him. "Elderberry wine, of the finest grade. It's a house specialty, very medicinal, and tasty. We take pride in fine things."

"Wine? I'm a whiskey man myself, it's more a man's

drink, but I'll try it." He knocked it back, then admired the glass. "Kind of fruity. I'm not sure I like it."

"Oh, it'll grow on you." I gave him a friendly pat on the arm. "A few more glasses, and you'll feel ten feet tall. What's your business in town, if I might ask?"

He pointed over his shoulder at the three women huddled in the corner. "I've come to take these women away. I'm starting a new coven."

Sarah stood staring at me with a strange expression that morphed into a smile as she met my gaze, while her sister and Etta Mae frantically drew designs on the floor with a piece of chalk.

"Wilhelm, did you know they're marking up your floor?"

"I saw that." He filled the glasses again and then stood, polishing the counter with a puzzled expression. "I ain't cleaning that up."

Turning back to my new drinking partner, I shrugged and picked up my glass. "You may as well drink up, Mr. Wolfe. I have some bad news for you."

After chugging our wine, I continued. "Those ladies over there are free to go where they choose, with whom they choose, and at any time they choose. What they are *not* allowed to do is go anywhere with you. That's a town rule."

He had the courtesy to look surprised. "You have a rule on that?"

"I just made it up, but I'm sure it'll pass at the next town council meeting."

He stood straight up in front of me, his right hand on his pistol. "That's ridiculous. Do you know who I am?"

A quick glance toward the ladies showed Sarah still shaking her head and staring at me, eyes pleading—what? Yes or no? Stop or go? The chalk pushers had drawn a circle around themselves. They looked a little smug for the amount of anxiety they'd been showing.

"Yessir, Mr. Wolfe. I do know who you are. You're a stranger in our town with a made-up name meaning a wolf that brings misery and grief—or some such. Your real name is probably Smith. If you were Mexican, it would be Gomez. Now, it is possible you're a legend somewhere. It's possible. But this is Bennett's Pass. It takes a lot to leave an impression here."

His smile was cold as he glanced at the ladies. "You don't understand. Do you know what I am?"

Tilting my hat back, I rubbed my forehead. Headaches seemed to come more frequent lately. "You're not meeting me halfway, Mr. Wolfe. Please try harder. I thought we covered who you are."

His stare was intense as he gave me his full attention. "I'm a warlock. I can bring fire and misery down on this entire town. I have the power to level this place."

Shaking my head, I shrugged at him. "Well, it's a free country. You can be whatever you want. If you want to be a...what was it...a warlock? More power to you. I'm all for free enterprise. But not in this town. You can go to the next county and warlock over there. Or up in Missouri. They might need that sort of thing."

With a snarl, he went for his guns. He must have practiced that growl because he did sound like a wolf. Or what I imagine a wolf would sound like. If I were ever close enough to hear a wolf growl, I'd be either running or shooting.

We stood close together, so when his first gun cleared leather, I took it and placed it on the countertop—the same for the second gun. I admired them for a moment. They sure were pretty. I wondered if my pay would allow such things. He stared at me, blinking slowly.

I couldn't help my grin. "Sorry, Mr. Wolfe. It must seem like we have a lot of rules around here, but we really don't. We're pretty much a do-what-you-want community. You're just hitting all the high points. We don't allow gun play here either, along with warlocking."

The man stood swaying as he watched me. We were both startled by the yell from the corner. Well, I was. His eyes widened some, but he didn't flinch.

"Yes!" Kate and Etta Mae came bounding over, grabbing the man by the arms. "It worked." I looked over their heads to see Sarah watching me with a strange expression. That little smile made me nervous.

They pushed the man down in a chair while he looked around, not struggling. Deputy Jones weaved his way between people and tables, finally standing next to me. I gestured toward Mr. Wolfe.

"How about you bundle this man up and take him north to the county line and then dump him? He's worn out his welcome here. Judging by his clothes, his horse is probably black with silver trim on the saddle. It'll be tied out front."

Sarah stood by me. How could she smell so fresh in a smoke-filled room? After the bit of tension, everyone seemed to light up a cigar or pipe. Her voice was soft in my ear as she leaned close. "You know he'll come back."

Jones met my gaze over the top of her head and nodded. I went back to getting lost in her eyes. "Mr. Wolfe, I don't think that will happen."

She stood against me, holding my arm, as the would-be bad man was dragged out the door by a couple of men, Jones trailing behind. "I can't believe they were able to ward off the warlock. I've never seen Kate come up with so many spells in so short a time. She was frightened half out of her mind."

I was thinking she wouldn't have that much to spare. Kate and Etta Mae were all smiles now that the crisis was over. Kate's voice came rapid-fire and high-pitched. "I knew we could do it. That man is evil and powerful, but no match for us." She hugged Etta May close to her. "We did it together."

I nodded to them, half listening as I dug in my pocket. I planned to look through the posters in the office. Something about him was familiar. But whether warlock or troublemaker, if Jones did his job, the man wouldn't be back. We tend to generate enough trouble on our own without outside help. But it was good to see the ladies happy. I flipped a gold piece to Wilhelm, and it disappeared into a pocket as if by magic, his hands hardly pausing from polishing glasses. The circus must be missing a juggler.

The bartender spoke over the returning noise. "I didn't think he'd take the drink. That elderberry wine did the trick."

Sarah stared at me. If she didn't start blinking occasionally, I was going to start running. "What was the gold piece for?"

No point in starting our budding relationship with a lie. "Laudanum."

Her laugh was more of a nervous bark. She glanced over her shoulder at her sister and then turned back to me. "You spiked his drink?"

"We did." I watched her to see how she'd take it. Some would call the act unfair. But the trick is to win a contest before the other man realizes there is one.

"Why? You're good with a gun...I've seen that." She just wouldn't let it go.

I gave her the first thing that came to mind. "He was aiming to take away my girl—"

Her smile was quick. "Your girl. I like that."

"—and that was not going to happen. Besides, why on earth would I want to trade bullets with some half-wit just because he thinks he's some kind of witch and a gun-slick? In a crowded room, several people would get hurt or killed. Makes no sense."

"He's not a witch but a warlock."

"Is he? Really?" I watched her mull that over a moment.

She shook her head, bouncing her curls. "It doesn't matter if he is or not. He thinks he is, and that's just as dangerous. It will lead him to do stupid things. Don't tell Kate and Etta Mae about your trick. They'd be devastated." Her giggle sounded more like pent-up nerves than mirth. "Laudanum."

The ladies headed for Etta Mae's place, given the late hour. I was glad. The trails were no place to be at night. Returning to the office, I fired up a coal-oil lamp and pulled out a stack of posters. Most were bad drawings, and the descriptions would match most of the men I knew, me included. Something niggled at my brain, but I couldn't bring it up. I rubbed my tired eyes and took my frustrated mind to the cot in the back of the office. Sleep was restless and full of dreams better left in those closed rooms in your mind that you try to keep nailed shut.

———

MORNING DID NOT START WELL. I fought to free myself from a tangled blanket when Deputy Jones came through the front door and stood staring at me. With his Adam's apple bobbing up and down, I figured he had a serious case of dry mouth. Uneasy at the fear showing in his eyes and throwing the offending blanket on the cot, I handed him a dipper of water.

He finally found his voice, still breathing hard as he watched me. "I'm sorry, Boss."

I'd read once that men plan, and gods laugh. Why do I keep being surprised at the things life puts in front of me? "All right. Things can't be all that bad. What happened?"

"We lost him. Me and those two boys that helped drag that Wolfe fella out of the saloon was about to the county line, just past Fiddler's Ford when he disappeared."

"Disappeared?" I felt mindless as a parrot repeating words that held no meaning for it.

"Yessir. He was tied to his saddle horn, and I was leading his horse. Jed and Lemuel rode behind him. We were going to get him to the county line, work him over a little, and then send him on up toward Joplin. He'd fit right in there.

"Then he just wasn't there. I don't know how I lost hold of the reins. Must be something wrong with my hands—didn't feel a thing. Anyway, we searched high and low...couldn't find him at all. Heard of a Creek medicine man doing that once, scared the hell out of people, but they found him under some bushes later. I'll get some men and go search some more. Now that it's light, we'll find him."

Disgusted, I sat in my roller chair. "Don't bother. I'm sure he'll be back." I gave him a hard look. "Just how drunk were your helpers?"

Jones grinned. "Hell, if they were sober, they wouldn't have gone out dragging a witchy man around in the dark. That was plumb crazy."

"He's not a witchy man. There's no such thing."

Jones straightened to his considerable height. "Then how'd he get away?"

I pointed toward a can resting on the desk. We kept some money handy for incidentals...like tipping bartenders. "How much money is in the kitty?"

"I need to leave." He bolted toward the back door. There was a thud and a frantic rattling of the handle. I'd put a couple of nails in it so the door wouldn't keep banging around. "That's a nasty trick, Billy."

I gazed idly out the window as footsteps approached, and he stood in front of my desk, pretending he'd never left.

His voice was hoarse. "Dunno."

"Oh, come on. Make a guess. You were looking in it the other day."

He sighed, glancing wistfully toward the front door. "About twenty dollars."

I nodded. "That's about right. Now. Here's the deal. You can have it all as a bonus if you can convince me you weren't asleep leading that man's horse."

He tried to stare me down. "I never—"

"Herkle, remember that little fishing trip we took? We left before daylight, and you fell out of the saddle before we ever got to the river."

"I got a smooth-gaited horse." His shoulders slumped. "I'm sorry, Boss."

"No." I held up my hand. "It's my fault for sending you. But you know, I figure you're paid pretty good for what you do, being this is a small town. Don't you think?"

I stared at him a moment as he watched the floor. When he didn't speak, I continued. "Don't lie to me again."

His head bobbed hard enough to jostle his hat. "Yessir."

He trudged out the door as Sarah came in. Maybe I should put on those batwing doors like you see in some saloons? Or charge a toll? I was getting a lot of traffic.

The sun was peeking over the top of the building across the street and followed Sarah through the door, blinding me as I rubbed my eyes. "Don't you people ever sleep?"

"What's going on, Billy? Your deputy looks as if he has a belly full of green apples, and the girls are restless and nervous."

I stared a moment and then shrugged. "Seems Mr. Wolfe disappeared last night."

She came around the desk and sat on the edge, watching me as she moved. Her legs swung idly for a moment as she nodded. We may as well have been discussing the weather. "What are you going to do?"

"Other than threatening abduction, the man's done nothing wrong." I held her gaze for a moment. "Still, it's my job to keep the peace, and that man did not strike me as being peaceful. He may need a little more help leaving the county."

That door would be worn out by the end of the day. Jones came stumbling back, followed by Kate and Etta Mae. I'd never seen his eyes so big. "They've got her, Billy. They got Emily!"

It was getting tiresome interrogating my own deputy. "Slow down and tell me."

"Tall rode into town and started banging on the front door of the Mountain Goat yelling he needed a drink badly. When I asked what was wrong, he said three men came to the house and took Emily. One of them he described sounded like that Wolfe fella. We gotta do something."

"What's Tall doing right now?"

Jones shrugged. "He broke in a window, so he's probably drunk already."

Sarah was herding the ladies out the door, and then she turned and looked at me. "Their trail would be easy to follow. It rained about sunup." Her smile was sugary sweet. "Not that you'd know, sleeping in like you were doing."

"I know what you're thinking, but forget it. You're not going." I glanced at my deputy. "And neither are you. You're too jumpy about this."

He pulled his pistol to check the loads. "I can shoot. You need me."

"Nope, you stay here in case he comes back this way. Besides, the last time we had target practice, all you hit was a boot—and I was wearing it."

———

TALL'S PLACE was close to town, and I arrived about a half hour later. The trail I needed was easy to find. I figured the tracks going in circles were Tall's. There were only two trails with access to his home buildings. Going any other direction would make you climb some mighty steep hills. The riders wouldn't go far. If the men wanted to use Emily, they wouldn't wait long to do it. But I didn't think that was the plan. I'd slighted that man, and now he wanted some payback.

I figured this was a trap, so I went slow. My deputy would have gone on a dead run—and wound up shot. I followed the churned earth with my shotgun across the saddle. About a half-mile from the farm buildings, the tracks turned away from the trail and went over a small rise. I knew where they were going.

Over the low hill and across a wet weather creek was an overhang of limestone, the underside more of a cut-out than a cave. At some point in the past, some enterprising soul used mud and gravel for mortar and walled up the opening with rocks. This land was rock-poor, so he had a lot to work with. Whether done for a home or hideout, it was ill-advised since the high-water mark was well above the ceiling of the cut—arguably how it was made in the first place. Still, it was a good camping spot in normal seasons.

I topped the rise and walked my horse down to the creek. I'd looked up and down the creek for someone with a rifle but didn't see anyone set up for an ambush. I wasn't surprised. That's not how anyone named Bane Wolfe would want to do it. Two strange men were leaning casually against trees, and I was glad of it. They were amateur wannabe bad men with no experience. To straighten and draw their pistols would take an extra second they wouldn't have. I'd known a few bad ones, and they'd have had their guns out already, maybe shooting when I came over the ridge.

A small, smokeless fire burned around a blackened coffeepot. Emily was tied with her back to a small tree, looking like the damsel in distress from some dime novel. Bane Wolfe sat on a rock next to the coffee, partially shielded by the woman. That didn't surprise me.

The off-key mockingbird had followed me from the other day, and I could see its gray and black form flitting between the scrub oak and juniper. When that bird shut up for a moment, things got quiet. The runoff water from the hill above splattered into the creek. It could have been peaceful. Seemed everyone was just waiting to breathe.

The day wasn't getting any better. Mistakes were made. I thought these men would talk. I really did. They thought I wouldn't be ready. We were both wrong. When I stepped down off the horse, the two men went for their pistols. Dropping down to one knee, I shot under the belly of my horse. Both barrels fired at once, a known problem with that Greener coach gun. The horse squealed, rose straight up, and then tore off down the creek for parts unknown, leaving me with an empty shotgun and no cover. I dropped the Greener and pulled my pistol.

The shotgun accounted for one of the men, and the other fired at me. He wasn't schooled in downhill shooting because he shot over my head. Uphill is easier. We traded shots again, and he went down cussing with a broken leg, tossing his pistol away. It went off again, the bullet notching the tree behind Emily.

Knowing I was out of time and expecting to take a bullet, I rolled on the rocks looking for cover and came up with my pistol pointing at Bane Wolfe. The look on his face made me think someone slipped him laudanum again. He stared behind me, and his face looked as white as the chalky limestone he stood by. When he glanced at me, only his eyes moved. His hands held pistols down by his side. I could see the strain on his corded forearms and neck as he tried to lift them, but the guns may as well have weighed a hundred pounds. He gripped his hands so hard one of the pistols went off into the ground at his feet, rock chips cutting his boot. The shot echoed between the rocks and assaulted my ringing ears. Blood oozed out of his boot.

His voice was shaky, and he seemed to plead as he looked at me. "I can't feel my arms."

I never got a chance to answer. Sarah dismounted and walked to me, putting her hand on my arm. She never stopped staring at Bane Wolfe as she spoke to me. "You're alright? Not hurt?"

I could see a tear coursing down Bane Wolfe's cheek as he struggled, leaving a muddy trail and collecting under his chin. He seemed to be having trouble breathing.

Nodding, trying to control my breathing, I replied, "I seem to be. Not sure yet. Lotsa bullets and rock chips flying around."

She stood close, rubbing my back and arms like I was a lost child she'd just found. "Sorry I was late, and you had to shoot those men. You shouldn't have had to do that. I missed the spot where you left the trail…had to backtrack."

Emily broke into my confused thoughts with a voice as calm as what's for dinner. "Could someone please untie me? I'm getting a cramp, and I gotta pee."

While Sarah took care of her, I ignored Bane Wolfe, who seemed to be frozen to his spot, and walked over to the wounded man. Blood covered his thigh, and it bent at an awkward angle. It didn't matter. Sometimes when the upper leg breaks, the splinters cut into the major blood vessel. He hadn't wasted time in joining his partner. Glancing back, the only movement from Bane Wolfe was his eyes as he tried to track movement around him. He was so stiff, I felt if I pushed him, he'd fall over, still at attention.

The women indulged in a long hug before Emily scampered behind a rock, and then Sarah stepped up to

Bane Wolfe. I drew my pistol again, just in case. "Sarah, don't get between us."

She glanced my way, smiled, and promptly ignored my advice.

"You may holster your pistols." Her voice came soft, barely heard over the wind sifting through the trees and the gurgling waterfall.

His hands moved, and my pistol came up, but he dropped his guns into their holsters. He flinched as he tried to grab Sarah, but his hands fell again to his sides. I could tell how hard he was trying to move by the sweat dripping off him.

She stared at him with an intensity I'd never seen. "Do you know what I am?"

Now that was curious. Not who, but what? Kind of like what he asked me the night before. The bigger question was—did I? He nodded to her, and for the first time, I saw fear in him...could smell it as he stared at her. If he could move, it would be a tossup whether he ran or fainted.

She put her hand on his chest, resting softly over his heart. It was an innocent gesture, and I felt a moment's jealousy at the intimate contact. But his face started turning red and then lost all color. The cords of his neck stood out as he fought for breath. I almost didn't catch her soft words.

"If I ever see you again, I'll take your heart and feed it to you. Do you understand?"

His nods came fast just before his eyes widened and he fainted. I almost did, too. Those words from that sweet, kissable mouth? Maybe I misunderstood?

Emily was gathering the dead men's horses—a good thing because I'm betting mine was still running. I'd lost a decent saddle and a good set of saddlebags.

I had to clear my throat a couple of times before I could speak. "Is he dead?"

Sarah glanced at Bane Wolfe. "Oh, he'll wake soon enough." Her gaze turned to me. "You can put your gun away."

I watched her close, wearing my surprise like a stepped-on frog, and had trouble closing my mouth. I'd seen some things in my life, strange things, but...

"I'm not sure about that. What just happened here?"

"I could never hurt you, Billy. Surely you know that."

We swapped gazes for a moment, and then she kissed me. It was just a quick peck on the lips, but it was enough to get my attention and holster my pistol.

"You didn't answer my question, Sarah."

Her head shook those black curls again. She watched Emily a moment before turning back to me. "Still don't believe?"

"It's a bit of a struggle. What I see and what I believe are at odds right now."

That mockingbird started trilling off key again, trying to imitate a pig squealing, until Sarah glanced its way, looking irritated. It cleaned up a strangled note and flew away. I was ever so thankful.

"Well." Sarah smiled at me. "Since you don't choose to believe, what happened is this—and I'll do my best Billy Bennett imitation. I was out looking for Emily when I came upon my man engaged in a fight for his life against someone of unknown abilities and intent. I rode up to the miscreant causing all the trouble and asked him politely to please stop. He grew agitated and then fainted. Will that work for you?"

"Your man?"

"You're being peckish, Billy."

I thought about it a moment, watching the man on

the ground. He was staring at the canopy of leaves above us, eyes open and unblinking like a dead man—still breathing while his fingers twitched.

One of the oldest instincts, right next to procreation, is self-preservation. I shrugged. "That sounds about right. And I do appreciate the help."

———

BENNETT'S PASS is quiet now. Our wedding went off without a hitch. It's a good thing, too. We have a baby on the way. She already knows it's a girl. Don't ask. I still don't know where the parson came from.

The Arnolds pulled foot and moved to Missouri. They never did get their bull back. I heard it died of exhaustion. Don't know if their Jersey started giving milk. Don't care.

Tall Johnson didn't die from a boil on his face. That was just his own superstition. He walked out of the Mountain Goat Saloon and Billiard Parlor, tripped on a loose board, and broke his neck on the hitching rail. Wilhelm claimed he was sober. I think he's lying. There are no witnesses who have ever seen Tall sober. Not ever.

And Herkle Jones had an alibi. He was busy putting two nails in that tipping horseshoe. I'm sure Emily helped.

Etta Mae still throws together a good breakfast, and we eat at her café most mornings with several of her women friends. I mostly ignore the conversation. I heard from a lawyer once to never ask a question if you don't already know the answer. And I do not know the answers.

We're getting a few more men moving into the county, so the womenfolk are happier now. Somehow all the carpetbaggers were run off—complaining of bad luck all the time and strange sounds during the night. One or two had large boils in strange places.

We don't see Kate much. She's busy doing things. I don't know what things and don't ask. It's none of my business. She still gives me the willies—even if she is Sarah's sister.

I make sure we have a barn dance once a month. In public. With clothes. I'm the sheriff of Bennett County, and I must put my foot down somewhere.

And Bane Wolfe? Never heard from him again. I can only assume he woke up from his faint—although, how he could be frightened of a beautiful woman like Sarah, I'll never know. Maybe he had a fever.

Life is good, so I don't meddle much. And a rarely beautiful woman who can straighten out a mockingbird and fry chicken the way she does? Time to settle in for the long haul.

And witches? Not in my county.

WHO SHOT JESUS?

Union soldiers showed up at my neglected ranch a day after I came home from the war and caught me trimming poles to repair the corral. There was a nice stand of white pine right close to the barn. The wood wouldn't last long, but it was handy, and pine trees are easy to cut.

The soldiers had a banker from Big Springs with them and a fancy-looking paper waving in my face that said they owned my place, because of my participation on the wrong side in the late difficulty between the states. I'd been expecting something like this, just not so soon. They must have thought me a dangerous individual to bring so many men.

My own fancy paper, a legal deed filed at the county seat, produced a bunch of guns pointed at me by kids playing at being a soldier, in uniforms that had never seen blood nor dirt, or any hard times at all. They were young, and I don't think they'd ever fired a gun at anything but a target. Bullets don't care who starts them in motion and have a common result, death or injury. I didn't want them to practice on me. All those new recruits were fidgety with their trigger-fingers, and that banker was grinning.

I figured this was no time to debate the subject, so I gathered my things. Me being dead would just make things easier for them. This was a game I couldn't win. The blue coats held all the cards, and it was time for me to throw in my hand. The Reconstructionists were stealing land right and left. It was pure thievery and everyone knew it. But this day and time, there wasn't much you could do about it.

Some of the local boys would stay and fight the best they could, especially the ones who'd been with Bloody Bill and the like, but I didn't see any future in that. I knew the Union was still fighting the war, only now they fought it with bankers and lawyers. A man once told me that when governments go to war, the people lose on both sides. I reckon he was right.

I'd seen enough killing. My idea was to raise horses, and I could do it somewhere else as well as here. I still had an Appaloosa stallion that I'd named Apple. A good neighbor kept him for me, and a couple of mares for a fresh start.

Those soldiers sat and watched as I gathered my horses from the corral, loaded what little belongings I had, and was ready to leave, except for a parting comment. I couldn't let it lay.

"You boys want the shirt off my back too? It's kind of faded, but the color won't run."

Somehow, they didn't think that was funny because, about then, that banker decided he needed my horses for interest on a loan I didn't have. I ignored his shouting and fist-shaking at me.

I'd taken a Spencer repeater off a Union soldier who

didn't need it anymore, along with a saddlebag full of Blakeslee loaders. I pointed that rifle casual like, right at the banker's belly. Since I was using my saddle and mount for a shield, all they could see of me was my rifle and hat. Losing my land was bad enough, although it was all rocks and brush. I wasn't about to give up my horses. Fighting was near enough in my past I still knew how to do it.

My voice was as hard as my resolve. "You may not know it, being a banker and always hiring your fighting done, but a .56 caliber ball makes a mighty big hole when it goes through a man. Most of your innards will be draped on those men behind you like Christmas tinsel."

That fine, beautiful morning got quiet, and I could hear a wren fussing under the porch. A crow called in the distance and somebody was getting nervous on his saddle because I could hear the leather creak. Finally, a grizzled sergeant worked his way through the troops and held up his hand. He rode his horse in front of the banker.

His voice was soft but carried where it needed to go. The soldiers were already putting away their rifles and turning away, relief showing on some of their faces.

"Blevins, you've taken enough from this man. Let it go. We're leaving."

I guess he wasn't so brave without the soldiers because that banker turned and followed them away, coattails flapping in the breeze. With a half-salute to the sergeant, a man I figured had a belly full of fighting, same as me, I grabbed the tether ropes and lit a shuck out of there. I hated to leave, and it stuck in my craw because it felt like running away, but dead men raise no horses.

It took a few days to work through the Ozark hills, dodging cavalry units along the way. I'd done nothing wrong, but having to explain that to every jack-leg bluebelly I met was not high up on my list of things to do. All I wanted was some wide-open country where I could live in peace.

Contrary to that wish, people told me there was work in Kansas City, maybe at the stockyards. Crowded places didn't interest me much, but money was scarce, and I'd need some to buy a place. It would take some doing, but I was determined to start over.

Folks couldn't get shut of me quick enough in Joplin, or Union as some called it. The marshal said I looked like a troublemaker and should keep moving. I didn't think I looked any worse than those boys working in the lead mines. Rough-looking or not, I was able to trade one of my mares for a pack full of supplies and ammunition for my pistol.

Two days out of Joplin, we were heading northwest into a miserable wind. When I saw that cabin, I nearly cried. It was bitter cold, and I was in trouble. I couldn't feel my hands or feet, and my face felt like stone. Anyone with half a brain would be sitting next to a fire, but here I was on the open prairie, freezing my tail off.

A sermon I'd heard came to mind. The preacher talked of the Seven Deadly Sins. I didn't remember it being mentioned, but stubbornness should have been included. I had an unhealthy dose of that.

The snow started yesterday. I'd camped early last night to gather enough firewood to keep warm, while I could still find it, and then rolled out at daybreak. Today, the weather turned from sleet to freezing rain and covered us in a sheet of ice. Down in the gullies, I could hear tree limbs breaking from the weight. A layer of ice covered the ground. If we hadn't had snow the night before, the horses wouldn't have been able to walk. I worried they'd cut up their legs, but so far hadn't seen any blood. The crunching sound of hooves breaking through ice sounded loud in a bitter cold, silent world.

That cabin I came upon looked deserted. The shuttered windows showed no light from within, and no smoke came from the chimney. A lean-to barn sat next to the house and I rode to the entrance. The rain had stopped, but the air was colder than before. I stumbled when I dismounted from Apple because I couldn't feel my feet. The reins stuck to my glove, and I had to pound my left hand against the saddle to break the ice away.

I looked around inside the barn and didn't see much. There was no tack at all, and the stalls didn't look used. Taking the saddle and pack off the horses, I left them out of the stalls, knowing they'd want to roll to get the ice off. There was a small stack of hay, mostly straw by the looks of it, and I pitched it down. Maybe they could eat the mice that came with it. Apple shook his head at it, and I shrugged. I was hungry too.

Grabbing my saddlebags, I put the pole across the entrance and went to the house. Light shone through some missing shingles on the roof of the porch, and I saw a broken board on the floor. The latchstring was out, meaning someone hadn't pulled it back from inside. It was a poor man's lock, but effective. I opened the door, thinking the house abandoned.

My face was stiff, and I was so cold I could barely walk. The clap of sound, tongue of flame, and bullet hit me as I stepped through the door. The bullet notched my shoulder on the top, putting a hole in my slicker I'd have to repair later. I stood there, nearly frozen and didn't think of going for my pistol. It rested under my coat, and my rifle was in the barn. It was a testament to how cold I was that I didn't move for a minute. I don't think I even flinched.

The small boy standing in front of me struggled to re-cock an old LeMat horse pistol that looked bigger than him. If he'd used the shotgun option from the center bore, pieces of my shoulder would be splattered all over the porch. He had on bulky mittens that kept getting in his way, fingers sticking from holes in the cloth. His breath fogged the space between us, and he looked to be near panic.

Ears ringing from the shot, I reached out and snatched that pistol away, laying it on a table.

"You shot Jesus!"

The voice came from a pile of coats and blankets next to a big cast iron stove, and that stove looked as cold as the bitter wind outside.

Shaking my head a moment, trying to get the cobwebs out, I turned and closed the front door. There wasn't much difference between inside and out, it was cold to the bone. Powder smoke and fog from our breathing filled the room. Looking around, all I saw were two kids and a door I guessed went to another room. The statement finally registered. I'd been called a lot of things, but not that.

It took two tries before I could speak. "Why do you think I'm Jesus?"

The shaky, high-pitched voice came again. "Mama said Jesus would come to save us."

The boy's face was pale from the cold, and I wondered how he could stand upright with all the clothes he had on. He was edging toward the gun, so I set it up high on a shelf. He must have had a dose of my stubbornness.

"Where's your fire?" My mind had slowed to a crawl by the bitter cold. I couldn't understand what I was seeing in the frozen house. Nothing made sense.

The little boy backed away from me. He didn't trust me, and I couldn't blame him. "It went out a few days ago. I couldn't find matches."

I looked around thinking no matter how bad things are for you, there's always someone worse off. The stove was big and had a flat top for cooking. When I opened the door to the fire chamber, I noticed sticks of wood were lying flat against each other. I jumbled them around a little so air could get in among the wood and then pulled out my waterproof skin of sulfur matches.

There was tinder in a box behind the stove and some that looked like a mouse nest, so I stuffed that in between the sticks. My fingers were shaking with the cold as I got that fire going. Finally, it caught hold, and after opening the damper to give it air, I closed the metal door.

I was afraid to ask, because I knew if the sound of that shot didn't bring someone running, they weren't coming at all.

"Where's your folks?"

The boy's eyes were big. He didn't say anything as he pointed and I opened the door to the other room. A woman lay on the bed, and she wasn't coming out. Ever.

She looked asleep and peaceful, with her hands folded across her stomach. They'd draped a faded blue dress over her like a cover, and her bright red hair was spread out and combed. It looked like someone had put black Sunday shoes on her, and they were polished.

Looking closer, I could see flecks of copper-colored

blood around her mouth and guessed she'd been cleaned up some. It looked like she had a hard time of it, and I hoped her kids hadn't seen it, but then my cold-addled mind corrected itself. Of course, they'd seen her. They must have washed her and took care of her. There was no one else around.

The little voice behind me broke my heart, and I've been called a hard man. "We did the best we could with her. She'd want that. I knew she'd want to look nice when Jesus came."

I turned to see a miniature version of the dead woman. She looked to be about five years old, dressed like the boy in every stitch of clothing they could find. Tears were frozen on her cheeks. Then whatever was left of my heart, she stomped on it.

"You took your sweet time getting here."

It was freezing cold in that room, and my mind just wouldn't keep up. Finally... "What are your names?"

The boy took over. "She's Josie and I'm Michael Kelly."

"What's your mama's name?"

"Moira." I looked toward the bed as he talked. "She always told us it was spelled with an oi, not just a plain old I. It was important to her."

I'd known a lot of Irish who fought for the South, so that didn't seem uncommon. "Your mama would be proud of you. What happened to her?"

Josie shrugged and sniffled. "She got sick. Every day she coughed more. She couldn't stop."

Michael was crying now. The little man was finally letting it go. "Few days ago, she could barely walk and went to bed, said she was tired. She'd been coughing something awful. I knew something was wrong. It was the middle of the day and supper wasn't fixed."

He wiped his hand across his nose. "I was scared and asked her not to go to bed, but she went anyway. She coughed really hard for a while and then went to sleep. We couldn't wake her up. Kept trying, but she just wouldn't."

———

I CLOSED the door to the bedroom and gathered the kids in front of the stove. It was turning red on the bottom and making a real difference in that room. I had the sudden thought that we'd have to move their mother's body outside soon.

"You kids start peeling your coats off. You'll be warm soon enough."

"Will we die, too?"

I could barely hear her voice. That question shocked me. I didn't know what to say. It was as if they'd accepted it. Things were simple for little kids, although I didn't have much experience. The important questions in their life were black or white, yes or no. I wished the world was that simple.

As soon as they shucked enough clothes, I gathered them to me. They hung back at first, reminding me of a couple of foals when I'd hold out treats to them, but I figured they needed someone to hold them.

"I'm sorry your mama died and you've had to go through this." I was still searching for the right things to say. "You're going to be alright now. I won't let anything happen to you. That's a promise."

They were both crying as I held them. I didn't have any experience with this. The last few years had left me a bitter man, and I never dreamed I'd be holding and comforting children.

A small voice came from against my chest. "I'm hungry."

Well, how stupid can I be? Of course, they were hungry. That should have been my first thought. I sat them on a bench close to the stove and grabbed the saddlebags I'd dropped near the door. There were some hardtack biscuits in there and pemmican trail mix. "Chew on this real slow. Not too fast or you'll get a belly-ache. I'll see about fixing something more to eat."

I went out to the lean-to and rummaged around in my pack until I found a side of salted pork. It was nearly frozen, so I brought the whole thing back inside to thaw a little so I could cut it. The horses were hungry, and I needed to find forage for them soon. A horse can take a lot, if it has food and water. Apple tried to stomp on my foot and bumped me as I went out, but it couldn't be helped. I was responsible for him and he knew it. I just didn't have feed to give them.

When I came back, those kids were leaning against each other, faces blank and just staring at the stove. I'd seen that sort of look before, worn by men on the battle-field. It was the look of defeat and being too tired and broken to breathe, and acceptance. Live or die, it didn't matter to them.

I fried up some meat, and then after I got a pot of clean snow, added the meat and hardtack to the melted water. I boiled that water first, something I learned the hard way. In the late conflict, dirty water killed more men than rifle balls. It was a makeshift stew and needed things in it that I didn't have, but the broth would be nourishing. I looked for food in the cupboards and didn't find any.

"Michael, what have you kids been eating?"

He looked at me a moment, still chewing on that trail

mix. "I found a couple pieces of bread. It had green stuff on it. Mama saved it to try and catch a mouse."

They were getting sleepy, so I made a pallet next to the stove out of all the extra clothes they'd worn. After I gave them a drink of water from my canteen, I laid them down. I think they were asleep before I stood up. That was all right with me. The stew would be ready when they woke.

More sticks in the stove made it cherry-red and pushed the cold into the corners. I realized I hadn't taken off my slicker and coat and still had my hat and gloves on, so I peeled them off.

This whole thing seemed as unlikely as any story I'd ever heard. With the cold, no telling how long since their mother died. And without decent food? Where did they get water? They just stayed here waiting for Jesus, like their mama told them.

And, for that matter, how close had I been to freezing? I couldn't remember much of the morning after I'd left that last camp. A sheet of ice covered us. It was a wonder I'd chanced upon that cabin.

Growing up, the only book in our cabin was a Bible. My mama would read it to Pa and me. I'll admit, the words were wasted most of the time. It was too bad, because these kids were going to be plumb disappointed with me. I remember someone called me a devil once, but never Jesus.

As soon as the kids woke, I'd feed them some more. Then, I'd find the nearest town and turn them over to the locals. Surely someone knew them.

I still had to keep an eye on that stew, so I sat and leaned on the table, and woke with Josie tugging on my sleeve.

"Mister, I need help." She was holding a pan with

snow in it. I hadn't heard her go outside. "I think that stew is going to burn if we don't add some water. I can't reach it."

"We'll have to boil the water first."

I had the thought that their mama must have tried to teach them everything she could before she died. The sadness and desperation must have been overwhelming. It was a testament to their mother's character, it showed up in her children. They were so young—and so old.

Once we took care of the stew, I sat down and she came and crawled up on my lap. She was studying my face as if she were memorizing it.

"Papa went away."

What do you say to that? "I'm sorry, Josie. Where did he go?"

She kept talking as if I hadn't interrupted. "Mama thought something bad happened to him or he'd have come back. He's been gone a while."

I looked at her. "You sure talk good for your age."

"I know. Mama teached me."

She was close to going to sleep again. I smiled at her misuse of the word. Many grownups I'd known didn't talk as well as her.

"You talk a lot, too."

Like most women I'd known, she ignored me. "Mama made us do lessons every day. Who's going to give me lessons?" Her shoulders shook a couple of times. "Mama died." She looked up at me. "I miss her. Should I die too? And be with her?"

Lord, help me.

"No. She'd want you to keep living. Look, we all die sometime. That's just the way God made us. But you and your brother are strong. And you won't die if I'm around. I promise."

That was the second promise I'd given. Are promises made to little girls the same as the ones made in the dark of night, to fade away at the break of dawn? I didn't know if I could keep them. Many a life was lost on the road of good intention.

It was getting light outside, and I could hear water dripping off the roof. The fickle weather was starting to turn warm. When the sun came up, we ate stew for breakfast. It wasn't good, but the children didn't seem to care. They were just skin and bones, and I wondered again how long it'd been since they had a good meal.

I went outside, saddled Apple, and set the pack on the mare. By the time I finished, the kids were on the porch watching me. They had their coats on and cloth wrapped around their hands and feet.

Michael spoke first in a tremulous voice. "Are you leaving?"

He held his sister's hand and wouldn't look at me. That was a brave little boy.

I lead the horses to the porch. "I'm not leaving you. It's warming up. There must be a town close by. You kids need to come with me. I need to get you somewhere safe."

"But, mama—"

I could see he still felt responsible. "She'd want you to go. We'll come back for her."

I banked the stove and made sure it wouldn't flare up and cause sparks. The last thing we needed was to burn down their house. We went outside and I mounted, and then put Michael behind me and Josie in front. I could see a lane now that the snow was gone, and some old, muddy tracks.

"Town that way?" I pointed, and Michael nodded.

We'd been riding a few minutes when Michael spoke. "I'm cold."

I reached around and grabbed him by the waist, pulling him to the front, and then scooted back behind the saddle to make room. "We'll hold Josie between us, that way, she'll be warm too." I had my arms around them, and they seemed content.

———

AN HOUR LATER, we came to a small town, just a few buildings down both sides of the street. Michael pointed to one building that had Sheriff painted on a sign. I wondered how he knew where to go but shouldn't have been. Kids always seem to know more than we suspect.

I reined Apple up to the hitching rail and slid off the horse. I didn't blame Michael for wanting to move earlier. Riding behind the saddle was no place to be.

A man stepped out of the building. "Looks like there's been trouble."

I just shrugged. "You could say that."

We got the kids off the saddle and took them inside by the fire while I told the story. He stuck his head in another room. "Zeke, you need to bundle up and go get Mary."

I heard what sounded like iron bars clacking together, and then a man came out shrugging into a patchwork coat. Slapping a hat on his head, he did a double take at all of us and then scurried out the door.

He turned back to me. "I'm Frank Bonner, the Sheriff of this county." Looking closely at me, he continued. "And you'd be?"

I hesitated a moment. "I'm Joe Cane."

He looked startled and was about to say something when the door burst open, letting in a blast of cold air.

It was my turn to look startled because it seemed the dead had come back to life. The woman shook her long red hair out of a scarf, glanced at me shortly, and then ran to the children.

"Aunt Mary!" Michael and Josie started chattering at her in hushed tones and started to cry again, her along with them as they huddled in a chair by the stove.

Well, that answered that. Pleased with the results, I turned to go.

"Not so fast." The sheriff's tone said it all. He wanted answers. "I'm sending some men and a wagon out to fetch Moira."

The woman turned and looked at me, listening to the exchange. I met her gaze a moment before the sheriff continued. "They're not going to find anything different from what you told us, are they?"

I looked at him, knowing a strange man showing up with a couple of kids could have gone a lot of different ways. That I'd found a relative of theirs was beyond luck.

"I'm not given to lying."

The sheriff watched me closely, but the decision seemed to come from the woman, spoken in a soft voice.

"Thanks for bringing in the children and taking care of them. I had no idea."

When I nodded and turned to leave, the children jumped from her lap and grabbed me by the legs. Trying to get them to turn loose, I said. "You'll be alright now. Your aunt will take care of you. She's family."

Mary put her hand on my arm. "Why don't you go over to the boarding house and get a good meal and rest."

When I started shaking my head, she insisted. "Look,

we owe you. You're tired, I can tell. The sheriff will take care of your horses, and you can get some rest. Another day lost on your journey won't hurt, will it?"

Well, looking into those eyes, it was hard to say no, but I was trying to manage it until the little girl spoke.

"Please, don't leave us. Mama said Jesus would come, and you did. You *can't* leave us now."

I looked into those eyes of hers and then glanced at Mary. "I ain't Jesus. Not by a long shot."

Josie spoke up again, and I was already learning she liked to argue. "If you're not, how come Michael shot you and you weren't hurt. I saw him shoot you."

Mary gave me a critical glance before reaching out and tousling the boy's hair. "You shot Jesus?"

"Papa told me to take care of Mama and Josie. I didn't know who was coming in the door." He was scuffing the floor with his rag-covered feet. He looked up at me. "I'm sorry."

I tried again, although it was beginning to feel as if I were on a runaway horse and had lost the reins. "I ain't Jesus, and the boy missed, although it was a good try. He notched me a little." I raised his chin so I could look at him. "It's all right. You did what you were supposed to do."

"That's it." Sheriff Bonner's voice was gruff, and I could tell he was trying not to laugh. "You stay until tomorrow until we can investigate this shooting."

My sigh was long and drawn out as I looked down at the two children holding onto my leg. The situation reminded me of a feral kitten I'd picked up once. Once they sink their claws into you, it's hard to let go. They stepped back as I knelt by them. "Listen to me. I'll stay until tomorrow and we can talk things over. You can trust me. Have I ever lied to you?" They both shook their heads. "You go with your Aunt Mary and let her take care of you. We'll meet up in the morning. I promise."

Mary gathered them up. "You can rest up over at the boarding house and get a good meal." She looked him up and down. "And I'd recommend a bath."

———

THE TROUBLE with getting warm and having a good meal is you get sleepy, and I'd been short on both those items for a while. The room had its own stove. They'd filled a metal tub with warm water, and I stripped and climbed in. After scrubbing all the grime off, I about drowned when I relaxed and went to sleep. Spluttering awake, I dressed in some clean clothes that had mysteriously appeared and made it to the bed. The next thing I remember is light coming in through the window.

The sheriff joined me for breakfast in the dining area. "We got the whole story from the kids, hell of a thing. They could have died out there and we wouldn't have known. You've made quite an impression on them."

I nodded, stuffing my face with the first biscuits and gravy I'd had in a long time. Pulling a slab of bacon off the platter and onto my plate, I poured gravy on that too.

"It was just luck I found them. Pure luck."

"Yeah. Maybe. Luck or providence, it makes no difference. Kids are usually good judges of character. They're rarely wrong." He took his hat off and ran his hand over his head before seating it again. "Well, the undertaker went out and got Moira. We'll get her buried when the ground thaws out enough to dig."

He looked pointedly at me. "Just so you know some more of the story, we found their father a couple of weeks ago. He'd been shot dead along the trail between here and his ranch. I figured it was a robbery."

"I think the kids suspect something like that. Have you told them?"

He looked down at the table and shook his head. "No, I haven't, and I'm not ashamed to say it. I hate to heap more grief on them. Their pa wasn't much. He gambled, wore fancy clothes, and always seemed to have plenty of money." He gave me a level stare. "You saw what their place looked like?"

I knew then why he didn't tell them. The place looked run down with no money spent on stuff that needed to be done, like a sick wife and hungry kids.

"It's a good thing I didn't know him. I might have shot him myself."

Frank just nodded and got up from the table. Looking down at me, he seemed to be debating something. "There was a sharp-shooter rode with the Texas Brigade during the recent difficulties. His name was bandied about quite a bit. Name of Joe Cane. He did a lot of damage."

Well, I just sighed and settled into my chair. "A lot of damage was done by both sides in that conflict, Sheriff."

I told him the story of losing my land.

The man nodded. "Sometimes when you win a war, it's hard to win the peace. It's unfortunate."

"Nobody won that war." I looked up at him. "Except the federal government, and they just wanted what we had. But, the war's over, and I'm not looking for trouble." I guess that was what he wanted to hear because he left after telling me my belongings were over at his office.

Breakfast finished, I loosened my belt a couple of notches, donned my coat, and wandered over to the sheriff's office. They'd saddled Apple, and he looked happy for once. The mare didn't look so pleased, she looked like Apple kept her up all night. I noticed my pack, along with a lot of other boxes and sacks, were in the back of a buckboard hitched to a mule. The way the mule and Apple were looking at each other, I could predict another war coming on.

I went inside and saw Mary and the kids. They all looked pleased about something, smiling at each other, and I thought about bolting out that door. There were a whole lot of people looking happy, and I wasn't one of them.

The sheriff pointed to a chair, and I sat down. As soon as I did, the kids came over and sat on my lap. Mary stood by the sheriff's desk and stared at me.

He spoke after a moment. "Joe, we have some problems here. Since I'm the proper authority in this county, this is how I'm going to solve them." He held up a piece of paper. "This here is all legal-like and signed by a judge. It makes you a co-guardian of Michael and Josephine Kelly."

I started to say something, but Josie elbowed me in the gut.

"The other guardian has to be Mary Kennon, since she is Moira's sister and the only living relative." He waved that paper at me again. "This has to happen because the kids won't let you go, and their well-being, so to speak, is the most important thing to consider here."

Once again, I started to speak. He stopped me by waving that paper. "You're not going against a legal court order, are you?"

I snatched that paper from his hand and looked at it. "You're the judge, too?"

"Handy, isn't it? It solves a lot of problems in a small

county. So, here's what is going to happen. That paper deeds the ranch and water rights to Michael and Josie. And there's quite a bit of it. As their guardian, you'll be legally required to take care of the ranch for them until they're old enough to assume ownership." He looked pointedly at me. "I figure a good man can grow that place into something special."

Stunned, I looked at Mary. "What's your part in all this?"

She tried to sound severe, but her smile ruined it. "You don't think I'm going to let you take those children out there all alone, do you? They need care, schooling, and a hundred things a man can't do while running a ranch."

I looked at her, shaking my head. "You don't know anything about me. All that could be done from town."

"We'll be starting even. You don't know anything about me, either. But the children seem to know you. That means a lot to me." Her gaze was steady on mine. "Mr. Cane, my husband didn't come back from the war. I had word recently that he died in Andersonville prison."

"He fought for the Union?"

She dropped her attention to her hands. "He did. There's not much a widow can do around here, and not a lot of decent men. With no money, I can't just leave and make a fresh start somewhere." She looked at me so long I got uncomfortable. "I don't want to be a burden on anyone, and I don't want to die a widow. With the right man, I want children of my own."

"That's a lot of wanting you're throwing out there." I looked at Frank, and he nodded his head.

"My wife and I took her in. She cooks, mends clothes, and works at the boarding house some. She's a friend. I'd take it as a favor."

"The favor is mine, Frank. I ain't much of a bargain."
My head snapped around. I was thinking of me asleep in
the bathtub. "Did you bring me new clothes?"

She colored up a might, but there was firmness in her
expression. "I'm a good woman, Mr. Cane."

"Well, I'm glad I was at least wearing my hat. And my
name is Joe."

"All right." She said, smiling. "Joe."

"So, you're going to be my...?"

"No." Startled, she shook her head. "We'll need an
extra room built just for me. Until then, I'll stay with the
children, and you can sleep in the barn. Just think of me
as their nanny." She smiled. "Besides, nothing can
happen between us until I'm convinced you aren't Jesus."

Everyone was grinning but me. They looked like a
bunch of gamblers that just pulled something on a green-
horn. But my deck of cards was different from theirs, or
at least, their expectations.

I looked at her and those kids, realizing I'd just drawn
a fistful of aces. "Well, now. That won't take long at all."

Her smile faded and she cast a wary look at me.

It was my turn to smile.

TYLER'S ROAD

I was just shy of seventeen when I killed Edward Tyler. He was my pa and a hard man. I didn't wake up that Thursday morning intending to kill him, but I surely did. I would take that memory to my grave, along with a question. Had there been another way? Could I have done something else?

He used to tell us stories of seafaring men and battles in lands far away. Some of those stories were hard to believe, but we listened anyway. It was a welcome change from sagebrush and dry, lifeless dirt. If he had to die, he'd be pleased to know that, like the Vikings of old, he would be borne to the afterlife on the backs of his enemies. He did not go alone.

The only headstone to mark his grave was the shovel stuck in the freshly turned earth. His final resting place was about four feet down. I hit sandstone, and that's as deep as I could go. Ma didn't have a headstone either, but there was a well-trodden path to where she lay. Pa had walked that path often, and they were together now.

With the sun high in the sky, the distant hills, shimmering and copper-hued, drew my gaze. Maybe this was how it felt to be in a frying pan, praying for a cool breeze or a drink of water—a fair description of hell. There would be a day when I got used to the heat of this country, but I figured I'd be dead and buried before it happened.

Looking at his grave, I wished there was more I could do. Maybe I'd come back and fix a proper headstone if I could figure out how. Ma's grave was covered with rocks, and I would do that for his on a cooler day. There wasn't much family to notify. From what he'd told me, most of our kinfolk were stretched out where they'd fallen along dusty trails and forest glens. They'd be lucky to have an unmarked grave, if buried at all. We had a wandering family, and Pa didn't talk like there were many of us left.

Proper words to say didn't come to mind as I stood over Pa's grave. At least nothing meaningful. No preacher would come this far out, even if I could find one. Words of love and respect were given to him while he was alive. Anything spoken now would be to comfort the living, and there was no comfort for what I'd done. For now? A shrug and *so long* would have to do—and a short prayer that he was in a better place. We had a Bible and read it often. It was full of hope, but guarantees were hard to come by. All we could do was take our chances.

Most boys my age do not think about death. My older brother, Tom, was that way. He was a well-setup man in search of women, fine horses, and a fancy saddle. It's all he talked about. None of which he'd ever find on our ranch. Our saddles were patched and worn thin, showing wood on the pommel, and our horses leaned toward being sturdy and fast. There wasn't a thoroughbred among them, but they'd go all day and be ready to go the next. We had a working ranch, not a showplace. Guess that's why he pulled foot and left.

It was understandable, at least for him. This was a hard land that didn't forgive the weak and timid. Under every rock, over every hill, something was waiting to take a bite out of you. You learned to pay attention or learned to nurse your wounds. But you learned—if you stayed alive.

The land looked flat from a distance but wasn't. It was mostly gullies cutting through sandy hills, peppered by sagebrush and scrub trees. There was good grass to be found. This time of year, it was cured on the stem by the hot sun and lack of water. A longhorn could survive on it and find water too. It was a good thing. We couldn't afford to lose any cattle.

North and east was the Red River, and New Mexico wasn't too far west. There were some big cattle outfits around, and Pa had once drawn our holdings out on a map for me. Equidistant between the ranches, he'd found a spring with good water and filed on it under the Homestead Act of 1866. There was some discussion if that law was allowed in Texas, but nobody seemed inclined to dispute it. That was some years ago, when Ma still had energy and Tom and I were small. Since then, we'd found more springs and filed on those. Water was gold in a dry land, and we did what we could to improve the springs for ourselves and the wildlife.

Ma was a schoolteacher in Carthage, Missouri. Pa rode by one day and saw her sitting on the front steps of the schoolhouse. She'd been fired and was mad enough to shoot somebody. The list of things a female school-teacher could and couldn't do was longer than the Declaration of Independence. They talked some about that, and when he mentioned he was going home to West

Texas, she stood and looked back at that school and then asked if he wanted company. They were married a week later.

Since our small ranch was a two-day ride to any settlement, there were no schoolhouses around. Ma taught us boys our numbers and how to read—more importantly, to understand what we read. She'd always tell anyone passing through to bring back a book of some kind, and she'd stake them to a home-cooked meal. Pa taught us the ways of men, cattle, and horses. I'll admit I took to that more than book learning.

Tom practiced with his pistol every chance he got, dry-firing because powder was scarce. He read books about faraway places, sitting on the porch with his feet up on the rail, staring at distant hills. Sometimes I think Pa blamed our mother for Tom getting ideas and wanting a finer life. I didn't care either way. My interest was in wide-open spaces and raising cattle. Tom wasn't much help with that, although he was a good hand when he tried.

When Ma died, it hit us all hard. One morning, she didn't get up to fix breakfast, and it shocked us all. Said she felt tired. Like usual, once set on a course, it didn't take her long to do it, and she didn't falter. The next day, she was gone. After we buried her, Pa tried to read over her from our Bible but couldn't pick out words through the tears.

We looked at each other, and I was ashamed to be thinking about who was going to cook our meals and sew our clothes. Had we depended on her so much we wore her out? I'll always carry that guilt and vowed to never treat a woman that way. If I ever found a woman who'd have me, she'd be a partner, not a servant.

Now I was alone in an empire of dry grass, rolling

hills, and valleys choked with brush. And I loved this land. We had a fair amount of cattle, if I could find them. But it would be a few more years of work before we could drive anything with a big T brand to market.

Maybe the harsh land suited me. I'd been mule stubborn since I could remember, and most visitors couldn't talk to me for more than a few minutes. After that, conversation would dry up and I'd lose interest, walking away to work on something. Hard work gave me peace, and I'd been doing it since I was big enough to ride. While most folks were talking and planning, I'd be doing.

Standing on the low hill above our cabin, all things seemed at peace. But I knew that was an illusion. Glancing around, I vowed to stop daydreaming. Otherwise, some Comanche would end my suffering. And there was no one left to dig my grave.

I wiped my head with a faded blue bandanna, putting the battered and stained hat back on my head. It was low-crowned and the color of the land around me. That was how I felt on this day. Used up and beat down.

———

IT's BEEN SAID life is not a sure thing, nor can we know what the next moment will bring. Everyone knows that. But it's not often we're brought up against it. If the future were known, Pa wouldn't have gone out that cabin door. I don't know what he was thinking. If it'd been Tom, I'd have said his head was in the clouds or some faraway land he'd read about. But Pa wasn't that way. He knew the dangers. And the biggest danger of all was being complacent.

Every day we woke up knowing we were on land

claimed by the Comanche, and they didn't like us being there one bit. Most of the different tribes of Comanche were moved to government land in the Oklahoma Territory. I didn't agree with that, but no one asked me. But enough of them stayed behind to make life interesting. They spent a good amount of their time riding into old Mexico. Selling captives was a big thing with them. I never figured out why they bothered with us. Pay ransom? We were too poor to buy back a chicken if they stole it.

We'd been here a few years, and most people we met knew we meant them no harm. We'd have families stop by on occasion, mostly Comanche and Kiowa, trading for sugar or rock candy. We kept it around because most Indians had a serious sweet tooth. We didn't begrudge a beef or two when they were hungry and told them that. And we tried to serve a meal when visitors came calling —provided they weren't shooting when they came. Most folks moving through were short on supplies and seemed to appreciate a good meal.

Our trouble came from young warriors out to make a name for themselves, and I sometimes wondered if some of those we fed on one day didn't launch arrows at us the next. Life is hard enough without making up hatred where none should be. But they still came against us on occasion.

Sometimes we exchanged shots, and they rode away whooping and hollering, having a grand time. The persistent ones stayed. We didn't bury them, that wasn't their custom. We'd drag the bodies up a hill, and they'd be gone in the morning. Several horsemen would come in the night, quiet but with enough noise to announce their presence. They'd bundle up the dead and leave. Being curious, I trailed enough of them to know they would head straight to a cave in the hills and place the body inside, covering it with rocks. One way of burial is as good as another. When out riding, if I came upon a hole or small cave covered in rocks, I knew enough not to go digging around.

———

THE ATTACK that morning shouldn't have been a surprise. We hadn't had visitors in months, so they were due. We'd talked about it some the night before in a casual way. Wasn't much we could do—it was like seeing lightning in the distance and waiting for thunder.

Pa left the house while dawn was just a promise over the hill. I was frying up potato slices and bacon with some wild onions I'd gathered at the spring. There was leftover fry bread to sop up the grease. Being only a passable cook, I had to pay attention to what I was doing and didn't see him leave.

They caught him trying to fill a bucket with water from the spring, and he never made it back to the house. His pistol was hanging on a rawhide string inside the doorway, and that was the only time I knew of that he broke our rule. We always went armed. Lessons in life cost money or blood. I figure Pa paid too much for this one.

He cried out—a hoarse, angry warning full of pain. Thinking he'd fallen, I set the skillet off the flame and looked out the door. Pa was down, and a cold knot formed in my throat as I tried to yell. I went out the door holding a double-barreled Greener shotgun. A pistol was stuck in my pants, but I didn't reach for it right away.

An Indian straddled Pa, knife raised for another blow, when I cut loose with that gun, aiming high. The buckshot took the Indian in the head, and he wound up under a bush, struggling to get his knees under him to rise. He didn't.

Dropping to one knee and pulling my pistol, I did a quick look around the clearing to make sure this was the only enemy. It wasn't like them to come alone. A sharp whistle came from the brush, cutting through the morning wind, and hoofbeats pounded away. They stopped about a hundred yards out. If they were coming back, it wouldn't take them long to decide.

Fearing what I would find, I turned to Pa and almost lost the breakfast I'd been sampling. They'd put two arrows in him. The first one must have dropped him and taken him side-to-side. The second nailed his shoulder to the post he leaned against. Either wound was a death sentence, but the deep slice across his belly made it a sure thing and was pure meanness. He tried to hold everything in, but it was no use, and his hands fell to his sides as he struggled to breathe.

His gaze met mine in a grimace of pain as he shook his head.

When I reached for him, he waved me away with a feeble, blood-soaked hand. "It's no use."

I kneeled by him, hands stopped in mid-air, not knowing what to do. I'd seen men die, but they'd been strangers—Indians we'd dusted up and cowmen who couldn't make it back to their home range. Men who'd been sick, gored, or had a horse roll on them. That was our violent world.

When Ma died, it was gentle-like. Not like this. It does something to you when you see someone you care for broken and used up, fighting pain with their last breath.

Pa coughed up blood and seemed disoriented a

moment before giving me a hard stare. "They'll be back. You get to the house so you're not caught out in the open. They can't get to you in there."

I knew he was right. The roof was sod and the walls were adobe and rock, but my head was shaking. "I can't leave you out here. Maybe we can—"

His bloody hand gripped my arm before falling away. "You can, and you will. I'm already dead, boy."

My answer was cut short by an arrow glancing off the post above us. He was panting like he was starving for air, a wild look in his eyes. "When it's over, bury me by your ma. I'll rest easy there. Then you go find your brother. Bring him home!" He paused for a moment, pain causing him to try and double over—but he couldn't. "Now hurry. I can't stand the pain. I can't. Give me release and get back to the house."

I glanced toward those Indians and then back at him, using time we didn't have. "What do you mean? Pa, I can't..."

Blood splattered my face as he tried to yell. "Dammit, boy. We ain't got time! They're coming. You going to leave me here to be tortured? You going to listen to me screaming while they throw my guts around for the dogs? I'm trying to go, but I can't die fast enough."

He gripped my arm again with weak fingers, slick with his own blood. "Son...I'd do it myself, but I can't hold a pistol. I can't."

Staring at him, I cursed the very God we prayed to every day. And then prayed for that same God to give me strength. But Pa was right. They were coming, and we were out of time. The hooting and screaming grew loud. They were circling and drawing near. I drew my pistol as he smiled at me, nodding and showing bloody teeth. He got his release with his eyes loving me until they went empty. Smoke from that pistol hid him for a moment, and I was grateful for that.

He knew what he asked of me and what it would cost. A good man gone who'd taught me everything about the world a man would need to know—a man with a vacant stare fixed on a brassy sky.

Lurching to my feet, I emptied the pistol into the brush, screaming and crying with a voice gone hoarse. Guns empty, I turned and stalked toward the cabin, and you'd think I had a charmed life. But I just didn't care. For a moment, I couldn't think of a reason to keep going. All I held dear was gone. When I got to the house, arrows hit all around me and bounced off the adobe bricks as I went inside. A lance adorned with feathers slammed into the wooden door as I closed it.

I was glad they weren't using rifles. Not that they didn't have them. Powder was scarce, and shells were usually saved for hunting game. Besides, Comanche liked their killing done up close and personal. Their ways might be different, but I'd never seen a coward among them.

Leaning against the heavy door, I turned and put the bar across. Safe for the moment in a house built like a fortress. Staring at my hands, I wiped my father's blood on my shirt, trying to get them clean. The tears might have helped some.

———

FINALLY GETTING my wits about me, I loaded all the weapons and waited. It wouldn't take long. I was the last, and they'd have a bloodlust to finish the job. Pa's pistol was better than mine, so I swapped. With two loaded pistols and the shotgun ready, I felt a little better. At least for the moment.

Four warriors rode into the yard, all holding lances decorated with hair. I'm sure they'd scouted us and thought of me as a young boy, hiding in the house and cowering in fear. They were partly right. Anyone not showing fear at this point was a fool. And I was young, but I've been doing a man's work since I could sit on a horse.

Watching them through the cracks in the shutters, I knew they'd give no mercy. Mercy was a Christian teaching, and I'd find no scripture in their medicine pouch.

It was tall odds for making it out of this alive, but I didn't care. A darkness was upon me, and only death could lift the veil. Theirs or mine. I took a deep, calming breath. It was useless. Ready as I could be and feeling hot all over, my breath quickened, preparing me for battle as I paced the floor. It startled me a moment. I looked forward to this—at least, the resolution.

We never harmed any man without provocation. But if they wanted it, I'd give them a belly full. And squatting on their land? They'd taken it from the Mexicans and the Kiowa. And those took it from the ones who lived here before.

It looked as if an older warrior was arguing with the younger men. Glancing between the house and the older man, they shook their lances and yelled at him until he shrugged, pulling his horse away. It made me wonder for a moment why he'd argue against attack—but he was wise to do it. I didn't know what they planned, but it wouldn't go the way they wanted.

Being in no mood for a long siege, I took the bar from the door—I wouldn't want it said I wasn't hospitable. When they dismounted and rushed screaming toward the door, I kicked it open for them. They were bunched up and surprised by the move, maybe thinking they'd break in the door by sheer weight of numbers. When I fired both barrels of the shotgun, buckshot cleared the porch, and they went down, wounded and dying. I emptied my pistol at the warrior on the horse, but he was riding away, dodging through the brush. I missed my shots and cursed myself for not bringing the rifle.

Looking around, still trying to catch my breath, my shoulders slumped. The three Indians lay in a pile in front of the porch. An arm jerked and then was still. I pointed my gun at them but wasn't concerned. The dead will do that on occasion, and these were long gone. The adrenaline of battle wore off and left me tired to the bone. But I couldn't stop. I had a mess to clean up and a burial to do.

It was going to be a hot day.

————

I KNEW WHAT PA WANTED. He died before I could make a promise I'd have trouble keeping. He taught us to keep our word, and that left me with a problem. I didn't give him the promise, but he gave me my marching orders. He wanted me to find Tom and bring him back to help run the ranch. But my brother Tom had no intention of coming back, and I wasn't sure about staying either.

Our ranch was about two-days ride to anywhere, or nowhere. Most of it was rolling hills and grassland. To make things interesting, there were brush-choked gullies and tree-lined valleys that used to have water—whenever it rained. West of the Red River, southwest of Amarillo, and east of New Mexico. Pa had a map he'd bought at the capitol that showed the location of our springs and home place. I don't know what he paid for something like that, but it was detailed and well done. That's what they used to file our claims on the springs. A few creeks were misplaced, but we drew those in when needed...even the dry ones.

Like most places, land was controlled by access to water. We had it if you could find the springs. The nearest place people congregated was a little town called Johnson Flats. I don't know who Johnson was, but it didn't take much imagination to call it flat—most of the country was.

Before leaving, I used a stub of a pencil and printed a note on a piece of paper I tore out of the back of our old Bible.

Gone for supplies. Use what you need. Leave it like you found it.

The butt of my pistol worked as a hammer as I tacked the note to the door. If someone rode by and was down on their luck, I hoped they could read it—I barely could, and I wrote it.

It was a tradition in the country to offer hospitality to travelers or those needing help. There was talk that it was the same if you came to an Indian camp—they'd not turn you away or do you harm if you were a guest. It wasn't something I'd bet my life on. Still, I'd never heard of the practice being abused. Most folks were honest enough. Those who would steal or take advantage were buried, or they left in a hurry.

We had a dry milk cow and a couple of pigs. Before we penned them up, those pigs collected more arrow wounds than Pa, but I guess they had thicker skin. Comanche or Mexican, it didn't make any difference. Those boys sure liked to shoot at our pigs. I opened the gate to the pen and pitched down what feed we had left from the loft. The animals would make do, or else the coyotes would. The chickens were on their own but wouldn't last, except maybe a couple of roosters that would fight the devil himself. Maybe I'd be back before the coyotes got all of them.

We had a solid house and decent barn, with a couple of lean-to sheds in the corral for the horses, but any place needs attention year-round. With one last look and feeling guilty at all the work that needed to be done, I gathered my duffel and saddled our last horse that hadn't been run off. I didn't blame anybody for not taking that horse, and the fact that the Indians didn't run off with him proved they watched us and didn't want him. He was a hammer-headed roan gelding that never forgave mankind for the cutting he got. He was docile enough until you got in the saddle. Then he'd crow-hop and swap ends a few times just for fun. The horse didn't disappoint or change his habit for this trip. Once he settled down, we followed my brother's trail toward Johnson Flats.

You couldn't call it a road, but enough horses and wagons had traveled the same trace to leave a well-defined trail. It was slow going, with me imagining Comanche behind every clump of scrubby trees and dark shadow. The second evening, I sat by a small fire, thinking of finding my brother and how to tell him about Pa—buying supplies and anything else that came to mind. I'd make it into town about mid-morning the next day.

What I thought of most was how to do the work on the ranch by myself with no money to hire help. Some hands will work for next to nothing—just food and a place to sleep. But they still liked to cut it up in town occasionally, and that takes money. There's nothing more pitiful than a cowhand sitting around with nowhere to go and no money for whiskey or the favors of a saloon girl—drinking free coffee and playing solitaire, maybe grabbing a free bite to eat when the bar served up sandwiches.

A metal contraption with three legs straddled the fire and suspended a pot full of beans and rabbit. I'd fried the rabbit first, then chopped up the meat and added it to the beans. The beans had been cooked several times, carried along in the pot with a tied-down lid. Along with some jerky added for the salt and fry bread—I was ready to chow down and turn in with a first-class belly ache. Except I had visitors.

I'd been listening to them for a few minutes as the shuffle of horses drew near. The ring of a horseshoe on rock told me they might be friendly—they weren't trying to sneak up on me and were coming in slow, or they didn't care. Most folks would have called out by now, and I had no reason to think these horses didn't have riders. Being cautious in nature made me take my shotgun and step behind an outcropping of rock hidden by a stunted tree.

A Comanche brave rode into the clearing, and he was big with a twisted look to him, like he couldn't decide whether to smile or scowl. He did both. The man was mostly naked but wore knee-length desert moccasins and a beat-up and dusty leather hat with a feather stuck in it. He led a horse, dragging a travois. I couldn't see what was in it, but I heard a woman groaning.

The third horse had a captive, a grown woman sporting a noose and a short rope tied around her neck. The end of the rope hung free, so her being a captive might be an assumption. Couldn't figure out the rope, though. Kind of an odd accessory. Men wore neckerchiefs around their necks. Never seen a rope worn.

She was as brown as a nut, with dark hair and a slim figure. I took her for an Indian or Mexican, but couldn't be sure. Not that it mattered. The light caught her eyes, and I had to look twice. There was something odd, but I couldn't tell from a distance.

The Comanche were disliked by pretty much everyone for their habit of stealing women and children and then selling or trading them back to their families, or to anyone else with something to trade. They gave young, pretty women back in a slightly used condition. I'd heard some of the women committed suicide soon after they returned, and I couldn't understand that. I may be young, but I knew that no woman would choose that to happen to them, so they deserved love and respect when they returned...just for surviving. This girl didn't look mistreated—but then, captivity is the pinnacle of mistreatment, no matter the circumstance.

When they stopped, she grabbed a small kettle off her horse and stepped to the spring to fill it with water, rope trailing after. When she came back, she put the kettle on the fire—moving my coffee pot. Now, that right there was a cow-camp sin. We'd have to talk about that.

The brave slid off his horse, looked once at my hiding spot, and walked to the fire, picking up a piece of fry bread. Wolfing it down in two bites, he spoke over his shoulder. "You can come out now. No need to be afraid."

Well now. Afraid? Only slightly surprised he spoke English, I stepped out, keeping the shotgun pointing at him. "That's right neighborly of you to invite me to my own fire. How's my supper? I've only had it three days in a row, and it was starting to be tiresome."

The girl spoke from the shadows. "Don't shoot, mister. We mean no harm. Please."

I'd seen a lot of harm done after speaking those

words and heard of a lot more, so I kept my gun pointed in the right direction. If this were a ruse meant to keep me off-balance and confused, they were doing a fair job of it. Not counting the raids on our place, attacks by the Comanche were getting few and far between. I'd heard it was worse south of us, but that was more of a Mexican problem. Maybe that's where they'd captured this girl.

I hoped my voice didn't show my confusion. "I'm not real sure what's going on here, and I don't know you people. Someone want to talk about why you invited yourselves into my camp and moved my coffee pot?"

The warrior's fingers buried themselves in my pot of beans. "You good cook. Make good squaw."

Well, that was damn insulting, but he said it in such a friendly fashion, it confused me more. If that was an example of Comanche humor, it was falling short. I could always shoot him later.

The girl turned on her heel and then went to check on the woman in the travois. She tossed the captive rope again so it hung down her back and she could walk around free. If that wasn't odd enough, a Comanche warrior sat at my fire, enjoying my supper, with his bow and rifle still on his horse, acting like we knew each other. I didn't put much faith in that, but I couldn't see an immediate threat. I knew what Pa would have done. He'd have shot him out of the saddle. Although I was considered the mean one of our family, I wasn't quite that quick on the shoot. But I'd thought of it.

I'd read about people playacting on a stage while an audience sat and watched. Ma talked of it some and about how much fun it was. Problem was, I didn't know the name of this play or what it was about. More importantly, how it was supposed to end.

The Comanche were fighters. Big as he was, this one

probably figured he could take me anytime he wanted. That might be true in a fair fight. Fair would be my last choice. I might surprise him, but that was not a chore I wanted to tackle. The woman on the travois groaned while the girl tended to her. It was a puzzle. My stomach grumbled.

"Well, hell." Shaking my head, I propped the shotgun against a rock and grabbed the tin plate and spoon I had situated, waiting for the meal to heat. "You mind if I eat some of my own supper?"

The man grinned with a bean-covered face and gestured toward the pot. I looked over toward the two women. "Y'all hungry?"

The girl glanced at me. Her voice had a strange accent, kind of musical. "Save me some. We're having a baby here, and I'm kind of busy right now."

A baby? Before I could comment on that, the Indian spoke. "You Tyler."

Now I'm wishing the shotgun was closer. I had my pistol stuck in my belt, but I'd be likely to shoot myself in the foot if I tried to get it out in a hurry or make myself into a steer. I'd do better to reach for my skinning knife.

"Now just how do you know my name?"

He shrugged and held up two fingers covered in bean juice before licking them clean. "Two days. Young warriors attacked your father. It was bad thing—no honor."

The memory was still raw in my mind and put anger in my voice. "Were they friends of yours?"

He considered that a moment, like he was trying to figure out what a friend was, and then shrugged. "Not so much."

I stared at him a moment, a spoon full of beans

halfway to my mouth, again wishing I had that shotgun. "Are you the one I shot at?"

He must have read my mind as he glanced at my pistol and grinned. He rubbed his shoulder. "You pretty good shot."

I was pondering a mystery. How could a Comanche brave wander into my camp and eat my supper without me shooting him? He surprised me again.

"You make big problem for me. Those men you killed had captive." He pointed his chin toward the women. "Now I have her. Big mouth. Talk all time. Could sell in Mexico but long way. Much talk on way. Maybe better to kill her."

I glanced toward the captive woman, but I didn't think she was listening. "Where'd you learn to speak English?"

"Mission school."

"Then talk normal. Those padres didn't teach you to speak like that."

The man shrugged. "Extra words waste of time."

The wailing of a new infant interrupted them. The girl held up the baby by the heels. "It's a boy. Tyler, would you bring that water here? It should be warm by now. And you're going to need a shovel."

Did everyone know my name?

He looked at me. "See? Bossy. Maybe better kill her."

I left him gorging on the bean stew, vowing to stay upwind of him from now on, and took the water to the girl. She'd untied the poles from the horse, and the Indian woman lay on the buffalo hide and among some blankets. Using most of the water to clean the baby, she put the kettle aside and kneaded the woman's stomach.

It was dark away from the fire, but the first thing I saw was a set of the bluest eyes I'd ever seen. Somewhere in her lineage, an Irishman was sneaking around. Those eyes pinned me a moment before turning back to the Indian woman. "Where's the shovel?"

"Lady, I'm not a prospector. I don't usually carry a pick and shovel with me."

That got me a long stare before she responded. "You know what afterbirth is?"

I nodded. "I've pulled a calf or two."

"Well? Don't just stand there staring. Are you addled? What's the first thing that happens after a calf is born? Coyotes and all manner of creatures smell it and come running. We need to bury it, or we'll spend the night fending off varmints."

She patted the woman on the leg and was rewarded with a smile. "Probably be about an hour. Gives a smart man like you time to think of something."

I turned and looked at the big Indian sitting by the fire. He gave me a bean-smile and shrugged.

"You'd better go get some chow." I looked again, shaking my head. That man sure loved my cooking. "If there's any left."

She nodded. "Let's drag this over by the fire. We don't want to leave her out in the dark. No telling what could happen."

Turned out it was easy to drag the skin and bedding since the woman stood and walked over to the fire carrying the baby. She sat, holding it in one arm, and started in on the stew with one hand. I always thought birthing would be harder on a woman.

"You folks starving? Seems a mighty Comanche warrior ought to be able to feed his family."

I scraped the bottom of the pot and ladled stew into a pan for the girl, proved I was quicker than Big Indian by grabbing the last of the bread before he could and handing it to her. I stood looking at my guests for a moment. There was jerky and some trail mix in my saddlebag if it wasn't full of bugs. Reckon I'd need it.

"You people got names?"

The girl nodded between bites. "He's White Bear, and his woman's name..."

"Nabuni." The woman's voice was soft, drawing the name out.

"...which means Dawn. My name is Mattie."

Dawn spoke again, pointing at her husband. "Tosaguara." She said it like it was supposed to mean something.

Mattie looked at me. "Don't let him fool you. He took me from those warriors before you killed them, not after. That was a fine piece of shooting, by the way. I've never seen anything like it. Anyway, these are good people. I trust them."

Well, that was fine and dandy. Did I trust her? I pondered that for a moment, glancing between them. Just because nobody was shooting yet wasn't a matter of trust.

"If they're such good people, why are you still wearing the captive rope?"

"No cut." White Bear spoke. "Tied with wet hide. When it dried, the knot is like iron—can't untie. The woman"—he pointed to Mattie—"she say to find rancher. You can make it soft again?"

"We could hold her under water until the leather softens." I could tell White Bear liked that idea. "Or I could use something else."

Digging around in my saddlebag, I pulled out a pair of wire cutters. We don't have fences, but half the ranch is held together by wire. This wouldn't be much different, except it was embedded into the skin of her neck.

"Hold still."

That rope was tight. I don't know how she kept breathing or why she put Dawn and the baby first before asking for help. The only thing saving her was she hadn't worn it long. If I listened closely, I could hear her breath whistling.

"The knot is so tight we can't undo it, and we can't get a knife under the—" She gasped as the thin rope came free. "How did you do that?"

I shrugged and grinned. "I took the simplest solution. The problem wasn't the rope but the knot, so I cut it off."

Rubbing her neck and then taking a deep breath, she whispered to me. "Thank you, from the bottom of my heart. We've been riding at night, so the sun wouldn't make the hide constrict any farther. Sweat helped a little. I don't know how much longer I could have lasted."

"You're a mighty brave girl. The men who captured you didn't mean for it to come loose." I was staring at White Bear. "Usually, the Comanche will put a wide, wet strip of hide around your head. When it dries, it kills you…real slow."

Ignoring him, White Bear walked to the spring and washed. Returning to the fire, he held out his hands for the baby and then looked at me. "The woman is strong. Being captive did not damage her spirit, only made her stronger." He grinned. "She is your woman now."

"Now, wait a minute—"

"You need to help them." Mattie stared at me a moment before continuing. "Since they helped me, it will be bad for them. They've nowhere to go. Their people will know they freed me, so now they have to wander around the country."

Dawn's voice cut in. "Those men were half-breeds."

Her hand made a slashing motion. "Kiowa and Comanche. No one will miss them. Still...we say no fight anymore. Our people tell us to go away. Whites tell us to go away. Where? This land is our home."

My sigh was long and drawn out as I wiped a hand down my face. Some of their problems were of their own making—well, we helped some. But things could change. I had an idea—a crazy one. No telling how it would turn out. I needed help and couldn't hire hands—at least not yet. Glancing at Mattie, she was already nodding encouragement. How'd she know I was thinking of something?

The solution was in front of me, but it was chancy. I had nothing to go on but a gut feeling of what was right and wrong. I glanced at White Bear. "Can a mighty Comanche warrior learn to work on a ranch?"

"He can," Dawn said. "I can help."

I tried to hide my smirk. "Your voice changed. Got higher."

White Bear shrugged, his voice mild. "Take woman for wife, man lose voice. Same everywhere."

Trouble could come from this alliance, but I could see some advantages. The hardest part would be to throw out my mistrust and anger over the death of my father. Earlier attacks I could forgive. The warriors paid more for those attacks than us. But it could not continue. If we were to have a workable ranch, it had to stop. Maybe this would help.

Holding out my hand, I held his gaze. He hesitated a moment, and then we shook on it. "I can't pay much. Hell, I can't pay anything for now. But you'll have a roof over your head and food to eat. I can't promise safety, we'll have to work on that. You'll have a home. It's about all I can offer."

Without thinking too much about it, I'd decided to

work at the ranch. Pa would be pleased. Maybe there was never a doubt—not too sure what he'd think about the hired hands. "I'm short on help and short on money, but we can make it pay after a few years."

My glance took in all of them. "If we don't die first."

White Bear picked up the empty bean pot and looked inside, running his finger along the rim. I started having second thoughts about feeding this man. I could tell there was something on his mind. Silence stretched for a minute or two before the Indian spoke.

"I know of others—tired of running from reservation to mountains and back again. Ride to Mexico. Ride to reservation. Soldiers always chase. Buffalo going away, antelope hard to find. There is much hunger. Children die. Families die."

He looked at Dawn for a moment, and I'd swear his eyes softened. Then he met my gaze. "We are much tired."

"Things always change, be it country or people. We must change too, both of us. It doesn't pay to be too stubborn. These others you mention, they'd be welcome. But men with families. No troublemakers. I got a real short temper with people who cause me trouble. Can we agree on that?"

White Bear nodded and shrugged. "We can try. Always trouble."

Everyone was smiling, even the baby. I'd been gently pushed along a path toward an uncertain end, and looking at Mattie, apparently by a master. But it felt right, and I wouldn't go back on it.

"Go on back tomorrow, you know the way. Try and gather as many of our animals that you can find, especially the chickens. We need the eggs." I chuckled as he made a face. "I bet you've never eaten a fried egg.

Anyway, you can use the house to live in until I get back. I must find my brother, and it may take some time. I'll have to break this deal to him real gentle-like." I'd been rummaging around in my possibles bag for my tally book. Tearing off a sheet, I wrote a note on it and handed it to him. "If anyone comes by, show them this paper. It says you work for the Tyler ranch."

I drew a big T on the page. "If you're hungry, find a beef with this mark on it to feed yourselves. But only this mark."

I looked at him until he returned my gaze. "This is important. If anyone comes and objects to you being there, don't make a fight of it. Take to the hills and wait for me. Once I'm home, we'll make our stand where needed with both Comanche and whites. If someone takes over the buildings and don't want to move, we'll move them. Some of the people on either side won't like what we're doing, but they'll have to learn to live with it."

He gave a grudging nod, and I could tell it took a little out of him. I doubted this man ever backed up for anybody. What seemed normal to me must be demeaning to him.

I tried to explain. "White Bear, you think about this. If you kill somebody while staying in our place, it'll just make things hard. Don't stir the pot. Give ground until you hear from me. You must not make yourself an enemy. Think of your family. That's the most important thing."

Dawn and Mattie had walked away from the fire. When they came back, Mattie looked at me. "Shovel?"

She returned my gaze with a smile and a quizzical look. Finally, I shook my head. "You're pushy."

"Let's call it spirited."

They'd wrapped the afterbirth in a piece of buckskin. I knew there was an old buffalo wallow not far away. The edge of the dirt could be caved in to bury the contents—barring rattlesnakes, rabid gophers, scorpions, coyotes, mountain lions, or an occasional jumping spider taking an interest in a young, not-so-bright rancher stumbling around in the dark. I was still trying to figure out how I'd gotten into this mess.

———

WHITE BEAR and his family had moved away from the dying fire and rolled up in blankets on the buffalo robe. I sat on a big, flat rock and listened to the night. Other than the rustle of the horses munching on thin grass by the spring, it was quiet.

Mattie wrapped a blanket around herself and joined me. "You're not sleeping?"

My gaze fixed on the darkness where the Indians were bedded down. She noticed where I looked. "I think you can trust them."

"It's hard. All I've ever done is fight them."

She grunted. "Same for them. They're taking a big chance siding with you."

I nodded. "What's your story, Mattie? How'd you happen to get captured? I've heard what happens to captive women. I'm sorry you had to endure that."

She leaned her head on my shoulder. "I appreciate the sentiment, but it never happened. Maybe because I'm not white. I don't know. And then White Bear took me away from them."

A low chuckle made me glance at her. "Not that they weren't getting around to it." She returned my gaze. "Seems the excitement of killing Johnny Tyler was more important than me. Are you that big of a prize? A mighty warrior?"

He snorted and shook his head. "Hardly. I think we were kind of the local entertainment. Why did White Bear take you away from them? Seems out of character for the Comanche."

"It is, but don't low-rate him. He's smart. I think he needed some way to gain your trust. I guess I'm his calling card. He may have thought you'd shoot first and ask questions later."

"He was right. I thought about it. You seem willing to help them."

"I am, to a point. There's no doubt he saved my life. For that, I'm grateful. But trust must be earned...by both sides."

"So, back to my first question. Where'd you come from? You talk better than anyone I know."

She sighed and snuggled into my shoulder. I wondered about her being so close, but I wasn't going to complain. "My parents were house servants and teachers."

When her voice stopped, I glanced down. Mattie was asleep, and my next problem was how to get comfortable without waking her.

But sleep did not come for me. My gaze went to the Comanche. Was White Bear asleep? Or was he guarding against some treachery...like me? A couple of days ago, I was fighting for my life and burying my father. It seemed the only rule between me and the Comanche Nation was to shoot on sight. Now they slept in my camp while I pondered the turn of events. Could this work? Did I want it to? There was much to gain and much to lose with the deal.

I sighed and settled back. Time would tell.

———

I SPOKE to Mattie the next morning. Sleep didn't come to me, so I came across as grumpy at best.

"Mattie, you've got a choice."

We'd broken camp, and I was ready to point my horse toward Johnson Flats. I had no fear of trying to explain the situation to my brother, provided I could find him. He wouldn't care less since the last I knew, he had no plans of coming back.

Her voice was neutral, like discussing the weather. "I like choices."

"You can go back to the ranch with White Bear and Dawn, maybe keep them on track while I'm gone. I'll make a place for you if you wish to stay. Or I can take you into town, and we'll see about sending you wherever you wish to go. I've little money, but I can spare enough for a few meals and travel."

She shrugged, giving me an irritated look. "Those aren't choices. I belong with you."

I wasn't sure how she meant that. We'd spent a good part of the night talking and rubbing shoulders around the campfire. That didn't seem like much of a courtship or commitment. I hadn't gotten her story yet, maybe she wasn't ready to give it. She probably had a few demons of her own to put away. Some might frown at her skin color, but make no mistake, this was a pretty lady. One thing I'd come to know in my young age, we all breathe the same air and bleed the same color.

When she saw my hesitation, she spoke again, staring into my eyes. "I can't make it any simpler, Johnny."

Simple? Maybe for her. I wished Ma was alive to give me some advice.

―――――

JOHNSON FLATS WAS BUILT on ground that wouldn't grow anything but rocks, mesquite, and cactus. Dust was an inch deep in the street and followed us like smoke from a slow-moving fire as we moved along. The one thing the town did have was a reliable spring. Someone built a rock wall around it to gather water, and they'd put a lot of work into it. It looked like they used red clay between the rocks to make it watertight, and that gave me some ideas about my own springs. It was cool water on any day. A gnarled oak grew nearby, giving shade to anyone needing rest. Knowing those old trees, I wondered who kept the trash out of the water.

It looked like a cattle outfit was in town, judging by the number of horses tied to the rails in front of the saloon. I noticed different brands. Maybe they were having a get-together of some kind.

After I filled both my canteens and we drank our fill from the spring, I watered the horses in the runoff trough below the spring. That water was sure sweet. Pa told me the town citizens hung a man once for letting his stock foul that drinking water. Seems extreme, but you never know. It was a commodity that couldn't easily be replaced and was worth more than gold.

The town started when there were enough ranches and homesteads close by that needed supplies. A few years back, some enterprising souls started hauling in wagonloads of goods to sell. Now, there was a dusty street with buildings along the sides.

The second thing built right after the mercantile must have been the saloon and bawdy house. It was the biggest building in town. Pa never would let me go in there. I hadn't been to town for a couple of seasons, and

I was older now. Looking at Mattie, I figured to get educated sooner or later—that bawdy house didn't have the draw it used to.

Looking along the weathered gray buildings, a red and white striped barber pole stood out. A sign advertised a professional barber and a bathhouse—ladies welcome. There's nothing like riding with a young woman who makes you aware of your own fragrance. It'd been a while since my last dip in the spring, and my clothes would stand in a corner even if I wasn't in them.

The barber shop would be a good place to find information about my brother, so I headed that way, Mattie trailing along behind. She hadn't said much once we got close to town, but I could tell she was nervous. I'd have to start calling her my shadow because she was staying close.

I figured the saloon and barber shop would have been the first two places Tom would have gone to when he arrived in town, and we could use some sprucing up ourselves.

Lettering on the door read, *M. Spence, Proprietor.* Moving through the door, the first thing I saw was a man sitting in a large, padded chair, reading a newspaper. Several wooden cane-backed chairs lined the walls, along with a couple of small tables. The few men playing checkers or cards stared at us as we stepped through the door. Conversation stopped in mid-sentence. Strangers must be in short supply. Of course, I'd already noticed myself getting tongue-tied around Mattie.

The man in the barber chair folded his paper and scrambled to his feet with a friendly smile. "Help you, folks? I'm Spence, and I own this shop."

I looked him over and then glanced at the men. Most of them just looked curious and then went on about their business. "Mr. Spence, reckon I could use a haircut, maybe a shave?"

Spence nodded. "Cost you seventy-five cents if you want a bath, otherwise two-bits will get it. Bay Rum, or that Jockey Club, will cost you extra. Smells nice, though."

I wasn't sure what all these cow-pushers would think of someone who smelled nice. "A bath would be good. It's been a while. How much extra for clean water?"

The man looked affronted. "We change the water with each bath, Mr....?"

"And the lady?"

Mattie had stepped around behind the barber chair, looking at the various combs and scissors. Hearing my comment, she looked startled for a moment, smiled, and then shrugged.

"Nothing to worry about, young man. We have complete privacy." Spence turned and yelled over his shoulder. "Mary?"

A short, portly woman walked in, wiping her hands on her embroidered apron. It looked fresh and clean, so I figured she'd keep the rest of the place the same way.

"Yes?"

Spence inclined his head toward Mattie. "This lady would like to have a bath."

"Certainly."

I stepped up to them and held out a gold piece to the woman. "The young lady has been a Comanche captive and will need some clothes and whatever else she can think of. Can you take care of that for her?"

"Oh, my." She glanced at Mattie and then back at me. With a smile, she nodded. "Of course. It'd be my pleasure to help the young lady. Your money won't be needed."

Startled and a little overwhelmed by her kindness, I finally found my voice. "We can pay our way, ma'am."

Mattie's voice interrupted. "Johnny?"

I turned, and she was holding up a comb with two fingers as she wrinkled her nose. "These have lice."

When I glanced at Spence, he shrugged. "Just had a bunch of drovers ride into town. They ain't the cleanest." Turning to Mattie, he continued. "Are you a barber?"

"If I wish to be." She shrugged. "You'll hold these over the fire before you use them on him? Maybe dip them in whiskey?"

Mary laughed, reaching out for Mattie's hand. "That would be a waste of good whiskey. Come with me, girl. And he'll clean them in alcohol, or he'll answer to me. Now, let's get you fixed up."

Conversation picked up as the ladies disappeared into the back rooms. The barber didn't have much to say as he worked me over. The smell of singed hair made me nervous. I guess if it was my head on fire, I'd know soon enough. Bits and pieces of information came to me as I sat in the chair, half-asleep. Mainly, the talk was of range conditions and some shenanigans at the bawdy house the night before. Seems someone fell out of a window and couldn't find his pants. There was no mention of whether he was pushed or thrown, but his effort to fly was unsuccessful.

The man gave me a good shave, and I got out of that chair with my face as smooth as a baby's butt, with no blood to show for it. He led me to a back room and closed the door behind me. There was no danger of falling asleep in the bathtub. It was hardly large enough for a grown man to get into. But I made do and scrubbed with lye soap until my skin hurt.

Stepping back into the main room, one of the men

playing checkers stood and came over with his hand out. "You look like your pa. I didn't notice until you'd cleaned up. Did Ed come to town?"

I shook his hand more from habit than friendliness. It'd be a while before I got over Pa's death, and it made me grumpy. "You writing a story for the newspaper?"

The reply was swift. "You disrespecting your elders?"

The older man stared at me until I decided I'd been chastised enough, so I stepped back and nodded. "I'm sorry. Sometimes my mouth spits words out before I get a chance to look them over. No disrespect intended. And you're right. I'm Johnny Tyler, Ed's son."

He nodded, giving me a slow smile. "I'm Joe Blakeley. Know your pa. He in town with you?"

"No, Sir. Some renegade Comanche got him a few days back. I'm in town looking for my brother, Tom. Have you seen him? If you recognized me, you'd surely do the same for him."

With a clouded look, Joe spoke softly. "Sorry about Ed. He was a good man. Hard, but so's the land. Don't know anything about your brother." He turned away. "I wish you well, young man. I truly do."

Well, that was odd. I hesitated, thinking to start after him for a better explanation, when Mattie walked into the room. Everything stopped, including my breath. I swear the clock stopped ticking on the wall because I couldn't hear it, and those Seth Thomas clocks are loud. For the second time, silence swept the room.

She wasn't dressed fancy. Just a divided riding skirt and blouse. A bonnet hung by its strings on the back of her neck. Given her experience with the captive rope, I was surprised she did that. Her entrance was like fresh air had blown into the room. She was that pretty.

Her gaze held mine. I don't know what she was

looking for. I was too stunned to talk. When she realized that, she smiled and walked toward me.

Mary got to me first and spoke softly, only for me. "Boy, I know that girl is mixed race. But don't you lose her. She's a gem."

Mattie was next to us by then, and I reached out for her hand. "You're beautiful."

She looked me up and down. "And you cleaned up well, though you could use some new clothes. You shouldn't have spent money on me."

I held the door open for her. "I'm thinking it was money well spent."

As we moved through the door, she paused, looking at the men lining the wall, nodding to them. "Gentlemen."

The spell broken—they were still scrambling to their feet as we left. We stood outside on the walk. A tall young man and a woman who could be a Spanish lady, an Indian princess, or an African queen with a splash of Irish. The only detractors from gentility were my shotgun and pistol, and I was sure she had a pistol stuffed in a side pocket. I was smitten and didn't care who knew it. Or know what to do about it.

"Mattie, I don't know what kind of place that saloon is, but I don't want to leave you alone out here. You could stay with Mary inside or come with me. Staying with her might be safer. There's something not sitting right about this town. The boys inside got a little squirmy when I asked about my brother. I've got a bad feeling about it."

She nudged me with her hip. "Thought we'd already talked about this. I belong with you. Let's go find out what you need to know. Take care of business, Johnny. Don't worry one bit about me."

I figured if anyone knew about my brother, they'd be in that saloon. Pa told me most saloons were places where people met and exchanged information. All a man had to do was sift through the exaggerations and downright lies to find the truth. Many deals and agreements happened in meeting places like that with nothing more than a handshake.

We walked together to that building. I glanced at Mattie, and she had a firm set to her chin. The door opened easily to my hand.

———

I DON'T KNOW what I expected since I'd never been in a place like that, but it wasn't what I got. Planks of lumber sat on up-ended whiskey barrels that ran along the back wall. I guess they called it a bar. That's what Pa called it when he described the place. Men were lined up and drinking whiskey, but mostly talking and smoking. Tables scattered around were full of bottles, shot glasses, and elbows. Lots of elbows. I have never seen so many people in one place. There were several women around, most of them occupied with one or several men, and they'd donned more paint than a Comanche war party.

The room went quiet when we stepped in. I didn't blame them, but it was curious that we seemed to be having that effect on people. Pa's old Dragoon Colt was strapped around my waist in what he'd called a belly holster. It was easier to get at when riding or sitting. The Greener hung down my right side by a piece of rawhide, right next to my skinning knife. I didn't know if it was polite to bring them inside, but I didn't want some thief taking them off my saddle. My store-bought and patched pants, held up by rawhide galluses, rode over scuffed boots. The shirt I wore used to be blue. Now it looked like the feed sack it was made from. It occurred to me I should have gotten myself a new outfit along with Mattie. Her opinion aside, I wasn't much to look at.

There was an empty table next to the bar, and I guided Mattie toward it. Holding her chair, I got her situated and turned toward the bar.

A man behind the bar spoke up. "Mister, we don't serve…"

Pa told me once that when you start backing up, it's hard to stop. I wasn't going to start now.

"You got a name, mister?"

It took him a moment to find his voice. "I'm the owner of this place. Name's Fred Barney."

I made up a rule on the spot. Never trust a man with two first names. "Well, Fred or Barney, seems to me I didn't ask for your opinion."

He studied me for a moment and then Mattie. His tone mellowed somewhat. "Are you her pimp then? She's a looker, but we don't allow independents in here. I'd buy her from you, but the blacks aren't worth much. You get a better price for China girls."

I hadn't thought of the consequences of bringing her in with me and was ashamed that I put her through this. Glancing at her, I said, "I'm sorry." She raised an eyebrow and looked amused.

"Mister, the lady is with me and is free to come and go as she pleases. That's a fact. You'll give her respect or answer to me. And it better be damned quick."

The man stared at me, and I guess he didn't like what he saw. He backed up, but I could tell he didn't like it. I decided to give him a moment to get his wits about him. It felt like every eye in the place was on us. My neck colored up some from all the scrutiny, and I found an empty place at the end of the bar, close to Mattie. She was watching me with a glow in her eyes. Kinda spooky, especially with those blue eyes.

A different man tending drinks moved up to me and asked what I wanted.

"Got anything cold?"

"This look like Delmonico's to you?" The man had a fat face to go along with his round body. The mutton-chop beard made him look like a badger as he smiled at me. He was friendly enough, and a few chuckles came from down the line. I never heard of Delmonico, but I figured in some other lingo, it meant he didn't have any.

I shrugged, ignoring the chuckles. "Well, maybe some information. I'm looking for my brother."

The man didn't look near as friendly once he saw I wasn't buying anything and busied himself polishing a glass, peering through it at one of the oil lanterns hanging from the ceiling. It was a wasted effort on something so pitted and stained, but he was giving it a fair try. He must have decided I wasn't going away, so he gave a long sigh and finally looked at me.

"This brother of yours have a name?"

"Yes, Sir. Name's Tyler. Tom Tyler. He's kind of a tall galoot, about my size. Got a scar that runs down his cheek." My finger traced a line from my right eye down to my chin. "He's usually clean-shaven, so you'd notice it."

Soon as I spoke his name and described him, the place got quiet. I seem to have a knack for that. Maybe everyone was just trying to remember, but mostly, they looked anywhere but at me. I had a bad feeling. The knot in my stomach that started at the barber shop was developing into a considerable bellyache.

A man about halfway down the bar leaned over so he could see me. "How'd he get the scar?"

An odd question, considering. But I chuckled and relaxed a moment, thinking of that. "We were busting a couple of longhorns, one of which was meaner than a bag of snakes, when Tom's cinch broke. He was riding a good cutting horse that turned on a dime and left Tom for change. Of course, he landed in the brush after the turn."

The man nodded like he'd seen it before, which he probably had. "Only problem, that was the same pile of brush that old mossy-horn was trying to hide in." Several men laughed at that. "I guess he was some upset already, what with the heat and heel flies after him. Anyway, they had themselves a little set-to before I finally got him out of there."

The man looked down at his drink. "So, he wasn't a troublemaker?"

"Him or that bull?" I checked on Mattie, and she was looking at me like she'd just discovered something.

The man smiled. "Your brother. We got that same bull over at our place, so I know all about him. We call ours Satan. When we get a fresh rider, we send him into the brush after that bull. If he comes back alive, we figure he'll make us a good hand. Don't matter if he brings the bull."

Shaking my head, I grinned at him. "That's a mighty hard way to land a job." I turned serious for a moment. "Tom's not likely to make trouble. He's a smart man, more apt to talk than fight. We're peaceful folk."

Mattie snorted and kind of chuckled. As I turned to look at her, the man spoke again. "Are you peaceful?"

I didn't like where this was going. "I figure to be like most folks. I'm peaceful when I can be. Besides, I ain't been off our place in a long time. I got no experience at causing trouble, wouldn't know where to start."

He seemed to contemplate that for a moment. "So, where are you from?"

Now, that wasn't a normal question. Anyone who came riding up to the ranch, we never asked where they were from and especially where they were going unless they offered. It just wasn't polite, so I played it cagey.

"We got a hard-scrabble place south of here. Comanche hit us the other day, and Pa cashed in his chips. I figure to find my brother and let him know."

"You take my advice and go home." The man tossed a coin on the counter. "Fred, give the man a beer...and the lady if she wants. He's just another rider down on his luck."

He looked at me. "You can pay me back sometime when my luck is gone." Then he turned his back on me, and I knew the conversation was over.

I thanked him anyway, along with the barkeep, and then tasted my first beer. I didn't like it but drank part of it anyway, to be polite.

Pa always said I was stubborn. I never disappointed him about that, never leaving a job until it was finished. I looked around the room, trying to get anyone to return my gaze.

"So, anyone here seen my brother?"

The sounds in the room never changed, but I could feel it. If I were out in brush country, I'd be looking for an ambush. Something was wrong, and my irritation was starting to show as my voice echoed in the room.

"Nobody?"

Then I got a surprise. "Johnny, you need to come over here and sit down." Mattie idly played with her bonnet strings as she watched me.

I was getting nowhere with the local drinking club, so I grabbed my beer along with hers and walked over.

Taking a deep, slow breath and leaning forward with her arms on the table, her head shook in slow cadence as her gaze pinned me. Her voice was soft, so I could barely hear. "Don't drink any more of that beer. There's something wrong, and you need your wits about you."

Well, she wasn't telling me anything I didn't know. I dropped into a chair next to her, letting the barrel of the Greener rest on my foot. She didn't seem inclined to stop talking, and I was too curious to stop listening.

"I found out about your brother from Mrs. Spence. She seemed to know all about it."

My gaze caught her for a moment, but I decided I wasn't mad at her. She must have had her reasons. "Why didn't you tell me before? What's happened?"

"I wasn't sure—"

Fred came over and interrupted. "Lady, you don't need to be talking out of turn. It'll bring you a lot of trouble. It's best if you don't repeat anything you've heard."

With my mouth hanging open, I probably looked like a stepped-on toad as I watched him. I couldn't believe he'd talk to her this way. But it's hard to take issue with someone who turns their back and walks away.

I took off my hat and set it on the chair beside me. Running fingers through my hair, I stared at the man a moment after he turned around behind the bar. "I'm still waiting on that apology, and you're running out of time. This is not one of your working girls."

The man at the bar who'd bought me the beer spoke to the bartender. "I think you'd better do as this man asks. You should know better. If he doesn't put a knot on your head, we just might. That was uncalled for, and you were out of line earlier."

Grumbling, the bartender spoke without raising his gaze from the floor. "Sorry, ma'am. It's been a long day."

Everyone ignored us, including the bartender, like this was an everyday occurrence. I turned back to her, but she was looking down again. She said something too soft to catch. I leaned toward her. "What?"

Tears coursed down her cheeks, and she sobbed once before seeming to brace herself. "I never told you how I got here."

She was stalling. We both knew it. But I knew whatever happened to my brother was bad, and getting in a hurry now wouldn't help anything. My voice was as gentle as I could make it. "I'd like to hear about that."

She shrugged, looking at the table again. "We'd been trying to make it to a place south of the border. My folks were house servants and free—"

"You were slaves?"

"I said we were free. You got to learn to listen better."

Someone snickered, but I ignored it.

"Anyway, after the war, we had to leave our home. It was the craziest thing. We worked for John and Mirabelle Gentry. I was a little girl then. It wasn't a big farm, not like some of the big plantations farther east. We were just across the Texas line into Louisiana—down by the coast. It was mostly swamp and pine trees, but they managed to make a good living. Had a beautiful home too, built up on a hill with the Sabine River down below."

She stared out the window as she talked. Looking around, I could see the men at the bar listening and trying not to be obvious about it. A good part of them probably couldn't read, but they'd listen to a story all day long.

"A couple of men came by," she continued. "Told everyone to gather around. When we'd done that, they told us we had to leave—that we were free now and had to go away. Folks told them if we're free, we'll just stay where we are. The Gentrys treated us like family, and we had a good home. The men laughed at us and said no southerner could own land anymore, so they had to leave too. Well, Mr. Gentry pulled his pistol and ran them off."

She reached out and snagged my glass of beer, drinking most of it. Hers was already gone. At my look, she smirked. "Never said I couldn't drink."

Wiping her lips with the back of her hand, she finished her story. "The next day, those two men came back with a bunch of Federal soldiers. Rode right up to the front porch. When the Gentrys came out, the soldiers shot them dead. Man and wife, right on the porch. Then those two men—someone called them carpetbaggers—walked right into the house like they owned it. After we buried the Gentrys, we loaded up a wagon with all we could take from our home, hitched up a couple of mules, and headed west looking for work."

I shook my head as I listened to her. If I had a life story to tell, she would make mine seem paltry. I couldn't imagine the hardship she'd endured.

"We bounced around from one odd job to another. Seems everybody was free, but we couldn't keep working where we were, nobody wanted us. We heard of a hacienda in old Mexico that needed someone to care for children and tutor them. Even if that job was already taken, we thought there might be others down there, so we headed in that direction. We paid a fare on a freight outfit to let us tag along since they were going that way.

Not too many miles from here, the Indians hit us. They killed my folks, and the pack train was busted up, so they turned back."

I decided that, given a chance, this girl could talk your leg off and make you enjoy every bit of it.

"Next thing I knew, those Indians put a noose around my neck and threw me on a horse. It's a good thing they were talkers. And they loved to brag about what they were going to do to me."

Her laugh was bitter as she looked around the room. "That's the first time I'd been a slave, and I didn't like it."

I gave her a moment before I spoke. "He's dead, isn't he?"

I was watching the men at the bar. On occasion, I'd catch one of them cutting a glance at me. You'd think they'd have better things to do. I took the thong off my pistol.

She sat with tears in her eyes. "Well, Johnny Tyler. I've been stalling long enough. Here's the long and short of it. Mary said your brother was here. He ran into trouble and got himself killed. Sorry to have to tell you that."

Her expression mirrored mine, and I knew she wasn't as tough as she put on. Her eyes were soft, and her hand was gentle on my arm. I couldn't get my mind to catch up with what she told me. Tom? Dead? He was almost as mean as Pa and practiced with his pistol all the time.

Me? Pa worked me on the ranch from can see to cain't, so I hadn't much time for anything. It didn't make sense.

I took a deep breath. "How did it happen?"

Mattie looked off toward the bartender, who was staring hard at her, and then at the front door. "Well, I hear they have a crazy sheriff, and he's kind of short-tempered."

"I guess I don't understand. Tom wouldn't break the law, at least not intentionally. He sure wouldn't be looking to shoot it out with a lawman. How'd he get in trouble?"

She shook her head, still gripping my arm with a soft touch. "He didn't have to break any laws. It was a matter of being in the wrong place. He was going out the front door of this place, and Mack Foster, that's the name of their sheriff, was coming in—he always goes busting through a door like he's trying to break it down. Anyway, they bumped into each other and had words. Mack pulled his gun and shot your brother and then went over to his table like he didn't have a care in the world. Called for whiskey and some of those meat sandwiches they serve here."

She continued like she couldn't believe her own story. "Anyway, he just sat there, calm as you please. Finally, some of the men dragged the body out and buried him in the cemetery on the hill behind the town."

I glanced over at the bar, but they all took a sudden interest in the countertop and tried to find the bottom of their shot glass. "When did all this happen?"

"About a week ago."

Even being a simple country boy, I could see the irony of it. I'd seen that word once in a book and had Pa explain it to me. Tom got killed about the same time as Pa. I didn't know whether to throw a good mad or just up and cry. If that girl hadn't been sitting there, I might have done the latter.

I ran my hand over my face. Now what? Pa always said gone is gone, and there ain't no use crying over something you can't help. But I can also remember him sitting on a rock out by where we'd buried Ma, and he'd be there a long time just staring at nothing.

All I had left to my name after being spruced up and buying Mattie some clothes was a couple of twenty-dollar gold pieces hidden in my hatband, some pocket money, and a ramshackle ranch in Comanche country—a ranch I'd never seen a title to. I guess Pa didn't expect to die anytime soon. I'm betting Tom didn't either.

Pa loved that ranch, and I know he wanted me to keep it going. I made no promises, but there wasn't time for him to ask. I knew at the time what he wanted me to do. What would I have said if he asked me? Deep down, I knew. And I'd already made that decision when I sent White Bear to the home place.

I had enough money for flour, beans, and such...not much extra. And then there was the matter of Tom's killing. That wasn't right. Those men at the bar kept glancing my way. I'm sure they were curious about what I'd do now that I knew of Tom's murder. Maybe they thought they'd have to bury me too and were just waiting.

Mattie watched me as I mulled it over—my mind miles away as I thought of things to do and how to get it done. We sat close to one another, close enough I could hear her breathe—as unlikely a pair as you'd ever find.

And the ranch? Pa wanted to see it grow, but one man can't do much. Improvements need to be made. There was no cash money to pay anyone to help. Even with the help of Comanche drovers, if that ever happened, it looked like my trail was about to end. If I felt any lower, I'd be sitting on the floor.

When you're young, you're just naturally smarter than anyone else. And bulletproof. Or so you think. Then circumstances change, time passes, and you realize what you don't know would make a thick book. For the first time I could remember, I was unsure about the road ahead.

————

I MUST HAVE JUMPED a foot high when the door to the saloon flung open, and a short, husky man marched in and sat at a corner table. He didn't look fat, just muscular, like he spent his time lifting whiskey barrels. He was dressed in black, head to foot, with shiny boots, and when I say marched, that's what I meant. If you didn't see or hear him, you'd feel the stomping across the floor. I guess he felt important. A badge was pinned to his vest, and it looked like he'd spent a week polishing it. Maybe he used it as a mirror to shave with. It was an education to see how fast the painted ladies moved away from him.

Mattie's hand clutched my arm again as I looked at the sheriff. Her voice was husky and low, like she had a secret to tell, as she leaned into me. "Don't do anything stupid. Mary said he's fast with that gun, and it's not just for show. He's wound up tight like a spring just waiting to let go."

I gave her a good, hard look. I don't know what she saw in me—I didn't know if I could measure up. Not that I was against the idea. We'd been joined at the hip since she saw me. I liked it, but it still made me nervous. Far as I knew, there were no rules on such things.

"I wonder what they consider stupid around here?"

She held my gaze, a small smile forming on her lips. "I figure what you're thinking will just about cover it."

I stared at the man until, like any wild animal, he felt my gaze and looked up at me. The kind of anger I felt right then wasn't something I'd experienced before, not even when Pa was killed. And it was hard to hide. I felt cold and alive, every nerve raw with feeling. Here was the man who'd killed my brother. Only thing is, I didn't know who the hunter was and who the prey was.

This was Mack Foster, and his name brought fear to the eyes of the men around me. I could see it. A man known for his temper, and he looked mad just sitting there. He dressed like one of those gunfighters you read about in a dime novel.

Mattie's hand on my arm was warm—it hadn't left since she started talking to me, but she seemed wise enough not to grip tight in case I had to move in a hurry. It was distracting in a way, but I liked it. We sat side by side and both faced the sheriff. Noise in the room seemed to trickle down to nothing, and the bartender gave a soft curse as he bumped over a glass on the countertop. It rolled and clinked against a bottle. Hard-heeled boots marked cadence as a group of men walked past on the rough planks that passed for a boardwalk outside the door and then yelled at someone farther down the street.

Mack tried to stare me down, but I didn't buy it. Giving that up, he lurched to his feet and marched toward me. Now, we were always dirt poor, but Pa didn't slight us on needful education. Ma passed years ago. Just kind of wore out, I guess. Pa said she was never healthy after I was born. She gave us a good foundation that Pa built on.

He taught us how to read and cipher—how to work cattle and survive on next to nothing. And he taught us about men. That's why I couldn't believe Tom was dead. He was older than me, and he'd been out and about some. He knew all the tricks. Well, maybe all but the one that tripped him up.

Just as the man stopped in front of our table, I moved the toe of my boot out and toward him a little bit. It still had the Greener resting on it. It was a small move, but it might make all the difference. He saw that and looked at my finger on the trigger guard. What made him step back was when I cocked both barrels. Nothing is louder than cocking a gun in a quiet, tension-filled room.

He was a man with a lot of bluster. I could see that right off, and he was used to pushing people around. His right hand was on the grip of his gun. His holster was cut away on the front and looked like real hard leather. I'd never seen one, but it looked like a fast draw rig, and by the way it was polished, he took pride in how it looked.

I let him stand a minute before speaking, never taking my gaze from his eyes. "That fancy gun rig won't help you none."

"Maybe. How would you know?" He glanced down at my foot. "You could blow your foot off that way."

I nodded slightly at him. "It's possible."

His bluster came out in full force. "Why are you staring at me? A man could take that the wrong way."

I didn't feel like it, but I conjured up a smile for him. "How you take it is none of my concern. I've never seen a dead man walk around before, so I was kind of curious."

Before he could bluster again, I continued. "I hear you killed my brother...for no reason at all." Mattie's hand left my arm, and I spoke without looking at her. "Girl, you best move away. I don't want you hurt."

She chuckled and leaned forward on the table. "Naw. I want to watch this. Nobody cares if I die."

It was hard to keep from being distracted, and Mack was looking between us like we were daft. Maybe we were. I spoke softly in that quiet room. "Mattie, that ain't rightly so. I don't know you at all, but you seem solid to me. I reckon you're just in a bad situation and doing the best you can. Happens to everyone from time to time. All we need to do is change your circumstances."

Mack seemed impatient and found his voice. "You look here, boy. I don't like strangers in this town. Especially mouthy ones like you. If that was your brother I killed the other day, he asked for it. Now you get out of here, or I'll plant you next to him."

Men started moving away, out of the line of fire. But they didn't go far. Maybe entertainment was in short supply.

His voice got loud, and I could see he was pumping himself up to do something. Casual-like, I kicked my foot up, and he was looking down the barrels of that shotgun. He'd just started his own move, and his gun was half out of the holster. Staring at me, he looked a little pale.

"Mr. Foster, you may have a lot of notches on the butt of your pistol, but my brother's will be the last."

He smirked at me, but his courage seemed forced. "I'm the sheriff here, boy. I run this town. You're under arrest."

"I don't think so." I watched his eyes, looking for any warning he was going to try and shoot me. "I think your arresting days are over."

Fred spoke from behind the bar. "Johnny, why don't you back up some? I'd just as soon not have any blood to clean off my floor. It gets down in the cracks, and I cain't get it out. Then it starts to smell."

I didn't take my gaze from the gunman as I shrugged. "You're going to have a bigger problem. Most of his head will be on the ceiling."

Mack stood rigid for a moment and then relaxed

when I didn't pull the triggers. His gaze wavered, and he looked around, tongue flicking over dry lips. His indecision was clear to everyone. This must have been new territory for him—someone not knuckling under. He was undecided about what to do. And he surely had to do something. He had to keep his pride intact.

I couldn't kill him in cold blood, though I dearly wanted to. That wasn't the way I was raised. I let him sweat and stew a minute before I spoke. "Why don't you get out of here? We're disturbing this man's business, and money is hard to come by. I'll come and take care of you when it's time."

Mack seemed glad of the chance, sighing as he backed up a couple of steps. "All right. If that's the way you want it. But you won't have to look for me. I'll be outside and waiting for you in the street. Let's see how brave you are then." With that little threat, he turned and marched out of the saloon.

I was in no hurry. It was hot outside, so I'd let him cook a while. The sheriff looked like a backshooter to me, someone who liked a sure thing. Pa would have called him *all hat and no cattle*. Trouble is, I didn't know what he could do, or, for that matter, what I could.

The noise picked up again, but most everybody was watching me. My hands were shaking, and I was real careful when I let those hammers down on the shotgun. Mattie must have seen it because she put her hand on mine. I know I was expected to go outside and fight the man, but I'm betting these cowhands wouldn't be so quick to do it either.

Besides, Pa always said those stories were hogwash, where two gunmen would square off in the street to see who was fastest. Unless both parties were drunk, and then it was usually the innocent bystanders that got

shot. Fair fights were just a lack of preparation on someone's part. And the only rule in a gunfight was to not get
shot.

I turned to Mattie. Words came out before I had a
chance to think about it.

"Reckon you'd be any good at ranching? It's a hard
life and lonely. I'm thinking I could use some help."

"Hard life?" She looked at me with those big eyes.
"Look around you. There's nothing easy anywhere you
look."

Shaking her head, she continued. "You don't want
anybody like me. I'd be a lot of trouble. You can do
better, Johnny Tyler."

"Well, the offer's open if you want it. In any case, you
won't get far talking yourself down like that."

We looked at each other for a moment, and a lot of
things went between us without a word being said. Her
eyes were the deepest blue I'd ever seen as she looked
me over.

I turned to Fred, still hanging out behind the bar.
"How'd you ever get a sheriff like that? I can't believe
you hired him."

He snorted, and a man at the bar laughed. "Hire him?
Hell, he just showed up one day and decided we needed
a sheriff. I don't think he's right in the head."

"Why do you pay him?"

"Well, we don't. I mean, not really. He takes what he
wants and don't pay for it. Food, whiskey, or the women
upstairs...don't matter. Folks stay out of his way."

I nodded at that. I'd never heard of anything more
unlikely, but then I didn't have any experience at such
things. Maybe the sheriff had cooked in the heat long
enough.

"You got a side door?"

He pointed, kind of surprised. I was expected to go out the front door and face the sheriff. Those men at the bar wouldn't look at me, figuring I was going to sneak out the back and run away. I didn't blame them for it. That was the smart thing to do. But a man's pride is worth something, and they'd not respect me if I pulled foot out of here. I wouldn't either.

I knew what was waiting outside, but Pa always told me not to fight anybody on their own terms or play their game—be it poker, roping a cow critter, or anything else. There was no such thing as fair in a fight. My job was to stay alive, and I wasn't about to give a crazy gunman a fair shake.

I put my hand on Mattie's shoulder, and she looked up at me, startled. I was surprised at the reaction we both had and at the softness of her expression. She had on perfume that addled me a moment.

"You got business to attend to, Johnny Tyler. Best see to it."

"I'll just be a minute. Then we need to talk some more."

"Oh, we're gonna talk. I'm counting on it."

Slipping out the back way, stepping carefully around the stacked crates, discarded bottles, and opened air tights, I moved around to the front of the building. Mack was sure enough standing in the middle of the street like he said he'd be and looked to be sweating a bit. His shirt was soaked, and he shifted his weight from one foot to the other. Guess he was high-strung, not used to waiting.

His gun was drawn and pointed at the front door of the saloon. It was short-barreled and one he could get out in a hurry. At that distance, I'd bet he'd miss the building. My fingers caressed the butt of my old Colt, but

I discarded that notion. It would take forever just to clear the holster if it came to that.

Seems he was primed to shoot me on sight, soon as I walked out that door. It was a wonder he didn't try to shoot me through the window, but I'd been watching for that. I was sure he wouldn't give me an even shake, and I'd lay odds he didn't give Tom much of a chance either.

But that was expected. My Greener wasn't exactly pointed at the ground, and I'd cocked it coming around the corner.

"Over here." My voice rapped out sharply and got the reaction I wanted.

The sheriff bleated like a startled calf and started to turn. As he did, something crashed through the front glass window of the saloon, and he whirled toward the sound. His gun went off, and the bullet hit the dirt by the hitch rail. Several horses broke the rein and bucked away, mine included.

By then, I was within a few feet of him. When his pistol came back around to point at me, I let go with both barrels. I dropped the shotgun on its string and pulled the Colt, but I didn't need to. A shotgun firing buckshot doesn't leave much to look at, and he'd about been lifted right out of his shiny, black boots.

As I stood in the dusty street, watching the man bleed out, I didn't know how to act. I tried to feel bad, but he'd killed my brother for no more reason than an innocent bump in a doorway. At least the Comanche thought they had a reason when they killed Pa.

Someone shouted they were coming out, and the saloon seemed to empty of people in a few seconds. I guess they were afraid I'd keep shooting if they didn't shout out to me. I didn't put away my pistol, not sure how they'd take to me killing their sheriff, but I needn't have worried. Most of the cowhands were grinning and didn't look too upset.

The man who'd bought me a beer stuck out his hand. "My name's John Davis. I can always use a good hand if you need a job. We're just down the road a piece at the Circle D."

Holstering my pistol, I shook his hand. "Meaning no disrespect, but this here is about the only road I've ever been on. I ain't sure I like where it took me."

"I can see how you'd feel that way, young man. It's not like this usually. Mostly this is a peaceful town."

Mattie came out and walked toward me. I didn't take my eyes off her smile as I spoke to John. "I figure to keep ranching. Pa would want it, and I ain't smart enough to know better."

John looked at Mattie approaching them. "Well. Looks like you've got things figured out. Best of luck to both of you. If I'm over your way sometime, I'll stop and see how you're doing." He slapped me on the shoulder with a grin. "You hold on to that girl, and you'll get educated."

"That's not a done deal yet." We started toward our horses, pleased that someone had gathered them. "You got a last name, Mattie?"

"My folks took the name Dubois. Not sure they didn't make it up."

"How does Tyler sound to you?"

She stopped and looked at me long enough that I got uncomfortable. "Sounds like we need to have a discussion."

A man came hustling toward them from the stable, leading Tom's horse, already saddled. His rifle was in the scabbard, and a pistol belt was slung over the pommel. A bedroll and slicker rested back of the saddle. It looked like Mattie had an outfit already.

"The sheriff was going to keep this horse and tack. That wasn't right."

I nodded to the man and thanked him. "That sheriff wasn't right about a lot of things."

The hostler glanced toward the body on the ground— a body no one seemed to care about. "Well, I guess he learned his lesson."

I got Mattie situated on Tom's horse since it was better than hers. Truth be told, she went into the saddle like one of them circus acrobats without using the stirrups. I guess that's what the divided dress was for. I never had the leg strength to do that.

Looking back over my saddle, I could see men wandering toward the shade while others watered their horses, getting ready to leave. Some of the saloon women stood on the boardwalk, waving. It looked like the town was going back to sleep and the Circle D was riding out. The wind picked up and blew down the street, covering Mack's body with a layer of dust. I wondered how long he'd lay there.

———

JOHN HAD the men from Circle D congregated under the shade next to the well. He wasn't giving them good news. I'd never seen a more dejected group of men. On impulse, I walked my horse over to them, followed by a startled Mattie. Conversation died out when I spoke. That knack was starting to get irritating.

"Mr. Davis, I heard some of your talk. Men at the barber shop talked about the range conditions and creeks drying up. Sounds like you're losing cattle."

"And you're not?" He gave me a hard look and then relented. "It hasn't rained in several weeks. You know that as well as me. Creeks are drying up, and it's a long drive to the Brazos or Red. Cows can go on light feed for a while, but they need water. So, yeah. We're losing cattle."

He glanced around at his men. Most were listening, while a few stared into the distance with disgusted looks. "Unfortunately, that means I have to let some men go. There's not enough work to go around."

Even as he spoke, a few were starting to leave, maybe wishing they'd saved their money instead of having a last fling in Johnson Flats. "If y'all would hold up a minute, I got a proposition for you. I know I'm young and inexperienced, but it might pay you to listen."

John looked at me a moment and then waved his men back. "Fair enough. Like you say, it can't hurt to listen. Lay it out."

Mattie watched as I squatted in the shade and took out my skinning knife. Finally, she rode up close behind me and hooked a leg over the saddle horn. When I glanced around, it seemed she was protecting my back. She was giving me support, and I was glad of it. After a curious look to see what I was doing, John stepped forward. Men crowded around.

I drew a circle in the dirt. "If this is the town, where would your ranch be?"

"Our headquarters is about five miles down the road."

He nodded approval as I drew a circle on the north side for his ranch.

The sound of empty canteens clanking together distracted me for a moment, and I was embarrassed to see Mattie climb down and head for the well—embarrassed I hadn't thought of it. I'd filled mine when we came, but not the extras.

Turning back to the matter at hand, I drew four squares about the same distance apart, south of the town. By then, a few more of his riders had joined us.

"Those are locations of springs my family registered and improved on."

One of the men snorted. "We been all over that country. Ain't no water out there."

I stared at the man for a moment until he looked uncomfortable. He'd just called me a liar in public. We both knew it, and he knew I'd just put down the sheriff. There'd been shootings for less reason, depending on the amount of whiskey consumed, although I felt he'd meant no insult and didn't push it. I turned to John. "Seems to me we both have a problem. I'm long on water and short on cattle. You've got the opposite problem."

He nodded, giving the man who'd doubted me a disapproving look. "How much water?"

"Well, sir. Three of these are small, including the one at our place. We've had some bad years, but they've never dried up that I can remember. Those I'll hold for myself."

He was staring at me. "And the fourth spring?"

"Now, that's the interesting one." I tapped the blade on the circle closest to his ranch and grinned at him. "That'll cost you."

John sighed, turning to watch Mattie return with the full canteens. "I figured that. How much? Cash money is in short supply."

"Not money, Mr. Davis, although I'm like you. I could sure use it. It wouldn't be neighborly. Here's the thing. This is a pretty big spring. Comes out of the ground and makes a little creek. The water goes out a hundred feet or so and then sinks into the ground. It's not a real big amount, but it's steady. The ground just sucks it down."

I glanced at the man who'd questioned me. "It doesn't show up from a distance because it gets lost in the rocks, and there's not much green foliage to look for. It's in a protected spot, and you have to about stumble onto it."

The change in color was always the first thing to look for. Available water usually meant grass and trees, and they could be seen from a distance.

A puncher spoke up. "How'd you find those springs? No disrespect, but we rode through that country and didn't see any sign of water."

"Bees. I got a sweet tooth and look for honey. If anything is blooming, there'll be bees working. Bees need water like everything else. Sit quiet and see where they go." I shrugged. "Takes a while. Doesn't always work."

John stood and looked at me. "I appreciate the thought, it's a kindness. But I don't see how that can help. Even with a little creek, it doesn't sound like the spring will support many cattle. What's your idea?"

Mattie put her hand on my shoulder, studying the dirt like it was a proclamation. After I gave her a smile, I turned back to the men.

"Sometime in the past, that spring had high water. Back when it rained on occasion." I looked at the sky. "I'm thinking way in the past. Anyway, on one side of the spring is a natural tank. It's all rock and clay with a gentle access on one side. Men could bring in maybe a hundred head at a time and water them. Drive them off and bring in the next bunch. If you culled your herd and only brought the best stock, it could hold you until next year."

"And the catch?"

"Well, it's a big one. The channel that took the water to that natural tank is plugged up with rocks, mud, and brush like nature made an adobe wall. It'd take some men with mules, wagons, and maybe a stoneboat to clear it out so water flows back into the pool instead of disappearing into the ground. It would be a lot of work." I grinned at the men fronting me. "I'm betting you've got some men sitting on their hands dreaming of being engineers."

He snorted. "My men are riders. If you could lasso a rock and pull it somewhere, they might help." He studied me for a moment. "And that's it? If we do this, you'll share? Seems unlikely."

"Mr. Davis, the weather affects all of us. It's water I'm not using, and it's the neighborly thing to do. I figure to be a good neighbor. Besides, you'll be doing most of the work, and in good times when you don't need the water, we'll have a nice natural water tank already built. Since I don't think we can dry it up, it'll help increase game animals, which will help everyone in the long run. You'll have to be a little judicious about how many cattle you water and how often, at least until that tank fills up."

His gaze moved from Mattie to me. "You talk a lot of sense, Johnny. How old are you?"

Mattie interrupted. "He's old enough, Mr. Davis. Sounds like he's talking sense to me too."

"You know anything about cattle, miss?"

"Not much. I'm more of a keep house and cook for the ranch hands kind of worker." She smiled. "But I'm a quick learner."

That brought a laugh from all of them. John nodded. "I bet you are."

I stood and brushed off the knees of my pants. "One

thing. I'll have some peaceful Comanche working for me." He glanced at Mattie. "At least, I hope they are. If you come over to the place and see them, don't start shooting."

John was shaking his head as I talked. "Mr. Tyler, a hard land is a great equalizer. What counts the most is, can you do the work and can you last? In this part of the country, you're likely to see an English lord riding next to a Mexican or a Black and more than a few half-breed Indians. We have men with wives and families. They come in all persuasions and colors. Our ranch looks like a small community, and I'm sure yours will too after a few years."

Looking past me, he tipped his hat. "Miss Mattie, barring the riff-raff running the saloon, I believe you'll feel quite welcome around here."

I grinned at him. "Do we have a deal?"

John shrugged. "I expect we do. I'll go back and talk it over with the boss—that'd be Emily, my wife. I can be back here tomorrow. That suit you?"

"I reckon we can stay a while. Might take me a few days to get organized. I got distracted and plumb forgot to buy supplies."

He glanced between Mattie and me and then smiled. "I can see how that could happen. A word of advice? Don't stay in the hotel. You'll find fewer bugs camping in the hills. And a lot more privacy."

IT WAS GETTING LATE in the day, so we took his advice. We set up camp about a half-mile outside of Johnson Flats. It was a dry camp, but we had plenty of water in the canteens. We worked together with no words spoken. After I got a fire going and dumped some coffee in the pot to boil, we sat with our backs to a boulder. A cooling breeze came through on occasion, and we were grateful.

"You surprised me today, Johnny."

Her head rested on my shoulder like it was her rightful place.

"How?"

"I reckon there's more to you than meets the eye. You're laying the foundation for a good life and maybe saving some others as you go along."

"Well, I doubt I'm saving them. That's a pretty savvy bunch." When I glanced down at her, she had a small smile. Maybe she knew something I didn't? "I'm just trying to do the right thing. Pa always said to roll with the punches and come up fighting. That's all I can do."

"What about us?" She turned a little, and her gaze locked on mine. "You got a girl in mind somewhere? Someone to share your life with?"

"Well, I'm a busy man." I gave her a side glance. "You know, being an up-and-coming rancher and all. Don't really have time for courting and such."

A sharp elbow about broke my ribs. "Are you scared of me, Johnny Tyler?"

She'd hit the nail on the head, so to speak. I was afraid. Not so much of her, but of what she represented —what she offered. And that woman packed a punch, so it was a matter of self-preservation that I let her off the hook.

"Mattie, I like you. I think it could grow into a lot more...hope it does. And I couldn't ask for anyone better. You're beautiful and smart. Given what you've been through, tough as nails. How about we get settled at the ranch and see how this goes?"

"Like a courtship? I get to flutter my eyelids and bake cookies for you? I don't think so. You're counting on a lot of tomorrows. This is a sudden land. We could be dead tomorrow or any day after."

"It's been a while, but I remember liking cookies."

She stood and faced me, bathed in soft, golden light. My jumbled mind tried to make words as her clothes started making a neat pile beside us.

"Mattie...you...uh...what're you...hey, that coffee is about ready."

"Hell with the coffee."

IF YOU LIKED THIS, YOU MAY ENJOY:

Shepherd's Fire

A FAST-PACED PRE-APOCALYPTIC THRILLER THAT EMBODIES TRUE HOPE FOR A BETTER LIFE.

Jim Lane is pulling himself together after burn-out from a rescue gone bad when his peaceful life on Stockton Lake is shattered. Jolted by betrayal, he survives an attempt on his life only to be drawn into a bloody turf war with the Russian mob.

But County Sheriff Rita Morris knows his history and isn't buying his explanation. Having lost her husband to a random shooting and unsure if she's ready to move on, Rita can't deny the connection she feels with Jim. It's a complication, but the pair form a united front with a simple message for the Russians —get out of Limestone County!

From the moment the first bullet flies, Jim steps into a whirlwind of twists and turns, new love, a bond with an old friend ready to hurtle to the end with an ally he never expected...and a blood debt that will keep him looking over his shoulder for the rest of his life.

AVAILABLE NOW

ACKNOWLEDGMENTS

Special thanks to Ellie Folden, editor-in-chief at My Brother's Editor. I've worked with many editors through the years, and she's the best—highly recommended. Thanks, E.

With that in mind, any mistakes found herein are my own.

While in the Navy, I operated radar, sonar, and radio. Seems I was always adjusting knobs. So our job's nickname came from twiddling, fidgeting, and fussing around with the gear. Yes, we were twidgets.

Any mistakes made are because I can't stop twidgiting, even after the editor lays a calming hand on my shoulder and says, "Stop."

ABOUT THE AUTHOR

Darrel Sparkman is an award-winning author of novels, novellas, and short stories. He's been included in three western anthologies, worked as a feature writer for *Saddlebag Dispatches* and blogged a short time for *Sundown Press*.

His ideas come from a diverse past of serving as a combat search and rescue helicopter crewman in Vietnam and volunteer Emergency Medical Technician First Responder. He has worked as a professional photographer, computer repair tech, and was once part-owner of a commercial greenhouse operation and flower shop.

Darrel is enjoying semi-retirement and finally has that job that wakes him up every day—with a smile on his face.

www.ingramcontent.com/pod-product-compliance
Lightning Source LLC
Chambersburg PA
CBHW011431240626
47153CB00011B/2935